# BODIE

# BODIE

Anne Sweazy-Kulju

TATE PUBLISHING
AND ENTERPRISES, LLC

Published by Tate Publishing & Enterprises, LLC
127 E. Trade Center Terrace | Mustang, Oklahoma 73064 USA
1.888.361.9473 | www.tatepublishing.com

Tate Publishing is committed to excellence in the publishing industry. The company reflects the philosophy established by the founders, based on Psalm 68:11,
*"The Lord gave the word and great was the company of those who published it."*

Published in the United States of America

ISBN: 978-1-62510-795-4
1. Fiction / Action & Adventure
2. Fiction / Mystery & Detective / Historical
13.07.12

# Dedication

I dedicate this novel to my dad, John Sweazy.

# Acknowledgments

My heartfelt thanks to Col. John T. Durkin, USMC—you are the best brother-in-law, ever. And to Lisa Durkin, my sister; I could not have done this without you two.

Special thanks to Myra Conway Hood, for sharing her regression with me (years *after* I'd written her/him into my story).

Many thanks to Joe Lushina, for giving me a beat I could work to.

Thank you Fire Chief Frank Douglas, for the great fish story!

Thank you, Donna McCabe, for "Claire."

My appreciation goes to The Friends of Bodie and the Bancroft Library, U. C. Berkeley, California, for the research.

"Whaaa? Whoa! Well—if this don't dunk my hat in the water." The tired old miner figured he'd managed to holler loud enough to scare off whatever landed on the shakedown of horse blankets he was using for a bedroll. He'd been snoozing nice and easy when something jumped onto his blankets and landed near his right thigh. Until that moment, his mule's trail saddle had made for a suitable pillow. But when he was jerked out of a sound sleep, he knocked the back of his head—*hard*, on the wood post horn. He rubbed the back of his head briefly and listened to the dark. The hollow thud which surprised him awake was followed by silence, dead silence in the moonlit desert. It was an ominous sound.

Lucius Ambert didn't want to admit it, but he was a tad nervous. Because whatever the critter was that had just jumped atop his makeshift bedroll, it wasn't frightened off by his hollering at all.

"My achin' back," he grumbled.

He reached out tentatively and knocked the object from the blankets. *Christ! It sure did stink terrible.* His hand had brushed against stringy hair and something worse—something thick and gummy. Now, Lucius was known as a man who never shied away from trouble of any sort. He'd fought Indians as a young man, had proved himself a soldier in the war, and had defended his few lucky claims against every rascal jumper. But, that didn't mean he was particularly anxious to investigate this disturbing matter of something strange and smelly, which had nearly jumped into his lap, and then apparently died right there.

Lucius reached out slowly, and his fingers took hold of the hairy thing. He scrambled quickly from the confines of his temporary bed beneath the Bodie Creek Bridge to get a better look. Even the bright moonlight wasn't much help to Lucius' failing eyesight, so he lifted the object directly in front of his face. In fifty-eight years of living, it was the first occasion Lucius Ambert had been known to scream. He made up for the lack by screaming again and again. But then it wasn't every day a severed head was dropped into a sleeping man's lap.

# Chapter 1

*Gold*, yellow glittering precious Gold. The baseness of man, and yet his antidote, his blessing and his curse. His happiness and his misery. His solace and his affliction. The forger of change, and manumitter. The pastor and the prison, and the releaser. The rich man's strength. The poor man's weakness.

—Bodie Standard, 1877

1 March, 1879
Bodie, California

Twenty-four Bay hooves thunder-drummed against the desert floor, their sound nearly drowned out by the crescendo of heaving lungs and flaring nostrils.

"Hyah!" the driver yelled and slapped his reins, stealing hurried glances over his shoulder at the devil on his tail.

A sign post just blurred passed him for Sweetwater. His horses knew this route to Carson City blindfolded.

"Hyah! Hyah!"

A shot rang out, and the driver felt something icy-hot whiz past his right cheek. His beloved horses were bleating in desperation; the six glorious beasts were work horses, large and strong. They were not bred to run, and they certainly were not made for speed. Conway worried their stout hearts might soon explode in their chests, and still he had no choice but to spur them on. Running was their only hope. *If they could out run the assassin, if they could survive for about ten more miles, they would be too close to the next town for*—thwack! The round hit the commercial buckboard near the driver's right foot. Conway shook the reins hard and snuck another hasty look back. He saw Touchstone's man, Parker, line up his aim at the lead horses.

"Shit," was all Conway managed before the last shot rang out.

Boston, the lead nineteen-hand quarter-horse, who was Conway's best friend in the world, went down. Brimstone and Barley toppled over him, followed a fraction of a second later by the rest of the horses, the driver, and the enormous wagon rolling end-over-end, in a spectacular, splintering crash.

For Conway, seconds slowed impossibly. He observed with morbid fascination, and a healthy measure of disbelief, a kaleidoscope of brown and black shoot passed; he then smiled at a churning blue sky and clouds of cotton candy; now his eyes widened at the tremendous sprays of bright red and stark white shards glittering in the high desert sun. *My horses are coming apart!* Conway realized with horror. And then he was floating and twirling with the kaleidoscope—blue sky, red sprays, unforgiving desert floor. The sounds were peculiar too: a rhythmic snapping and cracking of yoke and leather strap, and bone. Conway slammed into the ground with a concert of splintering bone and torn flesh, and his eyes came to rest on the lifeless eyes of Boston, his favorite horse. A sob choked on its way up Conway's throat.

"Bost…" he croaked as he forced his look away—and up, just in time to see his oversized buckboard flying straight at him.

Parker pulled a pouch from his vest and began rolling himself a cigarette as his horse, Clementine, circled the field of carnage—he had to be certain he had completed his assignment. He saw that a few of the horses, baring hideous injuries, were still laboring for final breaths. He sighed and pulled his revolver out, flipped open the cylinder and checked his ammunition supply. Three rounds. He dished two fingers into a pile of bullets in another pocket. He probably had a dozen or more rounds on him, and the beasts were suffering horribly. But, that wasn't really his problem, was it? A man can't afford to be wasting bullets in these badlands. He licked his cigarette paper closed, lit it up, and inhaled deeply. As he exhaled, he tipped his hat at the few still-breathing horses.

"Don't worry, you'll be dead 'fore the buzzards gather to pick at ya...*I think.*" He laughed cruelly, gave the grisly scene one last survey, and turned back toward Bodie, whistling a catchy tune. It promised to be another beautiful California day.

# Chapter 2

1 March, 1879
Bodie, California

She studied her reflection in the mirror, saving a lengthy examination for the crmine, sequins, and pearls. She hoped it wasn't too much for a widow. *No, you are not a widow tonight. You are not a widow, first-and-foremost, any longer*, she reminded herself. She had done right by Frank. She had mourned him proper. It had been three months, for Pete's sake. Surely that is long enough—especially if one considers how long Frank was sick. *I have a business to run, and my customers don't spend their paychecks to see women in high-necked frocks of black*, she gave herself bolster. Even so, those pesky little worry lines that had formed vertically between her brows wouldn't vanish, possibly because her choice of frock had little to do with what was really bothering her on this night.

True enough, Elise worried far too much what folks thought of her, an irritating trait she had no doubt gleaned from her mother at an early age; but no, this was all Parker's doing. Parker takes care of problems with a Colt 45, and just that afternoon

Parker informed Elise she had become a problem for him. She was warned to keep quiet, the message fairly unsubtle. But of course she could not. She owed that much to the friends and loved ones she had lost, and to Amanda, the best friend she knew she would be losing soon enough.

She wanted to sweep her long hair up. She did not tolerate the heat well, and her hair was thick and heavy. She stared at the large hair clip resting on the vanity; it was a gift from Amanda before she went to the hospital. It was not *so* gaudy. After all, Amanda had worn it often enough when she dealt Faro for the gamblers downstairs, and she swore it brought the house luck. Elise did not credit the hair clip as the lucky talisman; if anything, it was Amanda herself. She had a gift for gab and an even greater gift for listening; everyone loved her. She had brought good business to Elise's inn, that much was certain. Her eyes fell in sadness and her lips began to tremor. Elise said another silent prayer for her friend. She knew Amanda was dying, no matter what nonsense Doc gave as his official medical opinion.

Amanda was a desert ghost, like so many others, including Elise's late husband, Frank. She took a deep breath and pushed the lovely comb solidly into her twisted and rolled locks. She allowed herself to smile at what she saw.

"Well, if nothing more, this hair bobble is sure to gain me the attention of the men downstairs," she told her reflection. "Hmmm. It should not be garish, though, so as to have me looking like one of the working girls." She baited the reflection as she turned her head this way and that. She had never in her life worn such come-hither attire, and she blushed as she realized she was enjoying the feeling. "But, if I can look fetching enough, and get the men to pay attention to me, *maybe* they will pay attention to what I have to say." She smiled hopefully at her mirror, but her reflection and her nerves betrayed her.

The rising coolness, after a long day of oppressive heat, had a buoyant effect on the gamblers and women in the Swazey Hotel's modest casino. Elise fairly floated down the stairs, her skirts rustling against the floorboards and her heeled boots rap-rapping as she went. Elise Swazey was an attractive woman, seemingly composed and self-possessed. The latter came from the certainty she had nothing to fear in Bodie. While it is true, Bodie is a violent town which averaged a murder a day or more, even the worst characters showed respect to the decent and respectable women of the town. This absolute was due in part to the knowledge that death would surely follow any other course. Females were in short supply in Bodie. There were not enough whores to go around, and there were almost no women for marrying—even fewer of this last category held any aesthetic appeal. But in this area, Elise was well-endowed.

She glanced Jack's way and captivated him with her most engaging smile. Jack withdrew his faro bet from the table and slammed his chair back across the floorboards with a powerful screech. He smiled at Elise, working his muscular frame out of the small ladder-back chair as he straightened his snow-white shirt. Elise admired his tailored suit and polished boots. This was the uniform of the professional gambler, or "Sport."

The Swazey Hotel wasn't large or elegant, but her rooms were clean and tasteful. The whiskey was good and poured liberally, and the casino was directly across from the miner's union, which on paydays made it a popular spot for the gamblers to come and ply their trade. Elise could not keep herself from mentally comparing Jack to her late husband, Frank. Having been a rather luckless miner, her husband had never owned a Sunday's Best or expensive watch and cuff links. And although Frank had been mild-mannered until the disease began consuming his mind, too, he was never the gentleman that Jack was. Jack was a man of education and of experience. He'd been an Indian fighter before settling in Bodie, and as such had made near a legend of himself to both sides of the fight. He was a strapping man made even larger than life by his dignity, good character, and cool confidence.

---

Jack Gunn was Elise Swazey's one great love. But he also gave Elise a feeling of security—something she found herself sorely needing as of late. For Jack, Elise Swazey was the woman he had waited for all his forty years. He laid strong hands on Elise's slender waist and hefted her atop the bar. Elise winced inwardly at the sight of herself sitting on the bar like one of her saloon's working females. But, as she gazed at Jack's darkly handsome face she saw only adoration in his eyes, and she knew he had not meant to cheapen her. Silently, she wondered how long the Bodieites would expect a "respectable woman" to mourn before getting on with her life; she feared Jack Gunn would not wait forever.

They chatted about the upcoming wrestling match to be held at the miner's union. Jack had made a fortune at the last contest, billed as a Rough-and-Tumble, because the contestants were so woefully mismatched in size, and still the little man had won. Jack made a point of always booking for the man with the larger brainpower; he paid little attention to a competitor's size. He made a witty remark that sent Elise's pretty legs swinging as she giggled.

Men at the tables across the room grumbled at the couple, and one of the other sports rolled his eyes and made a jealous wisecrack. Then a door to an upstairs bedroom opened wide to reveal one of the town's more comely prostitutes, drunkenly weaving and laughing her way to the banister railing, her arms thrown around a Mexican who had recently gambled his wife away in a game of poker.

"He's done in, Jack, but I still got somethin' left for you, honey," she hollered playfully at Jack below.

"Is there not a woman in town immune to Jack Gunn's charm?" complained Carter Perkins, the town mortician. Although Perkins was an eminently successful business man, women cared little for his attentions. Perhaps it was because he rose to six foot two inches and was skinnier than a hitching post. He never strolled or sauntered anywhere, but instead was always paced rapid and purposeful, no matter where he was headed. He had quick, birdlike movements which, paired with his baneful stoop and the black uniform of the professional mortician, made folks think of a buzzard. Naturally, Perkins would be jealous of a man like Jack Gunn.

Jack saluted the drunken whore, laughing, and then turned seriously to Elise. "What does a man have to do to get a woman like you into one of those upstairs rooms?"

"Jack," Elise started. She didn't know how to go on. Wasn't her desire for him obvious? Didn't he know how often she had daydreamed about just that? It made color rise in her cheeks just thinking about the many times she had vividly imagined what their lovemaking would be like. "It hasn't been so long since I put my husband in the ground. What would the town folk think?"

"Who cares what they think, Elise?"

"I guess I do. I wish I didn't." She gave him a sad look. "I know you must've heard them talk, Jack. I know they think I'm light-headed as my husband was. But there's something to my questioning about why so many miners, and others too, are sick and dying. Svenson himself told me, Jack."

"Yes, and why would he do that, Elise? He's a lonely man, and he's sweet on you. Maybe he was trying to warn you, but more likely he is hoping to scare you into his arms. Svenson is a good-for-nothing who's not man enough to go to the newspaper or to call a town meeting and just *tell* everyone what he claims he knows. No, *he's* not man enough to call for an investigation against Touchstone—"

"He believes they would kill him, Jack," Elise interrupted him.

Jack set his jaw in response and continued, "but he is perfectly alright with laying his dangerous conspiracy at the feet of a ninety-pound, freshly-widowed mother of a young son." He reached out and touched her face lightly, tracing her fine features with his fingers. "I don't doubt you, Elise. But planting suggestions that it might be something other than bad whiskey that's causing all the sickness, ain't too popular a notion without any proof. And it could get *you* killed."

"Proof, Jack? Bodie is dying. I never heard of a gold-rush town having a hospital, let alone one the size of Bodie's. Why is it no other Bodieite finds its very existence, let alone the rate of occupancy, peculiar in the least? That hospital has five times the number of guests than my inn." She paused. "I'd hoped you would help me convince some of the folks here tonight to unite behind a call for investigation of Touchstone's mining practices. I told Morris Parker I was going to the newspaper, but Ezra says he's too threatened to run the piece. Then when Parker threatened me, I knew I had to—"

"He what?" Jack bristled and dropped his hand from her face. He grasped the bar on either side of Elise. With stiff arms and a taut expression, he demanded to know what Parker had said.

"It's fine, Jack. The light of day is Nature's most efficient disinfectant. The more people who know the truth, the safer I will be. This morning, in fact, I said something to Robert Conway, since Touchstone is now paying him to water down the streets for dust control. I have to say, he didn't require a lot of convincing. He told me he'd not been feeling well himself, as of late, and his other team driver is in the hospital with the sickness. But what really rattled Robert was worry for his horses—you know how he loves those horses. He said he was going straightaway to see the mining company's President and demand he shut down the Svenson-Processing of their gold tailings. At least until it can be determined whether it's responsible for Bodie's ghosts. He also promised me he would come tonight and help me talk to the other men." She looked around. "I'd rather hoped Robert would come early..."

Jack reached for her hand, his face etched with worry. "Elise, Conway was murdered this afternoon on the route to Carson City—Conway and his entire team of horses." Her frozen expression betrayed her fear; her words may have gotten a good man killed. Jack squeezed her hands for emphasis and went for broke. "Elise, I love you. I swear to you I have never said those words to another woman before. I want to take you away from here—now more than ever. I don't care if Bodie thinks me a coward for running from Parker's threat. I have seen plenty of trouble in my time, and if I've learned anything, I've learned not to go looking for it. Neither you nor I owe these people any heroics, Elise. They ain't worth it if they haven't got sense enough to question matters even when their horses drop dead in the street. Pay no attention to what these desert rats think of us. And to hell with Frank Swazey, too. He's gone, and I'm the man standing in front of you. I want you, Elise. I'm in love with you, and you're in love with me. Let's get the hell out of Bodie."

Jack mistook the blushing and silence as hesitation, and he hastened to convince Elise that they belonged together. "Elise, you know I can provide for you. Let your son run the inn, he's old enough now. Or burn the damn thing down and we'll all run away together—you, Frank Jr., and me. Say the word, Elise, and I'll take you from this hateful town tonight."

Elise was beginning to feel uncomfortably warm, and her head was swimming. *Robert Conway was murdered?* She knew Robert was sweet on her, and that was the reason she decided to approach him. *Did she use Robert like Svenson used her?* Robert was a dear friend, and Elise was beginning to believe his death was entirely her fault. The player-piano suddenly sounded fierce and pounding, and the noise level of laughing and shouting voices in the room seemed to rise impossibly. She wanted Jack to take her into his arms and hold her tightly. She wanted to lose herself in the smell of him. She wanted to run away with him more than anything.

The room began to spin. She could use some cool air, she told Jack. He winced with what he thought to be rejection, but nonetheless, he lifted her down from the counter. Elise hurried in the direction of the swinging doors but stopped short. She suspected she was making a grave mistake by leaving Jack at that moment. She ran back to Jack, throwing herself into his arms. His hug gave her tingly warmth that spurred her like an electric storm. Turning her lips to meet his, she kissed him on the mouth and asked, "Just to be sure, are you proposing marriage, Jack?"

"If you'll have me," he laughed and bowed lightly.

"Yes I will. I love you, Jack," she whispered. "And I don't care a stitch for this hotel. You and Frank Jr., are all I care about." She dabbed here and there at her hairline with a lace hanky and exclaimed, "Oh my, I am so uncomfortably warm." She wriggled in Jack's embrace and he grudgingly let her go. "I'm just going to catch a little air, and then we'll talk, I promise."

Jack tucked a wild tendril behind her ear and smiled after Elise as she pushed through the doors into the night.

# Chapter 3

9 March, 1993
Cloverdale, Oregon

*h...my...I'm having the dream*, she thought without waking. Willing herself to remain asleep, to see the dream to conclusion this time, Lara concentrated on staying with the dream.

The handsome man in the black suit is approaching her. He picks her up and swings her onto the bar, her royal blue dress swirling around her calves. She's very pretty. Her hair is a dark, shiny chestnut, most of it swept up with a clip of blue sequins and ermine. Her eyes are sparkling as she talks to the man. They are obviously in love. *I can't hear what he's saying to her. The music and the people at the gaming tables are too noisy.* She strains to hear them talk. She hears the woman on the bar laugh and swing her legs playfully. They both look up at a door opening on the second floor. A woman, appearing quite drunk, yells to the man below. He turns back to the woman on the bar, and soon the two of them look solemn. *Is she jealous? No, it's not that...I wish I knew what they were saying. Don't you dare wake up*, Lara willed herself.

He lifts her down, and she's walking to the doors. She turns to say something, then suddenly runs back to him, kisses him, and shrinks into his arms for a moment. Now she says something to make him respond with a smile and cute bow. She dabs at her hairline with a lacy kerchief and fans herself. She says something more, turns toward the saloon doors once again and…now she's out the swinging doors. *It's a little cool, but it feels good because she was getting so warm inside the hotel…*

Lara is no longer watching the woman in the dream. She has become the woman. She felt a swell of warm emotion and a little confusion at the same time. *The woman is most definitely in love with the handsome gentleman, and she seems to have come to an important decision.* She smiles with deep satisfaction as she removes a lace-trimmed kerchief from her cleavage and dabs her forehead daintily. Lively piano tunes and voices are carried out of the doors of Main Street establishments; the pleasant sounds lay like a soft flannel blanket over the town. The woman looks up to the heavens, admiring a clear night. The moon is not nearly full, but the stars cast shimmering white pinpoints of light here and there. It was magical.

*Any second now*, Lara thinks, asleep yet alert in her bed. *Don't you dare wake up until you see his face.* The woman lifts the hanky again, this time to wave a little of the fresh air into her face. She turns back toward the swinging doors and, "*Ohhh*," is all the woman could say before a large hand shoots out in front of her and firmly flattens against her mouth. At the same time, she is lifted off the verandah and around to the north side of the building.

Lara knew it was coming, but the woman in the dream is clearly surprised. Lara could feel the calluses of the assailant's palm against her smooth skin. She could taste sweat and whiskey and could smell obnoxious cologne. Her dark blue eyes grew wide with comprehension when she was slammed harshly against the building and something cold and oily was pressed behind her right ear. She knew it was the muzzle of a gun. *See who it is!*

---

Lara urges herself. *Hurry, there's not much time left!* The woman in the dream struggles earnestly against the man's hand, banging her head against the saloon's siding. Lara strained her eyes, in the dream's pitch black of night, to identify the man. All at once Lara felt the familiar fuzziness—an all-over sensation of life being drained, from her head to her toes. It was as though the dream were a television show being snapped off; the electricity withdrew to a single dot of diminishing power in the center of Lara's body, then *poof.* It was gone.

"Ding-dang-darn it all," she muttered in the dark.

"Hmm? What's wrong?" Lara's husband, Jeff, was roused awake by her restlessness. He couldn't see her apologetic look in the darkness as she turned toward him.

"I'm sorry I woke you. It was just the dream. It's nothing. Go back to sleep," she said.

"A bad one?" Jeff asked.

"Yeah. No. I mean, it wasn't *a* dream, it was *the* dream."

"Really?" That woke her husband up. He was fascinated with her recurring dream, but she had not had it in quite a while. Now he faced her in the dark, his lean, hard upper body propped up on one elbow, "so, could you change it? I mean, could you see anything else this time?"

"No. It was the same." She sighed with frustration. "I always know what's going to happen. I just wish I knew why." She pushed a sweaty lock of sunny chestnut hair from her forehead and gave her husband's shoulder a gentle squeeze. "Go back to sleep."

Wanting to go back to sleep herself—back to the dream if she could, Lara threw herself onto her side, punched her pillow into position, and concentrated intensely on the woman in the blue dress.

# Chapter 4

9 March, 1993
Neskowin, Oregon

Seven miles to Lara's south, her sister, Lainy, had also awakened from a repeating dream. She'd been curled in her favorite chair, hugging her knees in the darkness of her living room ever since. An attack was coming; one always followed, and she knew she could not be in her bed when it happened. Lainy was shivering even as sweat broke out about her hairline. It wasn't as if she believed she was in any real danger; she knew she wasn't. Her demons were in her long-ago past. But the dread she was left with when her reoccurring dream ended was a waking nightmare which always felt new and raw. Cold, heavy, steel balls in the pit of her stomach were sinking to her feet in waves of gentle nausea. Unpleasant images in too-bold colors were falling about her like a heavy cape, and she knew she had to put them away, or else they would suffocate her. *It can't hurt me. Remember it, then put it away,* she counseled herself.

So she thought about little seven-year-old Maddie, a much younger sister-in-foster, throwing a tantrum over being hungry. She had always been hungry, poor Maddie, and always scary-thin.

Lainy squeezed her arms around her legs a little tighter as she forced herself to sort through the events of that awful day, so long ago. Her foster-dad had made the mistake of pinning little Maddie down and "water-filling" her on the front lawn—a grave mistake, because when she died of water poisoning, it was an act witnessed by neighbors and other children in the home. In 1978, he was convicted of torturing and murdering the little girl. His wife was also arrested, tried, and convicted of multiple counts of child abuse and as an accessory to Maddie's torture and murder. Lainy allowed herself a tight-lipped smile as she remembered that.

Three years before Maddie's death, Lainy's foster dad had attempted to water-fill her when she was a younger child of ten. But her sister, Lara, only twelve years old herself, had grabbed a knife from a kitchen drawer and threatened to kill him if he didn't stop. He stopped. Then he and his wife put all the knives under lock-and-key. Lara was resourceful though, and loathe to believe their foster-dad would leave Lainy alone. Even though he seemed to have it out for Lainy, often teasing her because of her red hair and freckles with cruel name-calling, like Bozo and Freckle-freak, it seemed to Lara he tried to touch her sister too often and for too long. His eyes were always following her.

Lara should have been in seventh grade, but she was advanced a year. She had a boyfriend in the eighth grade, and he got Lara a folding knife that was wicked sharp. She either kept it on her or under her pillow at night.

Lainy shivered and snatched a Pendleton blanket that was folded over the back of the chair. She tucked it under her chin, and began rocking herself softly. Lara's worry had been spot-on. Not even a month following Lainy's water-filling incident and Lara's subsequent threat, their foster dad crept naked into their bedroom late one night and slipped into Lainy's bed while clamping his large, dirty hand tightly over her nose and mouth. Lara was awakened by her sister's struggling for air. She let her eyes adjust to the darkness as she reached beneath her pillow and clicked the knife open. She was quiet as a church mouse as she rose from her bed and snuck up behind her foster dad, who was grunting like a pig beneath the covers. She raised the knife and stabbed him with it.

The old man jumped from the bed and ran around the room in the dark, tripping over things, screaming, and slapping at his back, shouting, "What did you do? You little shit, what did you do?"

Lara turned on the bedroom light and faced the pervert in the room, who was looking rather green at the sight of his own blood leaking from his back; she wielded the knife, swinging it side-to-side just as Jeremy had shown her.

"If you ever go near my sister again, I will kill you in your sleep," Lara had told him. Neither she, nor her sister, were bothered after that, so neither of the girls said anything to Child Services about the incident.

"God, Maddie, I am so sorry," Lainy turned her face toward Heaven. They had not wanted to move to a new foster home and a whole new set of problems. And there was always the risk of getting split up. Also, maybe Lara could have gotten in trouble for the stabbing. If that had happened, and Lara had been sent to 'Juvie,' Lainy would have been alone and without protection.

Lainy's remembrances always jumped from Maddie's murder to the rape, and back to the image of little Maddie's lifeless body on the front lawn. Her pathetically frail body had looked even smaller in death. The sisters had not been present for the little girl's torture, but Lainy had no trouble imagining what happened. They had been at school when the murder occurred. The younger children were released from school much earlier in the day and were at the mercy of their foster parents until the older children arrived home. So they hadn't protected Maddie. Lainy knew both she and her sister harbored guilt over not reporting the foster parents to Child Services, since that would have saved little Maddie from her awful fate. Lainy didn't know if Lara still had waking nightmares about it fifteen years later.

She tossed the throw aside; she was starting to get too warm. Her anxiety attack was passing; her pulse didn't feel as thready and her stomach had settled. *Maybe I can get back to sleep now*, she thought. *Providing I have no more freaky reoccurring dreams that trigger the Maddie-nightmares!*

Chapter 5

Any other day, she would have been taking her morning hike with her husband. Instead, Lara sat at the island countertop in the kitchen of her Victorian farmhouse, sipping coffee and becoming absorbed once more in the details of her repeating dream. It took place in another time—the last century, it appeared to Lara. She thought it a little odd that she would dream so vividly of an old-fashioned inn, and it wasn't this one. *Yes, Lara, that's what is so odd about all of this.* She shook her head as she ridiculed herself. And yet, she *did* know that hotel in her dream from somewhere. And that time period; that felt right, too. She was not fondly drawn to that time and place in history, but she was drawn to it nonetheless.

She allowed her eyes to travel the perimeter of her big country-Victorian kitchen. The room, which she had painted in the palest of yellows, had ten-foot ceilings, original cabinetry and lots of double-hung windows that sprang from near-floor to near-ceiling, splashing the room with natural light. A single high shelf circled the room. On that shelf, sat a parade of antique cookie jars—over one hundred. Lara had begun collecting the pottery to decorate her parlor where the guests enjoyed breakfast, but the collection quickly overflowed into the kitchen. The jars were intended to serve as a conversation ice-breaker for the guests, and they always served their purpose. The pottery procession put a smile on most every travel-weary face that encountered them. Lara liked what they epitomized for her: a time in America's history—arguably a better time—when every kitchen had a cookie jar, and all were filled with a mother's freshly baked treats.

Lara imagined the excited, chattering children, fresh off their little yellow buses, washing their hands at the kitchen sink so they could dig with pudgy fingers into the cookie jar. So vivid was Lara's Rockwell-esque daydream that she could actually smell the cookies and feel the warmth of a kitchen well-used. She could even envision a young mother, pretty in pearls, pouring gleaming glasses of cold milk and admonishing, 'just one cookie, children. You don't want to be spoiling your supper.' She drew upon soapy television shows of old to concoct such daydreams, since she and Lainy never had a foster-mother who baked for them. Also within her idyllic imaginings, Lara never had to fight off a foster father with a knife, in order to protect her baby sister.

Their childhoods may have been something from a nightmare, but Lara's cookie jar parade encouraged lovely daydreams. *That* is why she began collecting them, and *that* is why she kept the one cookie jar on her countertop, filled. Before Lara knew it, she was receiving antique cookie jars for birthday, Christmas gifts and more.

There was one more bond between Lara and her turn-of-the-century kitchen; Lara was a bit of a gourmet cook, and the spacious old kitchen allowed her to turn out spectacular meals for her family and guests. When it came to cooking and cleaning, Lara knew she was a tad-bit obsessive-compulsive. That is the not-so-unexpected result of struggling for order in an early-life filled with revolving foster care doors.

But that was childhood, and her childhood was long in the past. She had a loving family and a beautiful home; it had been a lifelong dream come true, and Lara felt truly blessed. But the roots of their family tree were generation-shallow, and it was something that gnawed at Lara. She and Lainy knew nothing of their biological parents. Lara had vague memories—she knew her mother had long brown hair and her father's was strawberry-blonde with a beard and mustache. Beyond that, Lara would not know either of them if she passed them on the street. She sort of remembered sleeping in the back of an old station wagon, a beige Rambler, when she was just a toddler and Lainy was only two years old. Neither sister had any recollections beyond that. As far as they knew, they had no relatives, living or dead; it had always been Lainy and her against the world. Both girls harbored a hope they would someday learn of step-brothers and sisters, cousins, or even grandparents; some relative *somewhere* to show them where they belonged in the world. Lara wished for a family tree with roots.

Running the B&B was something Lara thought she could do happily for the rest of her life with her husband, that is, if they could make enough money doing it. She loved working from home and having the luxury of being "stay-home parents" to their young daughter, Claire. Their new lifestyle suited Lara perfectly—so much so, in fact, that Lara wondered if she had been an innkeeper in another life. She was reflecting on that possible previous life as she spoke on the phone to her sister.

"Do you promise you won't laugh?"

"No. Come on, Lara. What is it?"

Lara took in a deep breath and then blurted out, "I keep having this same dream over and over again. Isn't that weird?"

Lainy's sigh was audible, "Is that all? You have the same dream now and then? God, I thought it was something really important, like you found a lump, or our Phantom of the Opera tickets are counterfeit. You know, I have a dream that I've had over and over too. I don't think it's all that weird. I bet a lot of people have them."

"Oh, I don't know about that, Lainy." Lara considered again whether she should even involve her sister in this matter. She had a queer feeling about it. It was the same kind of dread she'd felt when she was graduating from Junior High School and she was invited to her first slumber party. Six of them, feeling all grown up, staying awake all night, playing pranks, eating junk food, and dabbling with the spirits of ax murderers, which had a few of the girls secretly wetting their baby dolls, had piled into the bathroom to repeat "Bloody Mary," four times in front of the mirror. For all of their bravado, not one of the girls ever uttered the name a fourth time. They giggled and jostled and dared each other to do so, but no one did. Even so, Lara had trouble sleeping that night. She'd tried to laugh off the dreadful feeling swirling in her stomach, way back then, as she tried now to no avail. There was something about involving Lainy in this dream business that felt like she was saying "Bloody Mary" for the fourth and final time. *That's just silly*, Lara admonished herself.

Through the phone she could hear Lainy raising her voice a bit. "I said, what is this dream about that it scares you so much?"

"I didn't say it scared me, Lainy. But I am getting tired of watching some woman get murdered in my head while I'm trying to sleep," Lara said with exasperation.

"A woman? Oh. I thought you meant nightmares about…you know. But, hey, I've had the same dream several times where I see a woman getting killed," Lainy said. "I know it's not me in the dream, so I don't even get the teeniest bit scared," she continued matter-of-factly. She took a sip of chilled Chardonnay. "I think it's kind of interesting. I find it hard to believe that you don't! Anyway, I'm not even sure the woman in my dream is actually murdered. The dream always ends the same way. I get this fuzzy feeling about me that is not at all unpleasant, and it just ends. I never get to see the whole thing."

*Bloody Mary.* Lara looked around the kitchen for an open window or something that would explain the cold chill that just skipped down her spine. Could it be that she and her sister were having the same repeating nightmare? Maybe. But Lara *knew* the woman in her dream was murdered.

"Lainy, does your dream look like it takes place in the late 1800s, and is the woman wearing a royal blue dress?"

Lainy had been relaxing in a thickly cushioned bamboo swivel chair with her legs tucked comfortably under her and her glass of wine casually bolstered against the arm cushion. At her sister's surprise conjecture, she jerked upright and splashed wine over the pillow.

"God, Lara! I hate it when you do that!"

She jumped up for a kitchen towel. Dabbing at the liquid which was, so far, sitting atop the fabric, Lainy chided her sister. "Could you please stop surprising me with your little voodoo ESP tricks? I just spilled wine all over my favorite chair."

Lara was suddenly aware that something truly unique was happening with these dreams; they weren't just repetitious, they were also shared between sisters. "Lainy, how long have you been having your dream?"

"Sheez, I don't know…I think I was still a teenager."

*Years! Her sister has had the same dream for years, too. Surely, this could not be a common occurrence. Surely, this must mean something… significant.*

"I'll bet your dream woman is in a saloon talking to a handsome guy, and then she walks outside to cool off and is grabbed by someone, taken around the side of the saloon and shot in the head…I'll bet that's when you wake up every time. Am I right, Lainy?"

Lainy had reclaimed her chair and tucked her feet up under her, even higher. She hugged herself for comfort and for warmth. *Was it her imagination, or did the sun just go behind a cloud?* Lara's voice on the phone took on a strange, echo-y quality. Lainy threw back the rest of her wine and swiped at her mouth rather sloppily.

Lara repeated her question a bit louder, "Isn't that right, Lainy?"

Lainy stared out the window at the beautifully-sunny day and answered a bit husky from the wine, "Yes. That's when I wake up...every time."

# Chapter 6

"You know you guys are causing a disturbance," Jeff joked, poking his head and shoulders out the verandah's side door. "You better hope you don't cause any accidents. I don't think we're covered for this."

The girls giggled.

"Hey, Jeff, I'm advertising for you!" Lainy shot back. "This is good for business."

He observed the empty bottle of champagne on the counter and the empty pitcher between their feet. "I'm not sure I can afford having you advertise for me, Lainy."

"Oh, you got me cheap. It's Andre."

"We *love* Andre," Lara piped in.

"I don't suppose you thought to leave some for me," he feigned hurt.

"You know, we didn't drink all of that…" Lainy teased.

Jeff gave his sister-in-law a funny look. "It looks empty to me."

"Hands did it again," Lainy giggled at the nickname and the inside joke; her sister talked with her hands, a lot. And she broke and spilled stuff, a lot; thus the nickname, Hands.

"Shut up," Lara threw a wadded up dish towel at her. "Anyway, only a tablespoon spilled out of the bottle when it tipped—"

"You mean *flew*, don't you?" Lainy interrupted.

"Because I swooped it up before it had a chance to go sloshing all over the countertop." Lara finished. She stuck her tongue out at her sister.

"Hands, you spilled all the champagne? Again?"

Lara gave her husband a seductive shoulder roll and batted her eyelashes. "Who are you gonna believe, baby? The girl giggling like her IQ fell forty points, or the woman who has another bottle chilling for you...for later?" She rose and gave her husband a sip of champagne from her glass. "Besides, you can't drink before work. You don't want to get into any *more* trouble," she winked at him.

"Huh? What trouble?" Lainy turned to look at her brother-in-law, noted his wry smile, and demanded to know what they were talking about.

"I'll tell you later," said Lara. "Anyway, I'm sure you'll hear all about it in the Neskowin gossip-mill."

"Oh my Gosh. You pulled another stunt in *Neskowin*? Where you have your bowel movement in the morning and everyone knows what color it was by noon?" Lainy laughed outright.

"My husband just can't seem to leave his wise-cracking at home, and some people don't appreciate his sense of humor, is all. Right, baby?" Lara kissed him, gripped his biceps and gave them flirty squeezes. "Come home early?" she whispered breathy and seductively in his ear.

"I'll see what I can do." He smiled, pulled her hands off of him, and placed them at her sides. "What are you trying to do to me, woman?"

"Hey, Jeff, where's my little Cornflake?" Lainy wanted to know.

"Uh, you won't believe this. Your niece is out in the blackberries collecting garden spiders while she listens to the Phantom of the Opera soundtrack on her Walkman," a hint of pride evident in his voice.

"Sheez, my niece is beautiful *and* brilliant," Lainy remarked, slurring her words ever-so-slightly, giving a hint to the amount of wine she had consumed.

He was going to say something, but another car honked in response to Lainy's toasting salute, and the girls giggled again. Jeff shook his head with a facetious air of hopelessness.

"I got a shift. I'm going."

"Okay. I love you," Lara said.

He kissed her quickly and whispered in her ear, "Be good."

"Always."

It was doing Lara good to unwind and enjoy her verandah. The day had turned out with surprisingly good weather after having rained all night. Everything as far as her eyes could see was rolling, lush, and green, and blanketed by a sky that looked like the crayon named for it. The smell of the woods was fresh and thickly seasoned with the pleasing scent of burning alder and apple wood from a neighboring property. A bevy of bird calls and the occasional moos from spotted cows in the pasture across the road completed an idyllic setting.

Lainy turned in her chair to look at Lara. "Spill it—not literally—what did he do?"

"It's killing you, huh?" Lara laughed.

"*Yes.* Spill it, Hands."

"Okay, okay. Well, he and his partner went to a "man-in-distress" call in the Neskowin village, and when they got there, this guy—he was wearing women's clothing, makeup, and wig—was in the front yard, jumping up and down, shrieking and pointing to the cottage. Anyway, he started pulling Mike, Jeff's partner, by the hand into the house and down a hallway, and all they could understand from the guy was that his boyfriend was in some sort of trouble. So, Mike went through the door first, looked, turned to Jeff, and said, 'whaddya say to that?' Jeff came through the door, and there was this naked guy on all fours on the bed, and he, uh, he had a, um, well, just the back end was all they could see—just the tail section to about half of the top fin—of a live fish wiggling in the guy's…"

"Ewww. Okay, that's enough. I snapped a mental picture, thank you very much." She took a sip of wine.

Lara giggled, "Okay, so, the question was, what do you say to that, and Jeff took one look, turned to the man's boyfriend, or whatever, and said, 'your friend really needs to chew his food better!'"

"Oh, Jeff," Lainy started laughing and couldn't stop.

Lara was laughing too. "Yeah, well, he's going to lose a whole week of shifts because of that remark, just as soon as all vacation requests are covered. I told him I wasn't certain we could afford his sense of humor."

They finally spent their laughter, but not before their sides ached. Another motorist honked at the women.

"This place is so beautiful," Lainy remarked.

"Mm-hmm," Lara offered vaguely. She hadn't been able to find reference of a single similar dream—that being a dream that is both repetitive *and* shared—in any of the materials she'd gotten from their tiny local library. *Boy, sometimes life in a small town could be aggravating.*

Lara had rushed through her share of cleaning the inn, so she could dart over to the library and find something that would help her to understand the dream. She didn't have a lot of time left to share her limited findings with her sister before guests began checking-in later in the afternoon. The first thing she wanted to go over with Lainy was a book full of paranormal dream case histories. According to the book, it was rare for dreams to be shared by persons. The author, a prominent psychologist and professor at a northeastern University, verified what Lara had already suspected. Their dream was a paranormal one; it most likely was revealing a past-life experience. But there was no explanation for why she and Lainy *both* experienced the recurring dream, and had apparently done so for many years.

She turned and studied Lainy, who was mesmerizing herself with the wriggling of her brightly painted toenails. She had kicked her remarkably high-heeled sandals off the moment she hopped up on the porch swing. They'd been swinging on the wrap-around verandah of the big Victorian, sharing a pitcher of cheap champagne with orange juice and peach schnapps, as they watched the procession of tourists' cars traveling south on 101, the Coast Highway. The sisters resembled each other in the face. But beyond that, they could not be more different from one another. Lara was tall and slender, with auburn-tinged blond hair that she kept above-shoulder length, but still long enough to pull into a banana clip when she was cleaning. Lainy, on the flip-side, was five-foot three inches short, and trim. Lainy had a luxurious long red mane cut in the old Farrah style. The cut apparently never went out of style where men are concerned. Lainy turned the head of every man she passed by.

When it came to makeup and adornments, Lara subscribed to 'less is more.' Not Lainy. A flirtatious flip of her hair revealed huge dangle earrings, which she described as "fun."

"Oh, you rotter! You went Goodwill hunting without me?" Lara eyed the newest additions to Lainy's dime store-addiction jewelry collection.

"Sorry." Lainy pouted her lips for emphasis. "I was in Lincoln City yesterday, so I stopped in. Do you like 'em?"

"Yes, they're super cute. I like your walking shorts and scarf, too."

"I know. They still had the store tags on them, from Jones New York. Six bucks I paid for these. Huge score. Whoo-hoo!" Lainy's hands did a raise-the-roof.

Lara smoothed self-conscious hands over her sweet, calf-length culottes in blue and white flowers. She wore nothing more than a pair of pearl studs in her ears.

Lainy spotted the self-conscious mannerism. She could remember a time when her sister had lived in blue jeans and cute tops. But now, Lara's style had to do double-duty; she didn't want to wear clothing too nice or shoes too uncomfortable, that she might ruin cooking breakfast and readying the inn's rooms in the morning. But she also had to be mindful not to look too casual when meeting her guests in the afternoon. No one, Lainy was certain, would ever guess that her sensibly-dressed, mild-mannered sister had a sealed juvenile record for joyriding in a stolen Spyder Fiat.

"Aw, sis, I know that you have to dress…conservatively to be an innkeeper."

"You called me Mother Theresa the last time we went shopping together. I would love to be able to wear shoes like those and earrings like those…" Lara pouted for her.

"Yeah, but you do rock that Mother Theresa look," Lainy giggled.

"Shut up," Lara said.

"Just tellin' you straight up," Lainy pushed off with her foot and got them swinging again. "Ya know? Keepin' it real."

"How 'bout keepin' it zipped?"

Lainy continued to raise her glass and wave at the cars, more often than not gaining a few quick beeps from their horns. Her legs swung jauntily from her seat as she giggled playfully, and Lara was struck with a sudden, strong wave of deja-vu.

Her thoughts drifted far away for a few moments. When she snapped out of it Lara told her sister, "I think I drank too much."

"That's good!"

"Listen, Lainy, this book I got from the library says the kind of dream we're having is really rare. The author is some power-that-be doctor in his field, which is…wait…first of all, how would you feel about hypnosis?"

"I'm okay with it. You are feeling very sleepy…"

"You're hilarious. Now listen, this doctor recommends it. I mean, if you want to try and get more *physical* details about your dream material, he can usually help you by putting you under a hypnotic regression." She hesitated. She did put a lot of stock in what her younger sister thought of her. She didn't want Lainy thinking she had lost her nut. Lara took a quick gulp of woodsy air and blurted, "I think I'd like to do it."

Lainy laughed at her older sister's serious tone and obvious reservations. "Well great!"

"So…let's go call the professor guy." She nudged her sister playfully. "You better do it before you sober up, or you won't do it at all. I know you, Lara."

Lara sighed and rose to collect the empty champagne flutes. Lainy knew her all right. The girls left the verandah to go inside and contact the university where the author/professor taught— while Lara was still loosened up with champagne. "And then I need to begin sobering up before my guests start arriving." She looked at her watch. "Oh no, check-in begins in less than an hour!"

The author/professor's department was happy to recommend a therapist-hypnotist in the Northwest. Lara was given the name of Dr. Rachel Carrell, in Longview, Washington, who was currently researching case histories involving psychic dreams of all types: prophetic, warning, survival, reincarnation, and out-of-body experiences. Lara thought Dr. Carrell sounded like she fit the ticket, all right. She tried to shake off the unwelcome imperceptions, that they were about to dabble in some pagan occult for which they will surely be condemned.

She hung up the phone and turned to Lainy, her face as taut as her pony tail. "I did it. I made an appointment for us to meet Doctor Rachel Carrell, in Long View, the day after tomorrow."

Even in her slightly-inebriated state, Lainy could see that something was really bugging her sister. "Hey, Sweetie…are you *that* afraid to be hypnotized? I mean, Lara, if—"

"No, no, I'm not afraid of hypnotism. I've been hypnotized before, Lainy; once in high school, and another time at a bachelorette party held at a Chippendale's. So, no, I think I always knew a day would come when I would want to investigate this dream. I just never had the time or the money."

"Well then what is it, Lara? Because you seem really freaked out right now."

"Lainy, okay, here's the thing. I wasn't worried when it was *my* dream. But ever since I found out you were having the same dream, I've had a bad feeling about it."

"Whaddya mean, like something bad will happen?"

"Exactly." Then Lara smiled. "I don't know, Lainy. It's just a feeling."

"Yeah, but it's one of *your* feelings." She sat down heavily on a bar stool at the kitchen island. "You know what, Lara? I think this time it's just heebie-jeebies. Honestly, *how* could a dream possibly hurt us? I think it *is* possible, though, even likely, that all of those Jesus-on-black-velvet paintings our foster mom had hanging all over the house, might have given you a hyper-aversion to all things—paranormal."

Lara sat too, hands immediately traveling to the knick knacks on the countertop, which she began straightening with precision as she tried to organize the thoughts in her head. She stopped fussing and turned to her sister with sarcasm, "Hyper-aversion, huh?"

"Shut up," Lainy grinned. "Or something bad *is* going to happen to you."

Lara laughed with her sister, but her head was full of Mother Cary's chickens, signaling, cautioning: *not me, Lainy. It's you. I'm afraid for you.*

# Chapter 7

10 March, 1993
Washington, D.C.

S he tipped the small pail toward her and looked inside. *Peanuts in the shell—now that's class. Guess I don't need to feel under the simulated wood-grain Formica to figure out how regular customers dispose of their chewing gum.*

There were dozens of establishments in Washington where the rich and powerful met to merchandise their advocacies. Spike's Tavern was not one of them, which is precisely why he had chosen it. Senator Cilla had to concede, she was not likely to be recognized in this dump. It was now a few minutes after 2:00 p.m., and she was beginning to feel uneasy. The bartender (no doubt the estimable Spike, himself), and two more unshaven men at the bar, kept eyeballing her and talking between themselves. From the looks she was getting, she surmised they probably didn't see many impeccably-dressed females with perfectly coifed hair walk through the doors. She assumed they were sizing her up as a possible one-nighter. *Yuk, I'd rather suck mud,* she thought to herself.

The men at the bar were indeed talking about her. Spike boasted that he could settle their argument over the horsy-faced matron, in under a minute. He broke up a few of his mint-flavored toothpicks under the bar and out of sight; then he lined them up even at the top and hid the rest of the picks in his meaty fist.

"Who's goin' first?"

Mike took off his ball cap, ran his greasy hand over his greasy hair, and replaced the cap. Finally, he reached over and grabbed one. He smiled. It was a whole toothpick. The little fella named Neil grabbed one of the remaining two. He smiled as well. He'd chosen a short one. He'd wanted to be the one to do it all along. He had two rounds bet on the old broad's sexual orientation. The customers both agreed she was a lesbian, while the bartender insisted she was straight, but a "really dry lay." Spike had asked which one of them was sauced enough to go ask her, and they decided they were all sauced enough. So they drew straws.

A loud burst of bawdy laughter broke out at the bar and Neil rose from his stool, prepared to teeter on over. Just then, a fifty-ish man with a pompous air, and wearing a charcoal suit and spit-shined shoes, approached the woman's table and sat down.

"Crap," muttered Neil as he fell back into his chair.

"Thank you, gentlemen." Spike collected the money and dropped it in his tip jar behind the register. The two customers were still muttering about the couple when he turned back around.

"They're boring…Forget about 'em."

"Bet she wears gloves when she gives him a hand job," Mike grumbled.

"Bet she don't give no hand jobs," Spike retorted. He reached under the bar and pulled out a cup with some dice in it. The men at the bar turned their attentions to Ship-Captain-Mate-Crew, wherein Spike proceeded to gamble away some of his beer profits.

Without preliminaries, the man with sharp features and sharp pant creases announced, "sixty-five days ago it was reintroduced by two Republicans from your State, Senator, on the very first day of the 103rd Congress. Since it passed the house last time, we feel it's bound for success. You know, it might well have passed the Senate had it not been for your filibuster lasting until Congress adjourned. But, it appears they are wasting no time this session."

She kept him waiting for an answer. She started in with her disgusting habit of digging into the inside corners of her eyes for eye-goo and rolling it between her fingers until the stuff disappeared. He grimaced and self-consciously adjusted his tie. He nervously crossed his legs, patted his thinning hair, and played with the knife-sharp creases of his trouser legs. Finally, eyeing him smugly above her stylish rose-colored frames she declared, "I believe I was just about to be propositioned by those three scum bags at the bar. You certainly took your time getting here, Vanderling."

All in all, the meeting had gone well; she was pleased with the results. Vanderling never even flinched at her price. Senator Cilla, a.k.a. God-cilla to her less than admiring Republican constituency, had reason to feel good. Globalesque Mining Company was offering an enormous amount of money in return for a cake-and-pie favor. When HR 230 passed the House this session, she was the single force who could kill it in the Senate. She would champion the positive effects that a mining operation would have on local economy. After all, it was her State, and she was merely looking out for its best interests. In her opinion, a boost to local economy is of far greater importance than the "historical integrity" of Bodie State Park, even if it is the most well-preserved ghost town in America.

Other than Vanderling and herself, there were only two other people on the planet who were aware of any existing adverse effects from previous mining exploration, for which HR 230 would mandate expensive clean-up operations. Heck, the "previous mining" in Bodie had petered out around 1880. Even that pain-in-the-ass grassroots organization, Friends of

Bodie, gave no thought to how the gold was mined over one hundred-plus years ago. Not one of them raised any concern with the clean-up portion of the proposed Bill. Their lawyers were preoccupied with the effects that blasting and tunneling would have on the historic town.

This little-bitty favor that was going to pay her *so* huge, was going to be a-piece-of-cake and easy-as-pie. All she had to do was see to it the Bill failed. So long as they removed any threat of detoxification expenditures, Globalesque would have no trouble selling their holdings at Bodie. Senator Cilla smiled wickedly to herself as she popped another hickory-flavored almond. She could make or break this thirty-five million dollar deal for Globalesque. They damn well ought to be grateful.

# Chapter 8

11 March, 1993
Longview, Washington

There were no wing chairs in soft leather, or cherry wood bookshelves stocked with tomes and pretensions surrounding the room. There wasn't even a couch. Rachel Carrell's office was not at all what the girls had envisioned: a poorly-lit, overstuffed office that would have suffocated with leather bindings and wood polish—pretty much all that they had gleaned from books and movies. Then the doctor stepped through the door bearing no resemblance to Sigmund Freud, whatsoever.

Doctor 'call-me-Rachel' Carrell was petite in form and fine-featured, with lively eyes of denim-blue and bourbon-colored hair, cut sassy and tousled. She opted for a comfortable, casual style of dress, yet still looked, as Lainy would phrase it, very put-together. Lainy guessed the doctor's closet was an army of classic pieces from Anne Taylor Loft, sneakers and bootie-style shoes—and Lainy was precisely on the mark. Rachel did not even own a conservative suit, and she would *never* sacrifice her dainty little feet to pinch-me-tight pumps.

Rachel shook hands with the sisters and introductions were made. She gestured to them to take a seat. The first thing Lainy noticed about the doctor was her bust line, which entered the room a second or two before the rest of her. The second thing was the doctor's earrings; they were simple hooks sporting rather large, highly-polished rectangles of abalone shell. Lainy liked the doctor right away, and she really liked those earrings.

Rachel offered the girls afternoon tea. "Earl Grey is all that I have. I'm really a morning coffee person myself," she explained.

Lainy declined with a slight wave of her hand. "Just had my teeth whitened."

Lara accepted.

While Rachel was fetching hot water for the tea, the girls surveyed the room.

"Nice taste," Lainy whispered.

"I know, I love it. And, my God, these chairs. I feel like I'm sitting in a cloud, don't you? The hypnotic-regression business must be booming," Lara joked. Then added more seriously, "I wonder what she uses for incense."

"I *know*! That smell is so...fam—you know what it reminds me of?"

"What?"

"SoCal, the orange groves. Remember when we used to be able to drive down the 405 freeway, and just before Irvine the air would be filled with the smell of all the orange groves?"

"Sure. But that was years ago, Lainy. We were little kids. Orange County doesn't have orange groves anymore."

"Kill joy." Lainy wrinkled her nose at her sister.

Rachel rolled a rattan and glass drink cart into the private office. The top section of her clever cart held an inset tray which Rachel lifted out and placed on the table. She asked everyone to help themselves, and as Lara reached for a packet of artificial sweetener, Lainy noticed how her hands shook. "Don't be scared, Lara."

A nervous laugh escaped her sister. "I guess I am a little nervous about this," she confessed.

Rachel smiled and settled deeply into her own chair. "That's understandable, Lara," she remarked. "You did say over the telephone that you have never before been hypnotized, correct?"

Lara shook her head as she sipped at the hot tea. "Actually, I have been hypnotized before. Twice, in fact. The first time was in a high school class, where we were all hypnotized to believe we received eight hours of sleep during half of an hour on the classroom floor. It sure worked for me. Wish I knew where that guy lives. The second time was in a nightclub. That was…I was hypnotized with nine other people, and apparently we all did some pretty embarrassing things, which I am *not* big on repeating." She stopped to switch her ever-present smile into a curt scowl at her sister, who had started giggling. Lainy knew 'the embarrassing things' that Lara was made to do under hypnosis. "Anyway, they tell me I'm a good subject." Lara stared at Lainy a moment, took a deep, exasperated breath and told the doctor, "My friends tell me I danced around on stage and sang as if I was Paula Abdul." Lainy and Rachel were both laughing. Lara reddened a little bit, but she laughed with them. She reached for a tall knick-knack on the table that was a Great Blue Heron standing on impossibly long legs, held the bird under her mouth as if it were a microphone and sang, "Straight up now tell me, is it gonna be you and me together, ah, ah, ah…" Lainy and Rachel giggled uncontrollably.

"Alright. Okay. You guys, seriously." She set the bird figurine down. It wobbled a little bit, so she reached out to steady it, and her hand knocked over the creamer. "Oh, I am so sorry." She blushed bright pink.

"Hands," Lainy teased.

Rachel set the creamer upright. It was a little stainless steel job like you see holding syrup on a table at Denny's; it had a hinged lid so only a few drops of cream actually leaked out onto the rattan tray, and Rachel dabbed it up with a napkin.

"That's nothing, Lara. Don't be nervous. You're with friends here. Continue, please," the therapist urged.

Lara waited a moment for everything to calm down. "What I said on the phone was that, I *uh*, I've never been to a therapist before," she glanced at Lainy for support.

Rachel smiled maternally at Lara, "I promise I won't make you act like a chicken, okay?" Lainy giggled. Rachel focused her attention on Lainy. "And you, Lainy? Are you comfortable with all of this?"

"Sure," Lainy shrugged. "I've never been hypnotized before, but I'm okay with it. I think I should warn you though, I can't dance or sing," she teased.

"Funny," Lara said, dryly. "You're a real stitch."

For more than an hour, Rachel Carrell took notes on her new subjects. She wanted to know about their childhoods, their educations, their current lives. She was especially interested in hearing about Lara's past psychic experiences and in the revelation that Lara's seven-year-old daughter, Claire, had begun to show some psychic ability. It seemed curiously evident to the sisters that Rachel was unperturbed, even relieved, to hear Lainy possessed no psychic abilities whatsoever.

"So, Lainy, you've never had a dream, or a part of a dream, that came true?"

"Nope."

"Good. Lara, when you had the premonition of your—who was it?" she referred to her notes, "Your college roommate's husband. When you first received the impression that something was wrong, were you asleep or awake?"

"I was awake. I was sick with a killer flu bug at the time, though. I don't know if that's significant, but every time I've ever had a psychic experience of any kind, it's always been when I was sick or extremely tired, or after I'd been under a lot of pressure. I was away from home at the time so I had to see a new doctor, and he gave me penicillin even though I told him I had developed a reaction to it once before. That night, I had a pretty severe reaction. And for a while, I just told myself it was the reaction that was making me feel so—anxious. It was such a horrible feeling, like dread; like something bad was going to happen, and I couldn't do a thing to stop it."

"I understand. That must have been awful. And for the other incidents? Were you awake or sleeping?"

"Sleeping. Except for the time I saw my friend's dad killed. Only he wasn't killed. I mean it turned out to be nothing, but the vision I got was really clear, and it happened while we were playing Clue in her living room."

"*Oh good.* Tell me about that one." She grabbed another ink pen from the table.

"Well, we were on the floor, and it was my turn. I had rolled the dice and was deciding which room I wanted to go to, and then this picture just flashed into my head."

"Tell me about the picture."

"It was black and white. And it was just his face and shoulders. It flashed into my head, then I saw glass shattering across the vision, then it was gone. But I was just a kid, and it upset me. So, I asked my friend where her father was, and she said he was away on business, that he'd had to fly to Chicago. She wanted to know why I asked so, like an idiot, I told her. Naturally, she got very upset. I was trying to calm her down, when we heard glass break. We were the only people in the house; her mom had taken her two younger sisters to gymnastics practice, so we were a little bit scared. We searched the house together. We looked from top to bottom, but we did not find anything that had broken."

"Very interesting."

"Well, we both had heard the sound of breaking glass. So, we were standing at the foot of the stairs trying to think of any place we forgot to check, when my eyes were sort of drawn to a door at the top of the stairs. So I asked Patty what was behind that door, and she said it was just a storage closet full of linens and old junk. It was the only place we hadn't looked, so we opened the closet, and there in the bottom of it was this old black and white headshot of her dad. For some reason, it had just fallen off the shelf and the glass had shattered."

Lainy leaned forward, "Look at the hair on my arms, you guys." It was standing straight up.

"It must have been a relief to see a shattered photograph, when you both were probably imagining the worst," Rachel offered.

"It was to me, because I was positive that's what I had seen. But my friend was a nervous wreck until her dad came home."

"And other than those two incidents, were there any others experiences while awake?"

"No. None."

"Okay. Let's move on to the dream."

Rachel asked Lara, then Lainy, to recount the dream in as much detail as each could remember.

"You both agree, then, that the woman in your dreams wore a blue dress?" Rachel asked. Both girls nodded in unison. "Ladies, that detail is a matter of great interest here." Rachel explained, "Dreams actually occur in black-and-white. The dreamer's consciousness actually assigns the colors to their dreams and fills in any other details, whenever they are asked to recount them. In your case, you each assigned the same colors. Not only that, but the dream is long-lasting. It has been scientifically proven dreams actually last mere seconds. So you see, in the details you girls match up. That's interesting," Rachel remarked. "So, what does the woman in your dream look like? Lainy?"

The question was a disarming one for Lainy, who was accustomed to describing the dream, but never the woman. "Well, now that you ask, I think she looks a lot like me. I think she has brown hair with red highlights instead of all red like mine, and her eyes are incredibly blue instead of green; maybe the royal blue dress enhances them, but they are really blue. Oh, and she definitely has Lara's long legs, not mine," she added, voicing a typical low self-esteem that foster care seems to evoke in children—girls, especially.

Lainy was a full four inches shorter than her sister's five-feet-eight-inches. And even though Lainy knew her sporty little figure was considered "cute" by men, she saw herself as stocky, with almost no waist. Possessed of humor and the usual proclivity to knock herself, Lainy used indelicate terms like "squatty-body" to describe her build.

Rachel turned to Lara with eyebrows raised. "Do you agree the woman in blue resembles Lainy?"

A frown created tiny parallel vertical lines between Lara's eyebrows as she considered Lainy's description. "You know, I always just assumed it was me in the dream. I mean, there is something of a resemblance. Yeah, she does look like Lainy. Maybe a little taller, and her hair is a little more brown than red, like mine. And she does have impossibly blue, almost violet eyes."

Rachel explained how she intended to take them both back in time, first to their childhoods, then gradually to the threshold of birth, and finally beyond and into a presumed earlier lifetime.

"We, we have some baggage—from when we were kids. Pretty bad stuff. I know I don't want to relive any of that. I'm pretty sure Lainy doesn't want to either." Lara said.

Lainy looked nervously from the doctor to her sister and back. "I, I really don't want to go there. Can we bypass all of that?"

There it was again. The look on Lainy's face reflected the something-or-other that both girls had been harboring a worry about, ever since they'd arrived. Any well-trained therapist could have recognized it; it was the sort of mask a survivor of child abuse wears: part guilt, part victor, part shame. Lainy faired better than most.

"Of course, Lainy. I'll ask your permission all along the way before we open any doors to your past. You have my word." Rachel looked to both sisters before continuing with just a hint of sadness in her honey'd voice. "What we're trying to achieve is called hypnotic regression."

Rachel explained that the hypnosis is actually performed in stages, providing both Lara and Lainy could be put into hypnotic states. If successful, they would be able to describe scenes and associations from their previous lives in greater detail than was possible through their genetically-shared dream. Rachel told them they might be able to bring to the surface some details of those lives, which could then be verified by conventional records.

# Chapter 9

Rachel's smooth voice rocked them back and forth. "Now you are souls waiting for the next life. You are on a bed of clouds, with sheer white curtains, that are curiously held up by nothing at all, and they are gently waving in the warm, gentle, summer breeze, like beautiful angles dancing. You are in the prettiest summer dress you can imagine. You are curled up on your very own clouds, sucking your thumbs, rocking, dreaming, patiently waiting for your next summons to mortal life."

"*Yes*," Lainy murmured softly.

"But wait," Rachel's soft lilting voice was just a perception stronger. "You've forgotten something, something quite important, actually. You can't go yet. You can't go yet, because once you do, you'll forget who you were before. So you must go back to your last day. Just for a few moments; just for the briefest time, go back for that last day, to find whatever it is you forgot."

"Okay," Lara's lip quivered, and her voice sounded childish.

"I promise it will be okay. You won't get into any trouble. You're just going back for a little while. And then you can go on." She paused and let them wrestle with the suggestion until their faces looked relaxed again. Rachel thought sadly that both girls seemed truly afraid of what someone of authority might do to them. She would be careful. "Sleep, Lainy."

"Uh-huh," she sighed.

"I'm talking to Lara. Where are you, Lara?"

"In Indiana."

"What are you doing?"

"I'm calling for Frank Junior. He's the third."

"Why are you looking for Frank, Lara?"

"He's my son. He drinks. He drinks too much."

"Do you know what it is you forgot, Lara?"

"Yes. I forgot to tell my son that I love him. I wanted to ask him to stop drinking. For the sake of his wife and two boys. Poor man lost his first wife and infant son to cholera. Frank's second wife is sick with tuberculosis. His boys need him."

"Do you remember the night when the woman in the blue dress was murdered?'

"Yes. I saw it. I could never forget it. I should have done something for her. I should have done something but I just stood there, frozen."

"What is your name in this life, Lara?"

"Frank. Frank Junior. I'm the second."

"What else can you tell me about that night, Lara?"

"Get out of Bodie. Get out of Bodie tonight."

"Where is Bodie, Frank Junior, and what night is it?"

"The desert. California. Never go there. Bad men in Bodie. Bad whiskey, bad weather, bad men, bad, bad…"

"What night did she die, Frank? What night was it?"

"March first."

"What year, Frank?"

Lara looked directly at Rachel with pure confusion. "1879, of course."

She tried more with Lara, but the poor soul was so frightened about getting back to her cloud. Rachel did not want to risk any emotional damage. She worked with Lainy, but she turned out to be as resistant as her sister. The two subjects validated each other, however. And Rachel did learn that Lainy was the woman in the dream. She was also able to get the dream woman's full name. Now they had something with which to do conventional research.

Her fingers snapped sharply and her soothing voice beckoned, "You should wake up now, girls."

Lara cast herself forward in her chair, complete surprise registering on her pretty face. Lainy smoothed her fingers across the skin beneath her eyes and blinked several times. The two sisters looked at each other a bit drowsily, then burst into laughter. Daylight that had been filtering through the shutters was now dim and wintry. Soft lights had been turned on around the room, and at some point Rachel had turned on music; relaxing, instrumental sounds that seemed to come from the ceiling tiles. Lara felt deliciously serene as though she'd had a long, luxurious nap. She couldn't help the yawn which escaped her. Meanwhile, Lainy was trying to remember just when they might have gone to sleep. She didn't remember much of anything beyond Rachel's talk of clouds and such. And of course, after the long drive to Washington, neither of the girls had a bit of trouble feeling sleepy.

The doctor reached over to the recorder on the coffee table and switched it off. Relaxing back in her chair, she announced, "It was very enlightening. My initial suspicion is that we are actually dealing with a reincarnation or genetic-memory dream from Lainy's previous lifetime." She noted the quick glance between the sisters and anticipated the question she knew was coming. "It's exactly what I would have expected. You see, those of us who have reincarnation dreams are rarely, if ever actually, psychic or show discernible talents with ESP in other areas.

"Early into the session, it became clear that the woman in blue, her name is Elise Swazey by the way, was actually Lainy in an earlier lifetime. And because you have psychic abilities, Lara, you were allowed to 'pick-up', if you will, on Lainy's recurrent dream. Lara, when I took you back, you told me you saw it. You were there, watching, but not a part of the incident. You could not tell me how you knew what went on inside the saloon, or how you knew what the woman in blue was feeling. Lainy could. Lainy was the woman in blue. But you could describe fully the scene that took place on the side of the building. When I asked you how it was you knew about that part so precisely, well, that's when you answered that you were there. Neither one of you dreams of a third person present at the side of the building. I don't know yet how Lara's past life relates to all this." She turned to Lara and said with humor, "You were a man in that life. I thought you might find that interesting."

The room was quiet enough to hear a pin drop. Then Rachel leaned forward eagerly, "It is an extraordinary case, ladies. I'll be honest with you, I would really like the opportunity to explore this further, ultimately with the hope of publishing your case. It would require a few more sessions, for which there would be no fee involved of course, but if you're agreeable to continuing sessions there is a good chance we can actually solve the mystery of Elisc Swazey and put the dreams to rest." Rachel tried to remain calm as she waited for the girls to accept her offer. Lara and Lainy were awed. And not just by the doctor's interpretation of the dream or by her proposal. They were stunned into silence by her revelation of the woman in blue's name.

"Could Lainy have lived before as, say, our great, great grandmother, Rachel?" Lara asked quietly.

Rachel looked thoughtful. She tapped her pencil against the notepad as she searched her memory for studies on genetic dreams. "Are you asking if Lainy could be having genetic dreams instead of reincarnation dreams? It's possible, and that is why I mentioned it. But I also tend to dismiss the idea, Lara, since genetic dreams almost always occur with persons who have displayed strong psychic abilities."

"I think what Lara meant, doctor, is could I be having both kinds of dreams—I mean, could I be having reincarnation dreams of a previous life, with that life being that of my great, great grandmother's?"

"Well, that would be *my* dream come true, but I honestly don't recall any such case history at all. What makes you ask?" she reached for her cup of tea.

"I know I asked you to keep our real names anonymous, so of course you wouldn't have asked, but...our maiden name is 'Swazey.'"

Rachel's mug trembled as she lifted it to her lips. *What on earth was going on here?* She wondered. She suddenly felt as though she had stepped through the looking glass; this case was getting curious and curious-er. She was going to need her mentor's help in order to understand the significance of this new wrinkle, but she couldn't stem the excitement racing through her.

"I don't know what import this revelation brings, girls. I assure you, I plan to spend a good deal of time and energy trying to untangle the mystery of it all. In the meantime, let's not expend too much of our energies on individual questions right now. We really need to focus on the total case and on getting to the heart of the memories which you dream about." She tried hard not to sound too eager or excited, but this was a rare and unique case, and Rachel wanted it in the worst way. She was certain that if handled correctly, it could make her famous in her profession; it could perhaps become a bestselling book.

Lainy was flush with intrigue as she nervously scratched at her nail polish, "Why am I having dreams about a past lifetime at all? I mean, why me?" she asked.

"Well, you're big girls, so I won't insult you by being delicate. Studies in this area indicate memories intrude most often when that previous life has been tragically cut short in some manner, or if there was some important, unfinished business. It is generally agreed that the experiences of those persons who lead full lives are never remembered in another, later life. In any case, the next life seems to be granted the memories as sort of a bonus. They can actually influence the present existence," she smiled. "You're lucky in a way, Lainy. This phenomenon grants you the lessons of a previous lifetime for you to learn from and to apply to your own life, or an opportunity to put past injustices right."

The therapist enlightened Lainy on the potential benefits of having reincarnation dreams, while Lara tried to shake a dreadful concern she was afraid she already knew the answer to. She bluntly interrupted their discussion. "Excuse me, Rachel, but you keep referring to the incident at the side of the saloon as a "scene." I want to know, was she murdered? I mean, Elise Swazey's life was cut tragically short, wasn't it?"

Rachel looked sadly at Lara, then at Lainy. "I'm sorry, Lara. Yes," she answered. "I believe we will soon be able to confirm she was violently murdered on March 1, in the year 1879. But I also believe she had some unfinished business, something serious, critical, and obviously dangerous. Whatever happened to Elise Swazey on that night, it went down in a gold-rush town named Bodie, in the California desert."

# Chapter 10

Something was wrong with Mommy. Claire knew her mother and her Aunt Lainy had gone a long way to see a special doctor about their dreams. Maybe the doctor told her she had a tumor. Claire interrupted her parents' quiet conversation to ask. Her parents burst into laughter.

Lara tried to sound like Arnold in Kindergarten Cop when she said, "It's not a toom-ah." This time, Claire laughed too. "No, really honey, there's nothing wrong with me. I'm a little sad because of what the doctor told me about the lady in my dream. She had the same name I had before I married your daddy, so she was probably my great, great Grandmother. I think it just makes me a little sad to know she died the way she did. And, I think there's something she's trying to tell me—something important. She needs me to help her, somehow, and I don't know how. But I'm fine, Cornflake. Okay?"

Claire's insights were usually far beyond what a seven-year-old should possess, and she surprised her parents once again when she told them, "But mommy, if a bad man killed your great, great gramma a long time ago, and you and Aunt Lainy have dreams about her because she wants to tell you something... mommy, maybe your great, great gramma is worried a bad man will hurt you, too."

"Oh, no-no, Cornflake. What you're referring to is something different from our dreams. They're called 'premonitions.' Premonitions are sort of like dreams, but you don't have to be asleep. They're usually, oh, like a slice of some future...event, I guess, that could happen unless someone changes it. But our dreams are about stuff that happened a long time ago. You see? It's not a premonition, at all."

"Cornflake, no one is going to hurt mommy," Jeff promised his pride-and-joy.

"So, you're just sad 'cause your great, great gramma died?"

Lara looked at Jeff and shrugged. "Yep."

"I'm sorry you're sad, Mommy." She reached for a Gala apple from the basket on the counter and bounded for the back door, hollering, "I'm glad it's not a 'premishun'! That dark man is really scary," over her shoulder as the screen door slammed shut.

"Geez," Jeff said dismally. "She's not just beautiful, she's smart too."

"Yeah, babe. You better starting polishing up the shotgun." Lara paused. "Hey? What did she say about a dark man?"

"I didn't hear that," Jeff said.

# Chapter 11

Lara could have sworn her daughter said something more, something about a premonition of a dark figure. She made a mental note to ask her daughter more about that later. She sighed. Their baby wasn't so much a baby anymore, she realized with a twinge of alarm. The pudgy baby fat was gone from Claire's cheeks and thighs. She was such a beautiful child. There had never been an awkward stage for her, lucky duck. But what truly made Claire a beautiful child was her disposition. Since the day of her birth she'd been as bright as a berry, inquisitive, and kind to every living thing.

Jeff and Lara watched their child as she played with Samantha, nicknamed 'Sammy,' their fiercely loyal Brittany Spaniel, in the back yard. Without warning, Lara was again ambushed by a wave of despair she couldn't explain. *Was something going to happen that could take her from her baby and the only man she had ever loved?*

"Well I guess there's nothing to worry about, Lara. Claire seems to have latched on to a healthy attitude toward this very old murder. I think we should both follow her lead," offered Jeff.

Lara walked around the island counter and slipped her arms around his lean waist. He was in the same good physical condition he'd been in when they were first dating. Jeff was not a big man. He was average height, quite fast, and what some called, 'wiry.' At seventeen, Jeff knew he would share his father's average build. When both of your parents die in a car accident, leaving no Will and no relatives, and you're suddenly plunked down in foster care to live out your final year as a minor, "average" is not an enviable size. It just so happened, he had come to the replacement foster home Lara and Lainy Swazey had been assigned, when their foster parents went to prison. He'd begun training in kick-boxing less than a week later, and shortly thereafter became the girls' protective "big brother" at the home. That was fifteen years ago. Lara lost track of the number of trophies her husband had won during kickboxing's heyday in the 1980s.

"I know I shouldn't really be worried. It's just…I haven't been able to shake this feeling that something's coming. It feels like learning about this old murder is going to cause some snowball effect on *our* lives, and not in a good way. I don't know, Jeff. Maybe I'm just bugged that this woman has turned out to be my great, great grandmother."

Jeff unwrapped her arms from him and held her at arms length, hands on her shoulders as though to observe her better. "Lara, let's put things in to perspective. Whatever may have happened, it was 114 years ago. Do you really think that it could possibly affect us now? I just don't see how. Except, maybe you'll find that you have family out there somewhere. Hasn't that been your dream-come-true forever?" he asked.

"Yes—," she trailed off.

Jeff gave Lara one of his lazy, crooked smiles. "Snowball, huh?" But on the inside, he was wondering if he should be worried. He had witnessed his wife's unsettling demonstrations before, and she was always right on the money. Like the times she would say, "I'll get it!" just *before* the phone would ring. So when something preyed on her mind the way this dream business did, there was probably a good reason for it.

Jeff had been present when she'd had a 'feeling' that one of her high school friends should not get on a motorcycle during a Super Bowl Sunday, many years back. Lara had felt ridiculous calling and warning him to stay off of any motorcycles for a few days, but she'd stowed her embarrassment and had called anyway. The friend must have forgotten her warning completely, or else he did not take it seriously. During half-time of the game, the guy had left the party and hopped on the back of someone's brand new motorcycle, just to take a quick spin. He died instantly when the bike went down and skidded into a fire hydrant.

For years worth of Super Bowl Sunday's, Jeff's wife could not shake the guilt that she hadn't done enough to warn her friend. He had seen first-hand why persons with psychic abilities rarely consider their special talent a 'gift.' He needed no convincing of his wife's strange feelings. In fact, Jeff was beginning to develop a feeling of his own; that they just might find some answers if they were to visit Bodie, California.

Late in the afternoon, as Lara sliced carrots and onions onto the plump sea bass filets in the poaching pan, her gaze drifted out to the pastures across the road. Absent-mindedly, she threw in the bay leaf and some seasonings and flipped the burner on before she grabbed her glass of Chianti and perched herself on the low sill of a large kitchen window. This is where Lara preferred to do her thinking. Observing the spotted cows always soothed her. *Those cows had life pretty tamed*, she thought.

Lara had never seen cows up close and personal while they had lived in Southern California. For that matter, she'd never watched a river otter slide through their front yard, or a deer snatch an apple right from her daughter's paper plate, or a black bear chase her husband out of the orchard (well, that incident kind of scared Lara, once she stopped laughing) until they moved to the Oregon Coast. True, she sometimes jokingly referred to her hometown as 'Hooterville', and now and then she would offer her husband hotcakes in a faux Hungarian accent, but the reality was, Lara genuinely loved the area and its lack of modernity. The small burgs were western in style; aged, yet preserved, and completely surrounded by virgin countryside and wild, beautiful beaches. The children that grew up in Cloverdale were unspoiled by shopping malls and video arcades. They tended to find greater interest in tree houses, 4H clubs and lizard hunts. A person actually knew his next door neighbor here, even if they were several miles away. And, yes, it was true that if you sneezed in your own bedroom, someone across town would probably hear about it soon enough to say, *God bless you*, but Lara thought Cloverdale was sanctuary. She didn't really want to leave, not even long enough to visit the California desert, as her husband had suggested. But, he was right; she could have family out there somewhere. It has been her dream to find blood relatives, to feel a connection to a network of half-siblings and cousins.

She was glad they had no business tonight, she admitted to herself. She just didn't feel like the gracious hostess all of the time, and ever since she'd seen Dr. Carrell, she'd had a lot weighing on her mind. She rose from the sill to refill her wine glass, and then she began preparing the sauce for the fish. She laughed to herself as she remembered her earlier conversation with her husband about the dinner preparations. She'd told him she thought she would whip up a light tomato-cream sauce reduction, with plenty of garlic, and she'd asked him if that sounded good.

Classic Jeff responded with, "That sounds like a lot of trouble, darlin.' Why don't you just pour some stew over it, stick it in the oven and call it good?" *That man and his canned stew…over Sea Bass filets? Ugh!* She shook her head and giggled some more.

Maybe some fettucini pasta on the side, Lara thought. And some garden fresh green beans. She loved preparing delicious meals for her family, but today she was busying herself with dinner preparations mostly as a distraction from considering Jeff's proposal. She wasn't even hungry; she had all the food for thought she needed. Earlier, her husband proposed they take a small vacation and visit Bodie. He'd reminded her he had a week off with no pay looming close. This was the same man who'd proposed pouring beef stew over Sea Bass, though, so not all of his proposals were the best ideas. She giggled. *Jeff and his Dinty Moore Beef Stew...*

To say she was a little apprehensive about a Bodie trip, would be the equivalent of saying Oregon gets a little rain. She'd argued they could not afford to close the inn, but once again her husband was right. In two weeks it would be April, and tourism on the Oregon Coast during April was absolutely dead. Chalk it up to rainy weather, income taxes, or the slow-down that followed Spring Break, but if someone fired a cannon down Coast Highway in April, chances are nothing would get hit for forty miles, maybe more. Besides, they had not taken a vacation in two years, and Lara knew Jeff was looking forward to some trout fishing in the Sierra mountains with Claire. He was just so darned positive that she and Lainy could have fun exploring Bodie State Park and put all their dream worries to rest. Lara thought it sounded like a pretty dull vacation.

# Chapter 12

And now my comrades all are gone;
Naught remains to toast.
They have left me here in my misery,
Like some poor wandering ghost.

—California Department
of Parks and Recreation

26 June, 1878
Bodie, California

The men watched as the burro shuffled at a rapid pace around the south end of the tailing ponds. They had been waiting with barely concealed tension for nearly two hours, having no way of knowing exactly when their man would ride in from the Carson Valley. Renick tossed his cheroot to the ground and violently hammered it into the dusty sand with the toe of his boot. Everything about Aaron Renick whispered violence. He was a small man, but hard and fibrous, and he carried an air of authority. He moved with startling alacrity; other men often found themselves flinching involuntarily whenever he was near. He had hair of steel—to say Renick's hair was merely gray did not suffice—like his features, which were not merely pointed, they were sharp. But it was Renick's eyes that made men jump. They were little more than scant shivers of black, slashed beneath frothing brows. And his eyes never just looked into another's, they pierced. Those eyes presently watched the horizon with a deathly calm.

By eight in the morning, the light chill and stony-hearted quiet of desert night had died, leaving rise to the glaring sunlight of common day. It was surface-of-the-sun hot. The men agreed to take turns squinting across the plain western desert. Since only sagebrush and bunchgrass decorated the slopes and coulees scattered around Bodie, the bouncing dust cloud that signified the rider was not difficult to distinguish. "There." Renick pointed southeast. The rider looked to be just a mile or so away, but no one could be certain. The temperature was withering, and heat waves distorted the image in the distance until it looked like a demon in a death dance. The stamp mill's office lacked even standing room for the five men, and so they had opted to stand outside in the shade of the small building. But the scarce shade had grown even scarcer, and so had Renick's patience.

The rider jumped from his saddle with legs so stiff he nearly went face-flat in the sand. He was wearing an odd looking cap he must have picked up during his stay overseas. He first extended his hand to Renick, then to the remaining three partners.

"I wouldn'na mind a drink, anyway," he announced. "Me throat's harborin' a nasty thirst, sirs."

Renick lit another cheroot, then growled, "Later."

The other men looked embarrassed. The good man probably ridden all night following his journey from overseas. Then he rented a mule in town, as instructed, and rode out to meet them here on the high grade. Drummond didn't doubt the poor man had a mouth full of pure Esmeralda dust. It didn't even make sense Renick wouldn't allow Svenson a drink before beginning his telling.

"Stop actin' like a jackass, Aaron." Drummond's second-guessing of Renick wasn't something most men would do. But John Drummond, a mountain of a man, was known to do as he pleased. He pleased himself to fetch a canteen from his mount and extend it to the weary agent. "I ain't gonna listen to an hour of croaking, Christ's sake. You just hold your horses, Aaron."

Svenson poured the crystal water at his mouth, slopping it greedily in and around, relishing it's coolness, it's wetness as it slaked down his throat. When he had drunk it all, he lifted the vessel above his face and shook it violently, wrenching loose a few more drops from the dark hole. Svenson wiped his chin across his forearm. The swipe left a single dirt free swath from his lower lip down, as though he and his razor had been interrupted after just the one stroke. The man handed the canteen back to Drummond with a grateful nod.

Renick was impatient. "What's the news," he demanded.

The rider looked at the apprehensive faces, "It's a simple process, Mr. Renick. I can do it for ya, and cheaply. But there's a problem."

Renick tipped his hat back to inspect the rider, then walked purposefully toward him until they were nearly toe-to-toe. He advised the man, real level and deliberate-like, "We paid a liberal sum to send you over oceans, clear to Germany. I don't even know where that is. You tell us you can do it, and do it cheap, I don't see how there can be a problem."

"Well, sir," Svenson reflexively took a step backward, clearly intimidated. "It's not the process with which lays a problem. It's what's to do with the poison when we're a'done with it." The more nervous Svenson got, the stronger his accent grew. "There's precious little water for treatin' the waste-cyanide, sir, an' it takes a frightful load of it. It would'a be a long haul to bring tha' much water out'ta here. I don' figure how we can dilute the poison, bein' so far removed from abundant fresh water, sir."

Renick glared. Then he lowered his head and shook it, disbelieving. Then he began to chuckle, and a couple of the others joined him because it was expected, though none got the joke. "Mr. Svenson," he began, "are you telling me you can do it, but you're afraid we might be corrupting this scenic landscape which surrounds us?" He asked facetiously, as he fanned his arm wide to unveil the desert. He hated this desert, and it hated him back.

Svenson looked uncomfortably from one partner to the next. "W-w-well, sir," Svenson stammered, "I, I don' think ya'r understandin' it clear. The cyanide is mortal dangerous to all livin' things. Ya can 'na just dump it some-where's. It must be disposed of proper. I been tryin' ta think a way to do it, an' come up empty." He fingered the cloth-covered button on the top of the tweed cap, which he now held in his nervous hands.

Renick laughed heartily and slapped the weary rider on his backside, nearly toppling him. "Don't you worry yourself about the poison, Svenson. The company will handle those matters. If we can't bring water for the cyanide, we'll bring the cyanide to water. On that you have my personal guarantee. Boys," He hollered expansively, "it's almost nine, and I believe I'll take my chances on a snake bite! Let's step inside the office and drink a toast to Svenson and the Touchstone Mining Company. Pard's, we have just hit pay dirt—*again*."

# Chapter 13

"How are the stocks today, Parker?" Demanded Aaron Renick as he stepped across the small office in two long strides, unbuckling and tossing his Peacemaker on the desk. Renick wore the gun on his trips out to the mill office, though he'd never had to use it. He had Morris Parker for that.

Men and women described Parker as "rather fine looking," with his half-breed complexion and large dark eyes. A curved scar bordering the left eye socket added a touch of elusive danger to his handsomeness. Certainly, his natural good looks could have earned him a position of respectability in a town like San Francisco, where image mattered. To Bodie residents, however, Parker's reputation was that of a fearsome assassin, rumored to having killed as many as ten men. Like most rumors, it was only half right and was not limited strictly to men.

He was currently employed as "negotiator" for Touchstone Mining Company. His duties required artful intimidation of other mining companies' executives whenever legal disputes arose, and he encouraged lone miners who strike a lucky vein, to see the benefit of selling out their claims to Touchstone before leaving town, usually in the middle of the night. Primarily, Parker was employed to oppose the hired guns of other mining companies, an area of his job description that he was particularly skilled in. Behind the veneer that was the second-most handsome face in Bodie, laid a pernicious mind and black heart. These were the chief assets which gained Parker such proficiency in his work.

Touchstone money allowed Morris Parker to live well. In his tailored suits and laundered shirts, he cut a handsome form. He could afford to dine at The Maison Doree, where the best quail in aspic in the whole Esmeralda region, was served. And he was a regular patron of Bodie's Philadelphia Beer Depot, though he drank cautiously and nearly always remained sober. For Parker, allowing himself to become intoxicated would be sheer foolishness and a grave danger.

Morris looked up from his newspaper, "San Francisco Stock Exchange quotes our shares selling at $48.00." He set the paper down and rocked back in the chair, placing his feet upon the desk. "Partner, that's radical." He referred to the extreme rise in share values over the last three months; they had been $0.50 a share in June, before cyanide processing was initiated.

"Yes, a radical rise." Renick mused. "Morris, I have a small matter that requires your, shall we say, aptitude for negotiation?" He paused before explaining, "Svenson is becoming a problem."

Parker nodded slowly, wickedly, as he stroked his holster, "Me and Lightning can have a talk with him," he offered, referring to his self-cocker.

Women were in short supply; less than ten percent of the men in Bodie had wives, and prostitutes were scarce. So, it was not surprising that lonely Tom Svenson welcomed Parker's affected friendship for him. After Sam Leon's Bar closed at about two o'clock in the morning, Svenson permitted himself to be led arm in arm up the street by his new chum, to the Sawdust Corner Saloon at Union and Main. He was too drunk to understand the danger he was in, and he allowed himself to be treated to a bit more whiskey. Finally, at half-past four, Svenson staggered out of the saloon and weaved from Main to Green Street, eventually heading east toward the rooming house that constituted his meager lodgings.

The barkeeper minded his own business when he noticed Morris Parker leave the bar after Svenson, and head in the same direction. The businessman knew Parker's prosperous home lay in the opposite direction, on the hill. Mere minutes later, as Svenson passed by the one-room school house, a shadow leaped from behind a woodpile and shot him directly through the head. A good part of his skull had been blown clean off, and some of his brains were spilling out the gaping hole, yet it still took Svenson an incredible two hours to die. The poor man had not the ability to speak during those final hours. His murderer was left unnamed.

# Chapter 14

H e dropped down the last sand hill on a direct course toward the unpainted, fairly ramshackle structure that jutted from the east end of Touchstone Mining Company's stamp mill. As he neared the office, he heard the tense voices of several men. Dismounting, he shuffled a bit before the door, more or less to alert those inside to his arrival; Parker was nothing if not careful.

He walked briskly through the doorway and was surprised to be met with the unfriendly stares of all four company executives. "Guess I'm interrupting—" he allowed the words to trail off in question.

"On the contrary, Morris," Renick muttered while putting the finishing touches on his cigarette and striking a match to the end. "You'll find this interesting. There's been a bit of trouble." Renick was perched leisurely on the corner of the desk, while another partner sat behind it and the other two positioned themselves reluctantly against the south wall. The room was no larger than a goat shed and only held but the one stick of furniture, several pokes of gold dust, and some twenty-dollar gold pieces. Gold was the only thing which remained bright, in the cramped office on that morning.

One window, in the north wall near the gunman, provided only a slight warm draft. But it was enough of a breeze that Parker could smell the ferment of the Touchstone partners.

"What trouble?" he posed nonchalant against the door opening.

"Just another dead man in Bodie. Done in from ambush with a self-cocker to the head, looks like. Nothin' you'd know anything about, right Parker?" asked Drummond, the next heaviest investor in the company, after Renick.

Drummond was a giant of a man, and self-made. He had earned his prosperity through silver mining the Virginia City strike for nearly a decade before hitting upon a rich vein. He was the only partner that Parker ever deferred to, grudgingly, and not because Drummond was a reputed gunfighter. On the contrary; Drummond could easily kill a man with his bare hands, before the other could release his holster snap.

Morris Parker stared him hard, trying to intimidate. But the angry Drummond maintained his slouched, crossed-arm position.

"Another murder in Bodie? Do we know who the man was?" Parker asked innocently.

"Yeah," replied Drummond, "we know him all right." Drummond was agitated. He paced the tiny room like a mountain lion with a prickly-foot, shooting Parker withering looks of despise.

"Well, is someone going to tell me who the man was?" asked Parker, with just the correct degree of concern.

Drummond stopped his pacing to scowl at Parker with an expression of double-distilled cussedness. "Somehow, I guessed you might already be privy to this ugly business."

Parker started to object, but Renick interfered with a gracious smile that was quite unbefitting the circumstances. "Now, now, gentlemen. Obviously, Mr. Svenson's untimely death was the work of our rivals. There's no cause to affect insult on Morris, here."

"I ain't too worried for Parker's feelings," Drummond growled. "I tell you all right here and now, I have never understood our need for the services of a hired gun. I want to know if murder is part of his designated duties, and if he was ordered to kill Svenson. As if we didn't know!"

"Hey, now!" Parker made a threatening move toward Drummond. The partner responded by eagerly taking a step forward himself, closing the gap between them. He smiled down. Parker realized too late that his six-shooter had just been neutralized; Drummond was standing too close for Parker to draw his gun.

Renick stood and casually stepped between the two men, puffing his cheroot Parker's way to get him to back off.

"Parker is our Negotiator. We need his services, all right. He's a gunman so yes, sometimes he kills." Renick shrugged his shoulders dramatically. "That ain't murder. That's business. He didn't kill Svenson, John. I can promise you that."

"Would that be akin to your promise of taking the cyanide to water, Aaron?"

"Whatever do you mean by that?"

"I mean, Svenson had my ear up. He said those horses of Josh Mitz's all died from the drinking water 'cause the poison is in it. He said you were having Parker dump the waste in Bodie Creek. Svenson was alarmed you might be poisoning the whole damned town. And now he's dead. Well, Aaron, that sort of fortuitous timing got me curious. I rose before dawn and I watched for our disposal wagon to leave for Mono Lake. That must have been one hell of a ride, Parker, 'cause I saw the same wagon come back just an hour later."

"Whaaat?" shouted one partner.

"What's this? What's this? Are we involved in murdering Bodie?" screeched Pierce Keefe. His wife and newly-born child lived in Bodie with him. *I must get my family out of here*, he spurred himself.

The tiny office was a cell of hollering, plaintive questions and outrage. "Now, now, gentlemen...gentlemen. Drummond, all the rest of you, how many times do I have to convince you? John, we have two wagons. You must be mistaken. Parker, did you take the wagon to Mono or didn't you?" Renick asked.

"'Course I did. Just got back."

"There, you see, John?" Renick eased off and resumed his seat on top the desk. "I'm sorry as anybody about Svenson. But it is important for us, as businessmen, to ensure that Svenson's absence is not going to harm this publicly-traded company. And it won't, so relax."

At Renick's callous disregard for a good man's exit from this world, Drummond abruptly turned and jerked his jacket off the wall rack. As he made for the door he growled in a low voice, "Ya'll seem a bit *too* relaxed with Svenson's murder for my tastes. I'll be going somewhere's I can be certain the neighborhood ain't tainted." He glared at Parker one last time, "Get out'a my way!"

At day's end, John Drummond stood in the doorway of the sizable cabin he'd built with his own sizeable hands. It sat on a sizable ranch just outside of town. No breeze existed on this warm September evening, but it was still a sight cooler on the front porch. He allowed a calloused hand to run up and down the smooth log that held up that end of his front porch, and he reminisced. Seattle was on his mind. When he'd left his boyhood home, with the pristine forests he'd logged for so many years to put food on his aging parents' table, he thought he had succeeded in leaving behind his passion for the northwest. But the air there, he reflected, wasn't so dry as to make your nose bleed. The sun over Seattle never cracked your skin or made you see things that weren't there. And he knew the water in Seattle was pure.

Drummond was thinking he should have gone back after he'd made his fortune in silver. He should have gone back and hunted up Melissa, seen if she was still free for marriage, and had himself eight or ten sons. How had he allowed himself to become so lonely a man?

The blare of the shotgun blast came from behind a nearby rock formation. The load of buckshot ripped into Drummond's side and groin, wounding him fatally. Since he lived alone, there was no one to hear the roar of the discharge. And no one heard the scornful words that were called out softly, yet arrived clearly at Drummond's ears before he surrendered to his maker, "there goes the neighborhood." And, there was no one to pull John Drummond inside the cabin, beyond the tearing claws and gnashing teeth of the desert's night predators.

The next morning a couple of Touchstone workers set out for Drummond's place to investigate the cause of all them circling carrion-eaters. Neither of the men could hold their coffee and grits as they scooped and wrapped the remnants that were John Drummond in a blanket for the undertaker.

That same afternoon, a third Touchstone Mining Company partner, Pierce Keefe, was cramming dishware and tools into flour sacks with reckless disregard for packing procedures.

His wife pleaded with him, "Pierce, you're scaring me. How can we just move to San Francisco like this? Why, we haven't a chance to settle affairs here. I want to say good-bye to the church ladies...Pierce?"

He didn't bother looking up from his frenzied loading of personal goods. "Go say your good-byes, and make them quick. I do not wish to spend the night here."

"Pierce, that man is a viper." Tears slipped down Helen Keefe's powdered cheeks. "He'll cheat us blind if we're not around to supervise our holdings. You must know that."

Finally, he looked up to meet the imploring eyes of his young wife. "I do know that, Helen," he said gravely. "And cheated is a sight better than dead."

The fourth Touchstone partner, Edward Calandra, was already in Virginia City putting his company shares up for sale on the exchange. *If they can do that to a bruiser like Drummond, what chance have I?* Thirty or so Bodie mining companies were listed on the San Francisco exchange, but not a one was pulling out as much gold and silver as Touchstone. With his holdings cashed out by noon, he proceeded to book passage for himself to New York.

# Chapter 15

In a packed house at the Miner's Union Hall, on a Saturday evening, Armstrong met Pheister for the pugilistic feud of the year. Billed as an all-out "rough-and-tumble," meaning that no holds were barred, the event appeared to be the cynosure of the entire population of Bodie. The sports were at ends giving odds on the fight, since the two contestants looked to be woefully mismatched. Armstrong was a much smaller man, and the crowd had been betting heavy on the other combatant. Jack Gunn was the only sport in Bodie who was booking any and all bets against the little man. If Armstrong emerged the victor, Gunn stood to make a "small" fortune, he'd joked.

But Jack wasn't a foolish man. He'd stipulated that all the little guy had to do was survive the fight conscious, and all bets would be called even. Since Armstrong was tiny and quick-footed, Jack guessed at worst he'd stay out of harm's way for the better part of the fight.

The men were squared off, and the bell was rung. Just as Jack had wagered, Pheister was sparring thin air as Armstrong darted this way and that. The Bodieites were well-watered and naturally disorderly with their raucous teasing, calling, and booing, when all at once, Little Man Armstrong quit his flitting and unleashed a blow that felled Pheister to the ground with his lights out. It was one for the history books, one newspaper man had later boasted, "Bodie fell silent on a Saturday night!" It had taken the drunken crowd a stunned few seconds to register that the little man had ended the fight. Then to everyone's further amazement, Armstrong let drop a rock he'd had concealed in his fist.

Many of the onlookers began protesting Armstrong's advantage, and it looked as though there would be several more fights to come. Aaron Renick climbed atop the bar and addressed the room. "The fight was perfectly fair," he'd assured the crowd. "After all, this fight was billed as a Rough-and-Tumble. So, hittin' Pheister with a stone, well, that was the rough part. And the little feller knocking him unconscious, that demonstrated the tumble."

Jack gladly collected his winnings. Some Bodieites grumbled and some cheered, but none left the Hall. They had come for a celebration of sorts, and no one was ready to call it a night just yet. An Irish miner named Sloan, who worked for Touchstone, clamored atop the bar beside Renick and announced to all, "It would be befittin' to drink a toast to Mr. Aaron Renick for the dust control he imparted over the long an' infernal summer. He did it fer no charge to us townsfolk, and made livin' in Bodie nearly tolerable," the soused miner praised.

Cheers were hailed and drinks were poured liberally, which is not the same as saying any of those present actually favored Renick. Fewer still trusted the man, but any excuse for another drink was a good one. Frank Swazey was perhaps the only miner present to have observed the cruel wink from Renick to his hired gun, and he found it disquietingly curious. Queerer still was the puzzle of Aaron Renick performing any good deed for the denizens of Bodie, especially free of charge.

Frank felt he would begin hyperventilating anew if he dwelled on that vile exchange of winks any longer. Matter of fact, his toes and fingers were again tingling as if a thousand toothless snakes were snapping at him. His fingernails looked dungaree blue, and the familiar ass-backward fireflies were swooping in front of his eyes, making him feel unsteady. These imaginary fireflies did not flash bright in the darkness. Instead, they cast pesky black spots throughout his fair vision. Frank urgently toppled his way through the crowd toward the cool brace of Autumn night.

A well-meaning, jolly miner punched Frank playfully and hollered after him, "Careful, Frank. It only takes a couple a' snorts of Bodie home-brew to craze a man of *ordinary* brainpower!"

# Chapter 16

October 31, 1878
Bodie, California

Unlike the other whores, Mustache Sally worked mostly days, since her regular john, one Morris Parker, did his principal work at night. True to her name, Sal was no beauty. She had a long horsey-looking mug that was covered with inordinately heavy facial fuzz over most of it, primarily above her upper lip, thus the nickname. She also sported a big mouth, in the harpy sense. Parker didn't visit Sally to admire her face, and he didn't much care to listen to her run off at the mouth, neither. But he got his afternoon visits free of charge, while he collected half the pay-off's Sal was getting from the other whores, China-men, and poor-luck gamblers, in return for the promise of protection supplied by the likes of Morris Parker.

Sal would spout off nonsense about the rights of such degenerates among the other town miserables, who comprised most of the Bodie citizenry. All that while she stole their money in the name of safety, but warned none of them about the poisoning, which her boyfriend Parker was largely responsible for. It was this latter character feature of Sally's, and nothing else, which Morris Parker found attractive.

Mustache Sally had only Morris and one other whore by the name of French Joe, who she would really call friends of any sort. French Joe was one of the busiest prostitutes in town, mainly because she was sort of pixie-cute and sort of clean, and that was unusual for a whore from the west side of town. Joe was a short little sass with dark hair and tiny features. She had a sizable rapper to rival Mustache Sally's, though, and it ceaselessly piped about nothing much. Parker could hear Joe snoring behind the coarse blanket divider as he buttoned up his black trousers. Sally remained sprawled on the stained mattress, sweat beading down her bony back. Parker could glimpse the tufts of dark hair peeking out from her underarm region. It matched the long dark roots at the base of Sally's peroxide-blonde hair. *The woman has a load of hair*, Parker thought fleetingly.

He counted through the money one more time on his way out, then turned and gave Sal a warning look. "Don't you go saying nothin' bout the—" He shot a glance toward the blanket curtain, "dumping. You hear me, Sal?" He patted his hat onto his head. "Damn but it's boilin' in here!"

The row of whore compartments was narrow. There was just room enough for a man to walk down the thin aisle which ran the length of the structure, past the foot of each bed. Privacy was installed via threadbare old army blankets hung between and at the foot of every cot or bed. Stingy windows that were cut into the wall opposite the headboards, one for every compartment, were the only means of new air. There was a single wood stove and no bed in the last compartment, and there was no bath inside the structure. Each working gal fetched her own pitcher of water for bathing. Sal's pitcher stood empty, Parker noticed. She wasn't too particular about sponging herself.

She sat up now with her legs crossed Indian style, and started digging her fingers around in her eyes, rubbing her thumb with her index finger whenever she found a sticky gob of sleep residue. It was a habit that made Parker grimace.

"I still say they got rights, Parker. And just think how much they'd be willing to pay to know when and where to drink the water? It could be our *own* little gold mine," she tempted, inspecting something on the end of her finger.

Parker fixed her with a glare so piercing she could actually feel it boring into her. She looked up to meet it defiantly. "Talk like that can get even a good whore killed. You say nothin', Sal. Nothin'." The door slammed shut behind him.

In the part of a minute it took for Parker to reach his tethered horse, Clementine, he'd made up his mind about the whore. He could do without his fifty-percent of Sal's extortion business, and there were other, fresher whores in town, to be sure. He'd have to muzzle Mustache Sally, permanently, maybe tonight. Maybe he'd tie her body to some big rocks and dump her in the creek, since she was so all fired up and concerned about the water. *Yeah.* He'd invite Sal to go swimming, he chuckled to himself. He slapped the reigns on Clementine's back quarter.

"Giddy up, partner. There's work to be done."

"Go fer a swim? At night? Did you turn crazy or somethin' Parker? I jus' saw you 'safternoon. I gotta sleep some," Sal whined.

"Are you turnin' me down, Sal? Fine, I'll go see what Joe's up to." He started to walk that way.

For Sal, it was close to a smack in the face. "Shit. Wait a minute, Morris. Will ya jus' wait a minute?"

He stopped walking and turned back to face her. "Okay," she sighed. "You wanna swim under the moonlight, we'll swim some under the moonlight. But don't you go gettin' yourself used to it. This is gonna be the last time for me; that water's cold!"

"Don't you know it," he smiled.

They were six miles south of town. Even in the desert, where night was so clear and so clean that sounds sliced through it like glass, carrying sharp shards of conversation or laughter for a mile, her screams wouldn't filter back so far as town. Perhaps an outsider or someone new to Bodie would worry for his own safety from the Indians, being they were so numerous in the Cal/Nevada desert, and seeing as he and Sal were so far out from the protection of the town. But Parker wasn't concerned. There had never been a report of a single Indian entering the town following its settlement. In fact, the desert Indians would ride a half-day out of their way to avoid accidentally stepping into any part of Bodie. They referred to the area as "killamema," or loosely translated, "land of much death."

They settled themselves on a wide portion of bank along Bodie Creek, where a sandy beach, cut from the landscape by ancestral waters, made the perfect spot for laying a blanket. Sal was overtly romantic in celebration of Parker's surprise affection for her, demonstrated so fancifully by his proposed date beneath the stars. She had even sponge-bathed for him. So, Sal was covering Parker with smooches under the scant moonlight, when she suddenly stopped.

"I'm reflectin' on all the times we been together, Morris, and I'm wonderin', just when was it you got soft on me?"

Morris turned her away from him and began rubbing her bony shoulders. "Well, Sal, you know I've always approved of your mind. Today, after our talk, that mind of yours convinced me it was time I took you to another level." He carefully slipped his tapered skinning knife from its sheath and set it beside him.

She smiled with conceit. "Well, I always know'd I was smarter than most whores. But, Parker, I had a thought 'twas my flesh what kept bringin' you back to my bed."

He looked around carefully for any sign they weren't alone; clear in all directions. He picked up the knife. *One last chance, Sal.*

"You been thinkin' any more about the poison and the dumpin', Sal?"

"Some," she replied cautiously, realizing maybe Morris was coming around to her idea.

He stopped rubbing her shoulders and reached his left arm around her. Gently, slowly, and sensuously, he rubbed his palm up her bony neck, which was stretched upward to admire the stars. When his hand reached her chin, he cupped it gently and rubbed her jaw line with his long fingers. His right hand brought the knife up to her waiting throat, and his left hand suddenly jerked her chin downward.

"Sorry, Sal. That was the wrong answer," he told her, as he dragged the razor-sharp knife sidewise across her neck, severing the major arteries in one fluid motion.

He'd done it with lightening fast speed and a good deal of his might. He'd hoped that by turning her away from him as he'd so cleverly done, he could avoid the warm gush of her blood from getting all over him. That best laid plan was spoiled. *Damn it*! Morris didn't know his own strength. He'd accidentally cut her neck near-clean through. Only a small flap of skin kept the head attached to the body. The splashing blood had come from all directions; it was unavoidable.

"Stinkin' filthy whore," he declared through clenched teeth, angry at Sally for soiling him. "Now I'm gonna have to take that swim after all, and that water's colder than a witch's tit."

Parker tied some stones to her body, under her arms, and around her legs. Then he dragged her out into the middle of the creek and sunk her corpse. He scrubbed himself a bit as he inspected the water from the surface. The water was still moving fairly swift, and it was deep enough that the body couldn't be seen. As it was growing late in the fall, Parker was relatively confident nobody would be dipping in the creek for at least eight months. He wasn't concerned about discovery of the body, but he still had to think of somewhere to ditch the head. If he buried it he risked animals digging it up by daybreak, and the danged thing wouldn't stay sunk. He looked around the nearly-vacant landscape and saw there was a small bridge which crossed Bodie Creek and led toward Aurora, just about a quarter-mile down the stream. He walked briskly down the creek bank with his grisly newsprint-wrapped package, and surveyed the bridge's underbelly. He saw something serviceable about the way the curved joists allowed for cubby holes between the lumber and the eroding earthen wall. He wedged the bloody package sidewise into a center gap, satisfied that the vultures would not be able to alert ground scavengers to it anytime soon. By the time some predator happened to sniff it out, the head would no longer be recognizable anyway.

"So long, Sal!" He tipped his hat rudely to the atrocity and rode away.

Something Morris Parker never thought of was how a head would shrink with decay in a dry desert heat. Flesh wrinkled, shrunk and darkened as the arid desert sucked all moisture from it. It wasn't too long before the gruesome aperture began to rock gently on its tiny ledge with every stirring current. Destined to occur eventually, the head toppled free of its makeshift tomb. But instead of rolling gently into the water, it landed squarely on top of the bedroll belonging to a seasoned miner by the name of Lucius Ambert. Lucius decided that having a severed head dropped on you during your first night in a new town, was a very bad omen, indeed. He quickly gathered up his pack of belongings and rode out to Virginia City, where saloon patrons laughed and bought him drinks the whole night long for bringing them another good story about the horrors of Bodie.

# Chapter 17

The two men drifted around the shoulder of the butte and quietly calculated to themselves the approximate depth of the abandoned mine shafts. They had been abandoned some years earlier when a company, Skeleton Flats, figured they'd been picked about as clean as bleached bones.

"So, the townsfolk don't reckon they need a dust suppressant any longer, eh?" asked Renick.

Parker moved his hat forward on his bowed head to combat the wind.

"No point in continuing. Someone's likely to find suspicion with us packing down dirt roads with oily water after the rain's already begun and snow's on its way. Most folks figured we needed to rid ourselves of the waste oil from the stamp mill. Nobody's objectin' none to our using it for tempering the dust in town free of charge, either. But then, ain't nobody suspectful of its being laced with cyanide."

"It ain't poison unless they consume it, and we ain't feedin' it to 'em. Get that through your stubborn skull," Renick told him.

Parker remained silent but his glare spoke volumes.

Renick never noticed Parker's slow-burning glower. He was deep in thought. He'd been thinking they should just start dumping the stuff into Bodie Creek in the middle of the night, and maybe rid of some more of it by offering cyanide-laced oil as heating fuel to the most destitute inhabitants of Bodie. Those who's misfortune it would be to accept the donation would otherwise probably risk their lives pilfering firewood come the winter anyway. Of course, those were still options worth considering, but dang if Parker didn't come up with a shinier idea in using the abandoned mine shafts.

"Ya just promoted yourself to a new position with Touchstone, Morris; Night Deposit Manager." Renick's laughter was cruel. "Son, I reckon you ain't just another pretty face after all."

November 9, 1878
Bodie, California

Seemingly bottomless. Serpentine and black. Icy cold like the river Styx. Hundreds of feet beneath the earth's surface, the caustic cyanide trickled deeper still, through hairline crevices and prehistoric rifts, merging with the subterranean currents which carried the water of life. Eventually, the ancient groundwater, desecrated now by the poisonous leachate, would emerge again in deceptively gentle pools to be released by men; tapped for bathing and drinking.

# Chapter 18

25 December, 1878
Bodie, California

A dozen beds in each ward, six wards between the two floors, and nearly every bed was occupied by a thin filthy body. Not one case of diphtheria or consumption existed in the bunch. This was some other plague; a mystery. One ward upstairs was half-filled with children and prostitutes suffering with the respiratory stage of the illness. The remainder of that ward bore women in anguish over miscarriages and stillborn deliveries of their pregnancies. Elise knew of only a single live birth, in a population of more than ten thousand souls, occurring in Bodie in more than a year; her friend, Helen Keefe, had given birth to a son a few months earlier. She'd had a Chinaman use his crystals to improve the vigor and health of her baby, and he had also given her a putrid smelling tea to drink each evening. Elise thought Helen's blessing was due at least in part to where she and Pierce lived, high on the west hill. Few people who lived on the hill were sick, it seemed. Elise whispered a hurried prayer and passed by the pitiful threshold quickly.

On this day, she and the boy, Frank Jr., had come to—no, celebrate would not have been an adequate word; they'd come to spend time with Frank on Christmas Day. She turned to warn her son of what condition his father might be in, but Frank Junior was no longer following, Elise realized. Well, she sighed quietly, who could blame her son if the misery within this hospital was too much for a boy to stomach.

She approached the upper north wing of the hospital hesitantly. She no longer had the advantage of anticipating and preparing for Frank's afflictions, since he was declining so quickly. Would he be asleep? She stole through the doorless opening and approached the first bed on the right. Quietly, she rested herself in the hard, rather uncomfortable chair next to the dressing table, and prepared to converse with Frank if he should awaken. The room was depressing, shadowy. The thin white muslin which hung between the beds offered little privacy, but redeemed a small advantage in allowing gray wintry light to creep toward Frank's end of the ward, from the sole window which faced Main Street. Elise's wool, felt-lined boots scraped softly against the unswept floorboards, and the jacquard cloth of her handsome holiday dress swished as she turned more directly toward her husband.

"If you can hear me, Frank, you should know it is Christmas Day. We asked the fellow who sometimes ministers at the schoolhouse on Sundays, I think you know him as the man who raises goats and chickens at the old Drummond place, and he's going to say a prayer for your recovery. A Christmas Day prayer, Frank! He promised us Doc Heilshorn don't have no more powerful medicine than that."

Her husband remained still. She looked at her bodice to see that it was properly pressed and straightened. "I'll send Frank Junior over after supper with a plate fixed for you. I'm achin' for you to try my sweet potato pie. I just know you'd like it." And she would send over a plate of fixings, after she runs everything through her meat grinder. Most of Frank's teeth had fallen out, completely of their own accord, over recent months.

She was thoroughly exhausted from minding the inn until late on Christmas Eve, not to mention the wear on her mental and physical capacities, to which months of ministering to her husband had contributed. Still, Elise had done her best to look fine on this day. Were he still able to possess an awareness, Elise was sure Frank would have loved the dress's fabric of emerald green ground with black figures, which she had made up into a rich shirt waist and full skirt.

She sat quiet next to her husband for a spell, and watched as Frank's sleep grew tremulous and agitated. Early on in the obscure disease's progression, the tremors that began in his hands and feet occurred only during the time he was awake. Now, they continued violently during sleep, not infrequently waking him. On the bedside table, Elise studied the menagerie of vials containing extracts made from the glands and organs of lower animals; renderings from the brain, spinal cord, heart, testicles, ovaries and some other organs, and parts of bullocks, rabbits, guinea pigs and other animals. Doc Heilshorn testified to the great efficacy of the extracts and their "invigorating influences," whence he injected them into her husband's tired veins. He'd claimed they would stop at once the progress of Frank's disease and turn the tide toward recovery. That was months ago, and Frank was still dying. But at least he was dying faster.

Elise rose heavily and reached for the bathing utensils, her muscles aching. She would need to give Amanda her sponge bath after she finished with Frank, and she still had so much work left to do at the inn that day. She wet the sternly bristled brush and proceeded to rasp the hard soap against it. The hospital had not enough nurses to see that each cadaverous patient received hygienic care, even though the physician believed the stiff brushing would encourage circulation and might rouse the extremities out of their paralysis. Elise also followed the doctor's advice when she manipulated her husband's arms and legs in order to exercise them, even though she feared she was making undue drafts upon his already weak body. To Elise, it seemed the regiment exhausted his little remaining capacity for power, instead of reinforcing it.

She applied the brush first to Frank's forearm, rubbing lightly in a circular motion. Her husband groaned, then jerkily turned his head in her direction. The arm she held began to spasm.

"What is it Frank, what can I do?" Elise looked around anxiously. Her eyes finally settled upon a vessel of water beside the bed, and she realized that he wanted a drink of water. "Here, Frank, let me help you sit up some," she volunteered. She needed to raise his chin from his breastbone for him so that he could take the drink, and still he swallowed with great difficulty. His thirst slaked, he sunk back down onto his pillows.

Elise watched him carefully for a few long, silent minutes, but he was not of a mind to say anything today. It had been so long since he'd been able to converse, or even to offer a 'hello' to his son. She sighed, picked up the scrubber again and continued with the brushing, careful to touch upon every part of his body. When she'd finished with Frank's scrub bath, Elise rolled up the pointed cuffs of her puff-top sleeves and positioned herself at the foot of the bed to begin leg exercises.

The ward was hushed, its inhabitants sedentary, and the suggestion of infirmity lay heavy on the air. It could be felt like heavy wool blankets, and it could be smelled, as in the ghastly tinctures and solutions of Doc Heilshorn's potions mixed with rubbing alcohol. Worse still, it could be heard. Labored breathing and thin shrieks of pain came from those patients still in the early stages of the mystery illness, and suffering the "lightening pains." The mix of cries were no more than so much background noise to Elise, so accustomed was she to the sounds. All of her ministerings were affected in silence, since Frank could not, or would not verbalize. It could not even be said that he was awake most of the time. Eventually, in the mute buzz of that frosty afternoon, with the fire bell tolling sepulchral in the distance for someone's passing, and horses clacking down the street as they carried drunken riders from one saloon to another, Elise gave in to daydreaming. On Christmas Day, 1878, her thoughts drifted from her ailing husband to another man, who was very much alive.

Months earlier, Frank's unknown ailment had manifested itself in his eyes, causing disturbances in his vision and affecting his balance. In walking, his movements were tottering like those of a man wholly intoxicated. His arms and legs became uncertain in any task, if Frank did not direct his complete attention to performing it. So although Frank did not drink much, everyone began regarding him a heavy boozer—understandably so, since the whiskey consumption in Bodie was legendary.

Elise remembered a story she'd heard not too long ago from some of the miners drinking at her establishment, about a contest held at Sam Leon's bar. A regular customer, who bragged he could identify every drink put to his lips while blindfolded, was challenged to prove it. When different types of whiskey, brandy, gin, rum and wine were tasted, he identified every one. But when water was given, so goes the account, he smacked his lips, swirled it around several times and swallowed, but eventually gave up in despair and admitted he was stumped. He could not identify Bodie's water. Elise was convinced that Bodie's water was not like drinking water anywhere else. She was convinced it was poison. Svenson had as much as told her so.

Fully a month before the fight at the Miner's Union Hall, when her husband had come home so terribly sick, Svenson had visited the Swazey Hotel and asked to speak to Frank. Elise informed Svenson she had already put her husband to bed with a small snifter of good brandy. It was the only means by which Frank could sleep, for by then he had begun having the night torments; the sweats, shivers, insomnia. So it was she who had met with Svenson in the downstairs saloon, and she'd bought him a drink for his trouble. It soon became evident it was not Svenson's first whiskey of the evening (according to the newspaper accounts the following morning, it had not been his last either).

Svenson had asked Elise many targeted questions about Frank's welfare, until she finally accused him of knowing more than he was telling. Normally, the kindly middle-aged man had a cheerful face, well-lined from the sun and not from worry. A rough, graying stubble belied the man's true gentle manner. Svenson wore the suntan and the customary pale lips and pale, watery eyes, of a miner of gold—the result of having a man's natural color somewhat bleached away through his work in the blazing desert sun. That night, Svenson's face was anything but cheerful. Confessing to Elise that he had unwittingly taken part in the blight of Bodie, he'd proceeded to explain through his tears the cyaniding process being employed by Touchstone, and the issue with disposing of the poisonous waste.

Svenson was dubious of Renick honoring the covenant to relocate the waste far from town, because so many of the townsfolk were becoming afflicted. And chickens, horses, and cattle were dying for reasons the animal doctor could not explain. Svenson was heart sick, he'd told her. Bodie was his mistress in this, his new country. He'd cherished her. He had admired her strength and moxie. To him, Bodie was a fiery lass, full of promise. Though sprung from the barren womb of desert, she flourished, nay, sparkled. With Bodie in his heart, he'd told Elise, he had believed wondrous things were possible. And yet, he'd had a hand in slaying her, a reality too painful for Svenson to endure.

By the finishing of his narrative, he was begging Elise for her forgiveness. The man's remorse was so naked, it could not have been untrue. Elise had believed every word. Before he left her that night, through hot, grievous tears, he vowed he would take his story to Ezra Phegley at the Bodie Standard, first thing in the morning. Perhaps he would have tried, but Svenson had been ambushed later that same night. He was shot through the head.

After hearing Svenson's confession, other earlier incidents began to make more sense to Elise. She allowed herself to ponder poor ol' Charlie Baker. A long-time miner at the Touchstone mill, he had reported to his fellow miners his ability to be drunk without drinking. He swore he woke each morning sober, and drank naught but water pumped from Bodie Creek the entire day. But by midday, Baker could feel himself growing gradually more intoxicated, and by late afternoon, he was roaring drunk. The town had nicknamed him, Goodtime Charlie; they had even written it on his marker.

Elise had another memory of Charlie. She remembered passing near him one day, on her way to delivering Frank's lunch at the mill. Charlie had commented on the enticing smells coming from her tied bundle. Elise survived poor beginnings in the Midwest during a time when food was scarce for her family. Whether stemming from a fear of becoming poor once again, or affirming she would *never* be poor again, it became Elise's way to always prepare "more than enough" food, which was to say, too much. But, since she owned an inn, extra food never went to waste. Elise untied the bandana and allowed Charlie to help himself to a few pieces of perfectly-golden fried chicken. He was such a grateful man for the favor. He'd praised her cooking and her generosity profusely as he relished every bite. A nice man, Elise remembered.

Charlie Baker had been an aging but sprightly man. He had a merry glint in those clear gray eyes of his, which hinted at his warm good humor. There was no drunkenness that Elise could identify at the time, but she had noticed how his hand shook when he'd lifted the chicken to his mouth, and how something in his right cheek kept twitching. She was unacquainted with those symptoms at the time and thought little of it, until those manifestations became evident in her husband's behavior just a short time later. Goodtime Charlie had been pronounced dead of alcohol poisoning many weeks ago. Since he was a bachelor who lived alone, no one could bear certain witness to his claims of sobriety.

Many stories like Charlie's were passed around the town of Bodie. Some of them were preposterous enough for retelling in the chronicles of other towns far away; stories that, while mostly true, were often embellished and served only to complement the notorious distinction Bodie had already gained. Many of the stories were considered hilarious or remarkable, or even puzzling, but no one seemed to find them particularly frightening, except Elise. She often wondered of late, and most times aloud and in the presence of other Touchstone miners, how many of their presumed town drunks, such as Charlie Baker and her own husband, were instead afflicted with a mysterious disease. Still, not one person seemed concerned. Well, that was not entirely true. There was one man who listened to Elise's *every* word.

Month's earlier, Frank's personality had begun to degenerate. Whether from pain or frustration, he took to shouting at Elise and their son, Frank Junior. On a few occasions, he even raised his hand to her. Sick man or not, she should have left him when the abuse started, but she'd been too timorous of becoming a lone woman with a child in a place like Bodie. In any case, the abuse stopped as abruptly as it had started. The last incident occurred in the saloon, and in the presence of customers. One of those customers was a professional gambler named Jack Gunn. That was the night Elise met Jack for the first time.

One evening, on miner's payday, Frank had returned home apparently drunk, and in a foul mood over being scathed at the mines by his supervisor for slacking in his work. Frank was a man who held a generally good reputation, yet he had fairly exploded over something as trivial as a lack of biscuits with his supper. He dashed Elise once with his palm, and lifted his hand to repeat the offense, promising the beating would continue pretty lively until she fetched him his biscuits. But a larger and more powerful hand caught Frank's on the downswing.

Elise had been bolstered for the blow that did not come, and looked up in surprise to see Jack Gunn, a handsome professional gambler who had been coming around of late on paydays. He had twisted her husband around by the arm to subdue him. Frank was immediately humiliated and his irrational rage played itself out. He glanced ashamedly at his delicate wife, mumbled something in the way of an apology, and weaved out of the saloon.

The gambler introduced himself to Elise, inquired about her state of being, and offered her the most engaging smile she had ever seen a man give a woman. Thinking back, Elise believed she had fallen in love with Jack Gunn at that very moment.

Jack Gunn visited the Swazey Hotel often after that night, and always took time to engage Elise in animated conversations. He was perhaps the only person in Bodie who shared Elise's concerns about the number of sick people the town was accumulating; mostly prostitutes who lived on the north side of town, on Bonanza Street, as well as many of the miners, whose cabins decorated the northeasterly hillside in the direction of Skeleton Flats, toward Aurora. One could only guess how many in Chinatown were affected by the disease that so few Bodieites had any awareness of. Doc Heilshorn agreed there were a staggering number of cases of palsy and ataxia in Bodie. But he asserted its development resulted from "over-indulgence of the animal and reproductive instincts, and too much whiskey."

# Chapter 19

One week following her lonely and silent visit to Frank in the hospital, Elise buried her husband in a marked grave inside the Miner's Union Cemetery. Although he'd been labeled a wife beater and a drunk, Bodieites found no shame in that. He had been accepted at his death as a respectable man.

Only Frank's closest buddies braved the cold sandpaper wind and snow to bow their heads over the pathetic coffin. The minister offered a quick set of sermons. Shortly thereafter, he too, abdicated for the warmth and whiskey of the town's saloons.

Elise huddled near the grave with her teen-aged boy, for just a few moments longer. She wanted to tell her husband she would remember him as a generally good and gentle man; that she and Frank Junior understood his behavior of the last few months was not really of his doing, but was the work of a mystery sickness. *I should probably make some declaration of love or longing for my dead husband, at least for the boy's sake,* Elise was wrestling with her emotions. She looked up suddenly.

"Frank, I hear Mr. Conway's horses coming from just one lane over. You go on down the hill and hitch a ride with him. Get yourself warm, darling boy, before you catch your death. I promise I'll just be a moment longer, myself."

Elise smiled through tears and gave her boy, her greatest gift from God, a gentle squeeze before patting him on the backside to get going. She had always, since the day of his birth, heard the faintest whisper in the back of her mind that she would never have enough time with her son. It was a nonsensical feeling, daffy, but nagging. So, she obliged to herself, she was a tich over-protective. Bodie was a dangerous place, after all. Frank Junior did not seem to mind receiving attention from his mother every free moment she had. Anyway, there was not an over-abundance of free moments in Elise's life, and there would be fewer still, now that her workload had doubled.

She watched him pick his way carefully down the snow-covered hillside, sniffed and turned back to her husband. He had never told Elise he loved her. Frank had told her often she was a looker; he had thanked her profusely for the son she bore him, and he'd worked hard to provide for them. But never once did Frank Swazey declare love for his wife. Elise had tried to love the husband who gave her a son, but it didn't take. *A woman can not be in love alone; we're just created differently,* Elise self-counseled. She'd stayed married to Frank anyway, just as her own parents had done. Elise believed her father had been in love alone in his marriage, too. Her mother had been beautiful and dutiful, but her heart was not deep. She'd had a finite amount of love to distribute, and she'd had to divide it among nine children and a husband. *Oh, how the mind wanders, and I can not feel my toes.* What was she to say over her husband's grave, then? What should be his wife's parting words? She had never loved Frank Swazey. But she had never promised too, either.

In 1864, she had started out with her large family from Fort Wayne, Indiana, in a covered wagon bearing the banner,

"California or Bust." Indiana had no real Indian problems until the government began forcing relocation of Shawnee, Muncie, and Illini Indians to reservations in Oklahoma. In some cases, the cavalry had been ruthless with the natives, and the natives in some areas were beginning to buck. That, as well as the war, had encouraged her mother and father to move their nine children west, to the land of milk and honey. Her father never made it, having died on the way across the plains at the second crossing of Ham's Fork. He'd been trampled by livestock when someone's weapon had accidentally discharged and the beasts stampeded. The family didn't want the Indians to dig him up for his clothing later, so they'd had the men of the wagon train bury him in the middle of the trail. Then they corralled the oxen over the spot for the night. By the next afternoon, after a few hundred wagons and the long strings of oxen and loose cattle had passed over it, Elise doubted they would ever locate the grave site again. Of course, they could not give him a marker.

Her mother made it to California with all nine of her children. She was an attractive woman in her late-thirties. The eldest of her brood, Elise, was sixteen years old, and a stunner. With no money to speak of, and ten mouths to feed, Elise and her mother began visiting mining sites to get laundry work to do. The men looked forward to the daily visits from the two handsome women— sometimes men gave them clean clothes to wash, just to ensure the ladies would keep coming back. Soon enough, they had all the dirty laundry they could handle.

They were pretty hard run to earn enough money for the family to live on, but somehow they got along. One day, a miner named Frank Swazey, offered to marry Elise. Elise's mother began thinking of all the miners she had taken a fancy to, who had looked her daughter's way instead. Elise was undeniably beautiful, yet her mother knew that she was a handsome woman in her own right. So, she was not jealous of her daughter, precisely. She simply realized she would never find another husband so long as Elise was in the wings. She'd told her daughter she had better take Frank Swazey. And so Elise did. He was fourteen years her senior.

Elise's choice was one of pragmatism. Saloons flourished. They went up anywhere there were enough drunks to make running one pay. During California's gold rush, that meant plenty of saloons. What could a young girl of sixteen do to protect herself from those men who drank most of the time, when she was visiting the roughest of them to collect their laundry? Frank Swazey promised her he didn't drink and never would, so she married him.

Both understood the arrangement was not for love; for Frank it was companionship and for Elise it was protection. He immediately began treating her like a servant, one he demanded sexual favors from every night. He was gentle enough, albeit uninspired. Frank took care of his need, rolled over, and promptly got to snoring. He did not love her, and he did not pretend to.

Within a year's time, Frank Swazey moved his young pregnant wife away from her family to the most dangerous town in the West, perhaps the whole country, Bodie, California. They'd scraped together enough to build a boarding house. They bought the lot across from the Union Hall and the Mortuary, which came cheap because of the neighbors. From there, they struggled hard to make the saloon and rooms-for-rent grant them a decent living.

She stared at the mound, already growing white with snow. She had so much love in her heart that she thought, unlike her mother's, her own may very well be bottomless. She gave every drop to her son, yet her heart always refilled. She was a terrible-lonely woman with a full heart. And yet, no man, other than her long-dead father, had ever loved her. She had so much love to give; she daydreamed of giving her heart to a man who would give his whole heart in return. She wondered if anyone ever really found such a love. Life in Bodie was hard, and since Frank became incapacitated, life had gotten much harder. But

Elise was of strong pioneer stock, forged of fortitude and fire. She would manage. She wondered fleetingly if she would quickly tire of meeting life alone. Would Jack Gunn perhaps step in to marry her? Jack Gunn was a man she could marry for both love *and* protection.

Elise tried hard to grieve for her husband's ending, but the ripple of excitement turning in her belly kept whispering at Elise that this could be a new beginning for her. The toes in her boots were too froze to wiggle in the slightest. They ached and burned with cold. Her nose was numb and beginning to run. When the icy wind blew, it seemed to pass clear through her winter coat. She lifted her head and looked down into the town from her place on the hill.

"Oh Frank, it's an astounding scene of great beauty. The painted desert of summer has changed into a winter wonderland. I pray you can see it." She gazed about, giving thanks for the pure white snow drifts, some right up to the tops of back doors.

The day following her visit from Svenson, Elise ordered a water cistern built behind her inn to catch rain water, or in this case snow. It was full to the top. She could rest assured her little man would already be covering it with its sailcloth and bunging it down. *He is such a good son; such a Blessing.* Elise gave the town a wistful smile. *I do wish the good Lord had seen fit to Bless me with more children—many more, just like him.*

Every morning, Frank Junior would shovel snow into an enormous cook-pot to melt it. The water would then be poured into a tank, which Elise had tapped for their drinking water. She'd decided, since Frank had the fire going anyway, that it could not hurt to fully boil the water, and then allow it to cool. "An education is never wasted," Elise's late father had often told her. She'd gotten quite an education cleaning all that laundry. She'd learned boiling is good for removing tough dirt from miners' clothing.

"The water we've captured in the cistern is to be our water for drinking and cooking, so cleaning it might be a real good idea," Elise had explained to her son.

The drifts sparkled wherever slivers of sunlight splashed. Severe in its simplicity, but with great integrity of emotion, Elise thought Bodie was beautiful. The snow had cleansed the town and purged the air with sweet tasting snowflakes that Elise tried to catch on her tongue; she could not help herself. She suddenly realized, as the crimson flushed up her cheeks, she looked a poor sight as a grieving widow. She was glad she had sent Frank Junior home. Chagrined by her lapse, she turned back to the grave and with glassy-eyed fatigue, she talked with her silent heart. Gradually, her ears became aware of what was then perhaps the loneliest sound in the world; the fire bell, off in the distance, tolling the age of her deceased husband. With growing regularity, it seemed to Elise, that bell rang long and often.

# Chapter 20

If the doors of perception were cleansed,
everything would appear to man as it is,
infinite. For man has closed himself up,
till he sees all things through narrow
chinks of his cavern.

—William Blake
18th Century Artist & Visionary

23 March, 1993
Longview, Washington

Rachel leaned back in the plastic patio chair and took in a deep and satisfying breath of fresh air. She looked radiant, her color enhanced by the filtered sunlight cast upon her through the table umbrella. Spring had shown impulsiveness this year by bursting into action with sunny days topping seventy degrees. Rachel embraced Spring's caprice by donning a pair of tan walking shorts, with Reeboks, and a Henley top which the dress shop advertised as nutmeg. It nearly matched her hair perfectly.

She knew she was early for the appointment with Peter, but the quaint little marketplace, slash gift shop, slash deli, offered rapturous espresso latte's with a wide variety of flavored syrups. Rachel had a fierce craving for one flavored with chocolate and hazelnut. Out the French doors in the back, was an enclosed courtyard with several blue-striped umbrella tables. The courtyard was surrounded by pretty flower borders and potted plants. She had decided to wait for Peter to arrive before ordering the deli's huge smoked turkey sandwiches for them. She closed her eyes and leaned back, face to the screened sun, and smiled with feline satisfaction. Mere moments passed and Rachel had a feeling she was being watched. She opened her eyes and in front of her stood Professor Peter Keefe.

"Just how long have you been standing there?" she asked coquettishly.

Peter was looking, well, like the psychology professor he was; dark suit, white shirt, executive tie. Not that the clothes didn't compliment him. They did. Peter avoided casual attire and sportswear, which was the uniform that other professors wore to their classes, because such attire only served to emphasize his doughy, rich-boy face and graying temples.

"Long enough to consider sneaking right back out of here before you noticed me. You failed to mention this little date was supposed to include a game of tennis," he nodded toward her shoes and shorts.

"Oh, of course not, Peter. I told you, I just want to talk to you about a case I'm involved in. And I thought we could enjoy an informal lunch, since we rarely get together anymore. As for the togs, don't you think you could lose that Eli suit of yours long enough to enjoy this fabulous weather?"

Peter just smiled indulgently and pulled out a chair for himself. "So, what's the poop?" he asked.

The Yalie-phrase, direct from 1956, earned him an involuntary grimace from Rachel, but it was vintage Peter. When Rachel was a fourth-year student, she had become intrigued with her professor and Student Advisor. Peter was a vain shell of a man who buried his heart and earnest conscience deep within. She found him delightfully eccentric; a personality so complex, no true therapist could resist him. And Peter had another attraction: Rachel knew his family had ties to gold mines in California. It was kismet. Peter could be a wealth of information—she smiled to herself at the pun and took another blissful sip of her latte, moaning with pleasure.

She set the paper cup down and leaned eagerly forward. "Peter, I think I've stumbled on to a case history that could make me the next Karen Horney."

She was referring to the pioneer analyst, Peter knew, who became notable by challenging Freudian interpretations of dreams with her own material, which included psychic elements.

"Well. That is some news. Tell your favorite teacher everything."

Rachel was talked out. She had relayed to Peter the whole story about the two sisters with an identical recurring dream. She did not use their real names. Lara and Lainy had requested anonymity, she'd explained when Peter had asked her for the girls' identities. Peter had taken some notes during the retelling, and the patio table was littered with his discarded steno paper. There was barely room for an elbow amidst their crumpled chip bags, empty paper cups, and green plastic baskets stuffed with the wadded tissue that had wrapped their sandwiches.

Rachel bent over and rubbed her flat palms quickly up and down her legs to warm them. She and Peter had been conferring in the courtyard for more than two hours, during which time the warm sun had blanched, and a cool breeze picked up now and then, raising goose bumps on Rachel's shapely legs.

Peter watched, mesmerized by Rachel's innocent sexuality. She was doe-like; graceful, alluring, and skittish. If he hinted even an inkling of attraction to her, she'd bolt. He cleared his throat and fixed his murky green eyes upon her, "So my dear, you want to publish this research as, what? A genetic memory, a past-life vision, or as a singularly unique psychic experience?"

"I'm not sure yet, Peter. I'll need to dig around in those dreams some more, but at the very least, *yes*, It most definitely is a singularly unique psychic experience, don't you think?"

Peter did not answer right away. He cradled his right elbow in his left hand and tapped at his lips with his forefinger. It was an affectation, she knew, but Rachel guessed he thought it made him look every bit the scholarly professor. Professor Peter Keefe neither published nor perished. He chose to focus on instructing undergraduates rather than offering any significant research. *Those who can't, teach.* Rachel thought Peter was a very capable academic. Ordinarily someone in Peter's position, lacking publication, would find themselves out of contention for the tenure-track. But Peter's family had connections at the university. Rachel hoped he could put those connections to work for her.

Finally, he spoke, "And you want the university to sponsor the research—help you facilitate progress through the field, and of course provide the funding for it. You'll need a fairly large grant to cover travel, I think. And, I'm guessing you want me to present it for you."

Rachel leaned forward and grabbed his hand hopefully, "Peter, you do have pull with them. Would you?"

Peter looked heavenward and sighed dramatically. "Madam, your wish shall be my command. It will be my pleasure to champion this research for you."

She was already out of her chair and hugging his head from behind him. "Oh, thank you, Peter. You won't be sorry. I'll be very thorough with the research. I think their story could become a significant bridge between parapsychology and psychoanalysis. It might just challenge the paradigm."

Peter could not see Rachel's face behind him, but he knew what expression it was wearing. She was flushed, exuberant, and smiling widely with straight, white teeth. Her smile would reach up into her eyes and spray some gleam into those mysterious green depths, and, oh, how they sparkled. Peter knew if he were to turn around and look, the vision would take his breath away.

Of course, Rachel could not see Peter's face, either. Or the dismay it revealed.

# Chapter 21

23 March, 1993
Longview, Washington

His office in the Psychology Department was rich, even though Peter was barely holding on to his family's dwindling wealth. At his own expense, Peter had covered the walls with teak paneling salvaged from a hundred-year-old courtroom; it had been demolished in the name of urban renewal some years earlier. The floor was covered with an eight-foot by eleven-foot Persian rug in Chinese red. Faux Tiffany lamps graced the desk and antique sideboard. Bookshelves, in neurotically-perfect order, were located behind his desk. The desk itself was an oversized secretary in the waterfall-pattern, which Peter had located during an antique hunt in Centralia, Washington. Peter knew it on first sight as a rare find, since the waterfall pattern was generally used in bedroom furniture design. Other pieces bearing the pattern were quite uncommon.

The door to his office opened just enough for a pretty female student to pop her head through.

"Professor Keefe?" The co-ed hesitated, "I don't mean to interrupt you, but I tried to find you during your scheduled office hours earlier today. I really need you to clarify your instructions on this term paper's objective and required format." She gave him a pleading, apologetic look.

"I'm sorry you had difficulty reaching me, Janet. Nevertheless, office hours are finished for today, and it's not a convenient time for me," he replied shortly, without bothering to glance up.

"But, if you could just answer a brief question? So that I can get started—"

"I'll have office hours again on Monday, Janet. You can try me then. Good day."

The co-ed was thinking how very much she would like to tell that smug bastard Keefe just what an arrogant ass everyone thought him to be. But the momentary joy it would bring wasn't worth expulsion from the program. She was burning mad. She had waited around campus all afternoon with the hope of clearing up the ambiguous instructions he had provided on the assignment sheet. Wasted time; time made possible only because she had given up her lunch shift on the busiest station at the most popular restaurant in town. Not that the hoity-toity Professor Keefe would give a rat's behind about her losing out on those bill-paying tips—it's not as if the minimum wage could pay her rent and tuition fees. No, Professor Keefe made a grandiose point of telling his students he did not *need* to work for a living. She closed the door quietly.

The student effectively shut out the hustle and hubbub from the departmental halls for Keefe, which differed discordantly with the womb-like atmosphere inside his office. Keefe knew he was not popular with the student body, or the staff for that matter. But he really couldn't care less. Had the family fortune not been squandered away by his shiftless, pretentious father, Peter would have afforded a private practice for himself, instead of a teaching career. He couldn't help it. Education was not his passion. *Passion.*

Peter knew he could be passionate for Rachel Carrell. He'd never been one to hold a fondness for a student—not in all his career as an educator. Rachel was the one exception. For some reason, and even Keefe couldn't be sure what the reason was, he would turn somersaults for Rachel. She was bright and beautiful, sure—and sporting double-D's. But there was much more to her than that. She possessed a singular ability to make Peter feel young and free—sensations he had never felt even when he was a young, free man. Rachel's lighthearted, unflappable demeanor was infectious. Peter suspected that, were he fifteen years younger, or if Rachel were to show the faintest romantic interest, he would be capable of making a sentimental ass of himself over her.

Finally, the telephone number he had been trying for the past half-hour was ringing through. Although the desk phone appeared to be an early 1900's princess phone, it was merely a reproduction with modern enhancements such as touch-tone, and the ever-important automatic re-dial.

"Vanderling," came the terse voice over the long-distance wire.

"It's Keefe. I have troubling news regarding Globalesque."

"Everything is splendid professor. Your frequent insecurities are becoming quite tiresome."

"No, no. I can assure you that things are not splendid. I just had an interesting luncheon with a therapist who was a former student of mine, Rachel Carrell. It appears she intends to publish a case history—one that involves a psychic dream shared by two sisters. It is a dream which reconstructs a certain woman's murder." A dramatic pause, then, "The woman was murdered in Bodie during the latter part of the 1800's."

"And this is relevant because..." the long distance voice snippily responded.

*Finally!* Keefe thought to himself. *I get to be the smug bastard that knows everything and you get to look stupid, Vanderling.* "I should think the significance would be obvious even to a layman such as yourself, Vanderling. Through hypnosis and conscious encounter, the events leading up to the murder can be uncovered. What events do you think may have led to the murder of an ordinary woman in Bodie during this particular period? I'm quite familiar with Bodie's history through and through, Vanderling. I can assure you that decent women never encountered violence. But there was one exception, as we both well know. The death of that innkeeper, with the highly questionable determination that it was a suicide. And we both know it was not a suicide, Vanderling. What happens when the therapist and the subjects also become well-versed in Bodie's history?"

The other voice paused, "I don't perceive a threat."

"Rachel Carrell is a fastidious analyst. She plans to uncover everything surrounding that murder; she intends to use regression therapy. And she hopes to publish. What if the...toxicity is revealed? What will that do for HR 230? I'm just giving you a heads-up, since you are quite obviously out of this loop. The vote must take place immediately, Vanderling. We must have the Senate vote moved up."

His petulant voice had been gaining volume, until the last exclamation came through the wire almost as a shout. Keefe was getting himself worked-up. His Globalesque stock was the only family investment he owned which offered any potential value. If it were to become worthless, Peter would have no more than a common teacher's salary, and later a meager pension, to rely upon. He would no longer enjoy his pretension of working merely for the stimulation. The silver spoon he was born with in elite San Francisco society would be yanked from his pouty mouth. He picked up a wooden stand holding eight antique silver baby spoons from around the world, and hurled it at the door.

The man on the other end of the phone call was silently contemplating the neurosis he sensed from the fussy professor. Still, there was a possibility his paranoia was justified this time. And if so, it would be a problem.

The company could ill afford any supposition about toxic wastes in the Bodie area, as a result of long-ago mining efforts, and it did not matter the number of years that have passed. *That* was their problem. The Bill should have had the standard boiler-plate clause about returning the affected land to its *current* condition, following open-pit excavation. Instead, the Bodie Bowl Senate Bill, HR 230, was all-inclusive; clean-up and *total* restoration of *any* mining efforts within Bodie Bowl would be required.

So far, only one geologist knew of the widespread cyanide pollution, and he had been encouraged, to the tune of fifty thousand dollars, to forget what he had learned.

The voice on the other end sighed dramatically. "Alright, Keefe. I'll take care of it. Clearly, the sacrifice of one good woman was not enough to satisfy the preservation of the old Touchstone mining rights..." Vanderling trailed off, pondering the narrow options. Finally he said, "I'm glad you brought this to our attention, Keefe. We shall begin making arrangements to, eradicate, shall we say, the possible interference."

Hundreds of miles distant from the voice in British Columbia, Keefe shot to his feet and reeled with the implication of Vanderling's last comment. "*No*. Good God, are you insane? I didn't mean for that. Move the vote up, that's all I am saying. You can't *kill* her!"

"Of course not, Keefe. I never suggested anything of the sort. And I would warn you not to propose such a plot over these very public international telephone wires. Now stop worrying yourself over the matter. I will see the problem is taken care of."

Keefe heard a click, and the call disconnected. His legs became limp as cooked spaghetti. He fell back into his wing chair feeling suddenly sick at his stomach. His bowels turned to water. Cold, prickly sweat broke out on his forehead. "What have I done?" he asked himself aloud. He ran for his private bathroom.

# Chapter 22

23 March, 1993
Howe Sound, British Columbia

Vanderling swiveled toward the wet bar, "I do not intend to let a self-promoting bitch-shrink screw up the sale of our Bodie mining rights, Jake."

With his back still to his boss while he fixed his James Bond martini, Jake shrugged his shoulders and replied simply, "Nope."

Vanderling always took his calls over the intercom and of course his problem-solver, Jake, had heard and absorbed everything. Jake turned with his drink in hand and walked to the chair on the opposite side of Vanderling's desk. He was a highly paid thug of lower-class beginnings, who had developed a penchant for the finer things in life. And Jake was willing to commit almost any act to preserve access to the things he wanted. That was just the sort of warped loyalty Vanderling had been looking for in an assistant, when he'd found Jake among his fruit-picking friends and relatives years earlier.

Jake wore his jet black hair slicked down and back. He also frequently dressed in black pants and custom-tailored, button-down shirts. He thought the attire gave him a swaggering 'Erik Estrada' look, who Jake assured him was an admired sex symbol in Mexico. Vanderling avoided taking Jake to Mexican restaurants, fearing someone might mistake him for a busboy.

"When ya want me to do her, this Rachel Carrell mujere?" Jake smiled above his elegantly poised glass.

"Be very careful, Jake. This needs to look like a doctor's office break-in, gone bad. And poor Ms. Carrell had the unfortunate luck to be present when the gang broke in. Keep an eye on her for a few days, and when you get the opportunity to get her alone, perhaps after hours, then do it. And, I'll want tapes, notes, anything that concerns those two sisters she's studying. We're going to need their real names, Jake. That is paramount," Vanderling instructed as he toyed with the regimental pleats in his slacks. "And Jake, it absolutely can not look like an assassination. It must look like an amateur gang of druggies got spooked and killed her—something along those lines. I can't have this traced back to Globalesque business."

"Sure, boss. I can make it a rape, too, if ya want."

"No, no. I couldn't trust Keefe to keep his mouth shut if the murder were to be brutal in any way. Keep it clean and quick, Jake. In and out, got it?"

"Got it."

# Chapter 23

"**L**isten to this, Lainy," Lara said. "This pamphlet on Bodie was mailed to me by the California State Park System. I thought it would be a good idea to learn a little about its history. It says, 'Nearly everyone has heard about the infamous Badman from Bodie. Some historians say that he was a real person by the name of Tom Adams. Others say his name was Washoe Pete. It seems more likely, however, that he was a composite. Bad men, like bad whiskey and bad climate, were endemic to the area.'" Lara whistled low. "Sounds like a wonderful vacation spot, don't you think?"

Lainy wasn't really listening to Lara as she read. She was concentrating, instead, on maneuvering her Camry along the seriously winding path of Highway 22. She was tired, and she had a fierce headache. Probably the result of a five-hour drive the day before, followed by hours of hypnosis in the afternoon, and another five-hour trek back to the Coast. To make matters worse, an early fog was setting in, and the damn windshield of her new car was slanted so extremely, that the defrost had to blast hot air like a furnace over her and Lara just to clear the window. Her eyeballs were being baked, and it was not making her headache feel any better. Lainy was furious about the obvious design flaw that, at the price she paid for the Camry, was simply unacceptable. On top of everything else, Lainy was distracted by the information they had gleaned from the afternoon's session with Rachel.

"Anyway, the town eventually became a hang out for Hari Krishnas to train together in solicitation techniques at California airports, and that was right about the time the town of Bodie ceased to be considered as a gold mining area," Lara joked. She looked over at her frowning sister who was slouched low in her seat and peering out a sliver of clear windshield just above the steering wheel. "You're not listening to me at all, are you?" Lara asked. Then, with a touch of concern she asked, "Do you want me to drive for awhile, Lainy?"

"Huh? Oh…no," Lainy answered as she squinted out the windshield on the lookout for deer along the roadside. Rarely a day went by that she didn't see a stiff and bloated doe discarded along the shoulder, a result of tourists, mostly, who did not keep an eye out for deer feeding close to the road's edge.

Lainy was careful in her driving, and she was careful about her new car. It was the first thing she'd ever earned and paid for herself, and she was immensely proud of that. She'd gotten herself a job at a small dress shop. It was one in a chain of four. It was the first "adult" job Lainy had ever held, since she'd married her first husband while still in high school. Later, she went back for her G.E.D. As it turned out, Lainy had some real talent in fashion. Her manager had Lainy decorate the store windows, earning her a raise after just three weeks. Her sales were higher than everyone else's in no time at all. After a few short months, the owner of the chain made Lainy the manager of the Lincoln City shop, and the Buyer for all four stores in the chain.

Her soon-to-be-ex-husband was from a wealthy family. He'd told her he was appalled to have his wife working for a living. Lainy knew he was offended by the realization she no longer needed him. She reminded him she would no longer be his wife in a matter of days, so he need not concern himself with her personal *or* professional life.

Ray had always held his fat bank book over her pretty little head as a means of keeping her dependent upon him. But Lainy learned, in short order, that Ray's mother held the family purse-strings, and she'd held *her* money over *Ray's* head.

Lainy's new car was her act of effectively snipping those purse strings, and she had become almost emotionally attached to the car. To Lainy, it was as if her life has been saved by the car. So, in return, she vowed to always take care of it. She felt *that* attached to her new freedom-on-wheels. She really didn't want anyone else, not even Lara, driving it.

They were both quiet for a few moments, and then Lainy blurted, "I can't believe our great, great grandmother was murdered in a gold rush town. I mean, now that we know a little something about her, now that I know she was a real person, I'm so chilled by how she was murdered in my, our, dream. All I can think about now is how terrified she looked in that dream." Lainy glanced at Lara briefly, "I don't want to ever see that in her eyes again. I don't want to have that dream ever again, Lara."

"I know. Whenever I was having the dream, I usually just considered it interesting, like a puzzle, I guess. But now it's become depressing. I mean, we have no family except for each other, and I have always wanted to know what kind of family we came from. I can't help worrying that we may never know who our family was." Lara said.

"She was so pretty and she looked so happy in the dream's beginning. And how about that hunk she was kissing? He must have been her boyfriend. It looked to me like they were in love. I bet they had their future together all planned. And then she's murdered like that. Hey, she ran an inn like you do, Lara. Doesn't that make you feel kind of weird? It's like a part of history repeating itself."

"Thanks a lot, Lainy. I guess I better not venture out to the verandah at night alone anymore, huh?"

Lainy took her eyes off the looping, cloud-covered road long enough to shoot Lara a you-shouldn't-tempt-fate-with-remarks-like-that look. "It's scary," was all she could say. It was probably all the weird similarities between Elise Swazey's life and their lives that had begun making Lainy uneasy. She was certain Lara felt the same. They drove in silence for awhile.

"Want to hear some more?" Lara offered.

"Sure."

"Okay. 'By 1879 Bodie boasted a population of about ten thousand'—*ten thousand*, that's huge." Lara exclaimed. "'And was second to none for wickedness, badmen, and the worst climate out of doors. One little girl, whose family was taking her to the remote and infamous town, wrote in her diary, 'Good-bye, God. I'm going to Bodie.' The phrase came to be known throughout the west.' Wow." Lara exhaled loudly, "What a place to have to live in." She shook her head.

"What a place to have to die in," came Lainy's quiet reply.

# Chapter 24

L ara was surprised to see the "No Vacancy" sign hanging when they pulled in. "Hey, not bad for a Thursday night in April," she said to her husband. She entered the kitchen through the service door on the porch, between the main house and the carriage house. Jeff was sitting on a bar stool at the island, reading another Patterson book.

"Seriously, that's not an April Fool's joke, we have a full house? How did that happen?" Lara said as she tossed her overnight bag on the floor to wrap her arms around her husband's waist.

"Well, I've got good news and bad news," he smiled as he placed a marker in his book and got up to give Lara a kiss. "Everything go okay?"

"Yeah. I'll tell you all about it, but I think hypnosis is giving Lainy and me headaches. I've got to take a couple Advil first." Lara kissed him back and headed for the medicine cabinet. "What's the good news?"

"All four rooms are full."

"I know that already. Uh-oh. What's the bad news?"

Jeff grimaced, "One of the guests, the guy from Seattle, smokes. He was not ecstatic with our no-smoking policy, and I got the distinct impression he intends to ignore it, if he hasn't already."

Lara groaned, "Maybe I should make that three Advil." Just then, someone knocked on the closed kitchen door, loudly. Jeff walked over to unlatch and pull open the solid door, but not before the impatient knocker had opportunity to bang just a little harder. After the solid door, which was kept locked at night and whenever Jeff and Lara were away, came a set of saloon-type swinging doors set into the middle of the opening. Jeff began to look over the top of these, when a man on the other side pushed them inward forcibly enough for the right-sided door to hit the wall with a bang. Then, without apology, and more importantly, without invitation, the man pushed his way into the kitchen.

"Need to borrow your phone," he explained as he stalked around like a bull in a china shop looking for the telephone. Jeff indicated the shelf as he backed up all the way to where Lara was standing. He turned toward her and moved his head up and down one time to indicate this was their smoker. Jeff noticed Lara swallowed three Advil tablets before she left the room to go next door.

"You know what?" Lara asked her husband when he joined her next door at their quarters. "I'm actually beginning to look forward to our trip to Bodie. I think I need to get away from here." Jeff's disciplinary leave without pay was to begin the following week. They were scheduled to leave for Bodie on Saturday, just two days away.

"Good. I think it's gonna be fun. Claire can not wait to go fishing." Jeff said.

"Good. You know what else? I'm totally spitting in that guy's eggs tomorrow."

Jeff started laughing. "No you're not," he tried to shoot her a stern look.

"No, I'm not," Lara giggled. "But my mouth is watering at the thought of it."

She wouldn't waste any more of her time or energy worrying about her rude guest. She would just keep the security deposit they made if there was any evidence of smoking in their room. She smiled.

In two days, she was off on vacation, where she knew the bad men were all in their graves.

# Chapter 25

"You're breaking a hard-n-fast rule, you know," he huffed as he tried his best to keep up with her. "You said you never worked weekends, remember? You said 'me' time was important for everyone. You said—"

"Okay, Mark, okay." She hollered over her shoulder at him. She was rounding the west end of the river. Ducks saw the joggers stampeding toward them and flitted in all directions, protesting loudly. It was time to stop jogging and begin the slow-down walk the rest of the way to the office. She stopped and bent over at the waist, stretching, waiting for Mark to catch up with her. They headed for the row of brick office buildings which lined the north end of the river. Beautiful shade trees and a popular jogging path passed directly beneath Rachel's second-floor windows. She found herself thinking, not for the first time, how fortunate she was to have found this office space. Each day following the last session, she and Mark would go for a half-hour jog around the small waterway and review cases.

"You're going to be a really good therapist someday, Mark. You're frustratingly persistent," she laughed at her third-year student intern's serious face. "You know, Mark, I may not say it often enough, but you really are going to be an excellent therapist." She winked at him. "Look, this won't be like work. I had nothing planned for Saturday anyway." She looked up and said a quick "hi" to a stranger standing under her building's covered entrance. It was not at all unusual to have lots of people, both locals and tourists, loitering about this breath-taking Longview park. Rachel always made an effort to say hello to anyone she met. Mark stopped her at the door.

"Rachel, I just, I'm sorry but I've already made plans to go skiing tomorrow; I told you about the trip, remember? So, I won't be able to help you."

"*Really*, it's okay, Mark. I need to work on this case alone, anyway. I mean no offense, but the sisters have asked for complete confidentiality. And it's such an unusual and exciting case that I'm really looking forward to it," she said brightly. She noticed the man she'd greeted was still standing there and seemed to be listening to their conversation. Rachel smiled politely, grabbed Mark's arm and they walked through the entrance doors to her building.

"That guy was watching you, Rachel. I don't like the looks of him."

"C'mon, Mark." She patted his hand affectionately. "You're such a mother hen."

# Chapter 26

Lainy frowned as she pulled her car into her driveway and parked behind her soon-to-be ex-husband's work truck. It was a pretty day out and Ray had a construction job through his family's company, pouring foundations. He should have been working. *When was he going to get it, that he does not live here anymore?* Lainy griped to herself. Then aloud, she murmured, "Just a few more days to go, Lainy."

She came through the kitchen entry via the garage, which was standing wide open, and laid her keys in the basket on the counter. "Ray?" she hollered for him.

No answer. *Must have just parked here and walked down to the beach*, Lainy thought. She walked passed the family room and halfway down the hall to the master bedroom, but stopped when she saw the door to her guest bath was closed. Bending over to peer at the gap between threshold and door, she could see the light was on. *Damn!* She tapped on the door, putting her ear close. She heard rustling and hurried whispers.

"Ray? Is there someone in there with you?" She asked.

No answer. She could hear someone moving around, and she wasn't about to walk away without knowing who it was that was in her house. A little louder and speaking into the door jam, she asked him, "*What* are you doing? And, why are you here at all? You don't live here anymore." She sing-song'd the last part. The door swung open with a *whoosh!* surprising Lainy to jump back a couple of feet.

"Whoa!" A very large, smiling man with dirty brown hair and unkempt mustache, stood before her, wearing a sweat-stained wife-beater tee and hard-worn jeans. Bare dirty feet completed the image.

"Hey, Ray, does the carpet match the drapes?" he asked over his shoulder as he gaped at Lainy.

Ray looked over at his wife and sneered, "Yeah."

Startled silent for a beat or two, Lainy took in the scene; her new shower curtain was tied in a knot and tucked inside the tub. Ray sat on the tub's edge with a crack pipe in his hand. Someone had rinsed dirty hands, clearly without benefit of soap, and dried them all over her new cream towels. Some were wadded up on the counter top and in the sink. Lainy found her voice.

"Get out!"

"Still my house, too, for three more days," Ray mumbled as the pipe reached his lips.

"Ray, you know you're not allowed here, and, are you *actually* smoking crack in my bathroom?"

"My bathroom," he wheezed through his inhale.

"Get out!" Lainy yelled at him.

"Seriously, dude. This is your wife? She's hot." The dirty man licked his lips and scrutinized her up and down.

The men were carrying on as if Lainy had not spoken, let alone yelled at them to leave. *Twice.*

The filthy bum turned to look at Ray. "Hey, asshole, I'm talking to you," he growled.

"*What?*"

"She still belongs to you for three more days?"

Lainy bristled, "*Belong* to him? I have never belonged to anyone, thank you very much, and certainly not *that* waste-of-space." She nodded in Ray's direction, then turned to walk away. But the man reached out and grabbed her upper arm.

Gripping it roughly, he turned to Ray again. "Whaddaya say, Ray? Share?"

Lainy was getting scared. She shirked his hand away and walked hastily to the nearest telephone. She quickly dialed 9-1-1, and to her surprise the call connected immediately. *Thank you, rural Oregon*, Lainy thought to herself with relief.

"9-1-1, what's your emergency?" The voice asked.

"I'm Lainy Erickson. Can you tell where I am calling from?" Lainy hurriedly asked the dispatcher.

"Yes, Ms. Erickson. What is your emergency?"

"There is a strange man in my bathroom smoking a crack pipe, and he is threatening me," she told him.

Ray walked into the family room and leaned on the island countertop that separated it from the kitchen. He smiled benignly at her. "You're not really talking to 9-1-1," he accused.

"Okay, Ms. Erickson, I have a unit in the area, and they are in route. Stay on the line with me. Did the man break-in to your home, ma'am?"

"I think he may have come in with my estranged husband, who must have broken in because he no longer has a key. When I came home, the door was wide open."

"So, your husband is also in the house with you?" the dispatcher asked.

"Yes, but he shouldn't be; I have a restraining order. Our divorce is final in three days."

"Now I know you're full of shit, Lainy! You're not talking to anyone," Ray lunged across the countertop and made a grab for the phone in her hand. He missed, but he'd gotten close enough to hear a voice on the other end asking Lainy if she was alright. Ray stood up ramrod-straight and stared at her, glassy-eyed.

"You bitch! You called the cops on me? I'm gonna F you up!"

The dispatcher on the phone could be heard shouting something. At just that moment, a *whoop-whoop* from a police car siren sounded, and Ray whipped his view around to the family room sliders. A black-and-white police car with lights whirling, was parked in front of the house.

"The stupid bitch called the cops, Daryl. They're already here. Get rid of it," Ray yelled as he went running for the bathroom; he stopped short when he saw his good buddy Daryl had already bugged out through the window. Ray hesitated just a split-second before he followed.

The police did a quick walk through the house and assured Lainy that her estranged husband and his friend had vacated the property. They left Lainy with a promise they would patrol past her house a few times each day and night to keep her husband away. One of the officers handed her a business card. She had to thank the officers through tears of relief and gratitude.

Lainy checked the locks on all of the windows and doors, and then she poured herself a glass of wine; a very big glass. She stood at the large picture window and watched as the waves in the distance crashed against the rocks. This was the part of Oregon she loved most—the raw, rocky outcroppings that worked in tandem with waves, to shoot impressive 'rooster tail' sprays of whitewater high into the air, often times to be backlit by a raging, color-changing sky. Lainy loved storm-watching. She stood mesmerized as she sipped a fruity, lightly-dry Riesling she had picked up at a small winery in the valley. Perhaps she had been more afraid than she'd allowed herself to believe, and was now shedding tears of relief. Or maybe she was cyclic and moody, and the overflowing tears running down her cheeks were cathartic.

Maybe it was both, and so much more. She hung her head a moment and tried to quell her decent into depression. But to do that, she had to convince herself there was a reason to be joyful, and she just couldn't think of *anything*.

Lainy raised her head up toward the sky. "Why, God? Why can't anyone love *me*? I know my sister does, and I know Jeff does, too. And I'm grateful, Lord. But I want someone to love, like they have in each other. I *need* someone to love *me*." She sniffed and reached for a tissue. Men had always buzzed around her like honey bees to nectar. They would tell her she was pretty, and they would buy her expensive gifts. But none of them were interested in loving her, cherishing her, or sharing his dreams with her. It was about sex. Once a man scored, he either wanted to possess her and tuck her away so no one else could have her, or he ran for the hills. Her two marriages had been the 'possessive' sort. Both were cold and devoid of genuine affection, empty of even a real friendship. How young and stupid had she been, marrying not one time but twice, to men who only wanted to put her on a shelf? She knew it wasn't really a matter of stupidity. *I'd been starved for affection and praise. That's why I fell for their…bullshit,* Lainy thought sadly.

Lainy's neighbor across the street was pulling her garbage can out to the curb. She saw Lainy and waved. Lainy waved back. Janey was one of the women she and Lara played Bunko with, once a month. They'd been doing it forever. *Janey thinks she knows who I am, but she doesn't. Not really. She doesn't know how lonely I am. She knows my sister and I grew up in foster care, but no one ever discussed it. The Bunko girls must have figured out that was a sore subject. I bet they would be surprised to know that I have not been on a date with a man since I met Ray.*

Like any other woman, Lainy dressed and did her hair and makeup to garner attention from men. And she got attention from men—plenty of it. But she always turned them down, opting instead for her man Clint and a big bowl of buttered popcorn.

Having been a red-headed child growing up in foster care, hers was not a child-beauty-queen story. It was quite the opposite. With her pale skin and freckles and bright orange-red hair, all of the children called her ugly names and said she had 'cooties.' She remembered when a foster father had told the entire household over dinner one night that red-haired people were mentally defective. "Like that orange cat that's missin' a chromosome, or something," he'd asserted. Lara had stood up for her, as she always did, but it mattered little. The entire household treated her as though she were mentally-impaired. Then they placed her in remedial classes at school, which bored her to tears. Thank goodness her big sister tutored her in just about everything, so that Lainy got a pretty good education, albeit one that was two grade levels ahead.

Lainy's first husband had broken her heart; she had believed he loved her. She'd loved him. But once the honeymoon was over, sweet compliments and random flowers ceased. Fresh-cut flowers were a luxury, though. Perhaps he was just being frugal with money and saving for their future. Maybe he'd been nervous about their savings because she had recently told him the happy news—they were pregnant. They had talked about children. They both wanted them; she had wanted lots of them. But her rationalizations did not explain why, drastically sudden, the compliments, good manners, and even basic thoughtfulness, went the way of the dinosaurs. She'd begun to wonder if he was unhappy being married, or if he was not truly happy about the baby. And then her wonder turned to a nasty, nagging worry that began nibbling around the edges of her idyllic life.

Nine weeks into their new life together something happened that answered Lainy's doubts, and she worried no more. They were stopped behind a school bus when a large truck towing an RV, slammed into them from behind. She had lost consciousness for a few seconds because she'd "woke" to the sound of her husband screaming that he had broken his back. She'd been able to turn her neck only marginally before pains shot through her head, but she could see her husband was hunched over the steering wheel. She'd felt like her back was broken as well, and panic was rising about the health of her baby. For some reason, Lainy couldn't talk right away. It was several long, insufferable minutes before Lainy found her voice, and told her husband she thought her back might be broken, too—not that he had asked if she was alright. But it was Lainy's heart that had broken into a million pieces, when her newlywed husband's reply was, "Really? Wow, Lainy, this could take care of all of our debt and then some."

Lainy took a bigger swallow of wine than was wise, and it caused a coughing fit. Conjuring up the hurtful words in her mind, even after all of these years and another worthless husband later, made tears flow freely down her cheeks. She had lost the baby. Her back had been fractured in several places, as well as her jaw, and she endured years of physical therapy. The State of Oregon did not allow auto accident victims to sue for pain and suffering at the time. All that could be recovered were the actual medical expenses that had accumulated over two years, as Allstate dragged their feet. They'd had no choice but to settle with them, and when they did, her ex-husband received five thousand dollars for his sprained wrist; he did not have a broken back after all, and Lainy received the rest. The money was just enough for Lainy to put a down payment on a small condo. The marriage had quickly disintegrated. But there was a happy ending; The State of Oregon was also a "no fault" divorce state, so hers was quick and easy. Several months later, when her brother-in-law had run into Lainy's first husband at a beach event, her ex had been accommodating enough to make a wisecrack about Lainy, the avoidance of stretch marks, and a reference to the baby she'd lost. Jeff put his lights out. She loved Jeff like a blood-brother. She allowed herself a teeny smile.

With two divorces under her belt, Lainy could determine with relative authority that whatever her marriages were, they were not about love. She shuddered. *If she hadn't called 9-1-1, would Ray have allowed that filthy degenerate to rape her?* She had zero faith in her soon-to-be-ex. She was glad she didn't have to find out the answer to that question.

Taking another sip as lazy tears flowed, Lainy genuflected and continued her sad soliloquy. "Thank you, Lord, for protecting me." She sipped for awhile and watched the waves crash. She wanted to know what it felt like to have a man tell her he loved her and believe that he meant it. "Am I just not loveable?" Her voice broke. She listened to the quiet and stared out the window. "I feel unfinished, Lord; incomplete. I am so lonely for someone to share my life with. Please—" She sobbed a little, hugged herself. "Isn't there *anyone* who would feel fortunate to be loved by me? Someone who would feel *lucky*? Please, send me a good man, Lord, one who would love me back. I just can't be in love all alone. Done that, Lord knows," she half-laughed, half-sobbed. She wiped her eyes, sniffed, straightened up and drained her glass. Lainy genuflected again. "Did you hear how I qualified that last part with 'good man.' Lord? Maybe I'm getting smarter. I love you, Lord. In Jesus' name, I pray. Amen."

She laid the empty wine glass on the counter top. "I have to pee," Lainy announced to an empty room; she hadn't eaten all day and the wine had gone instantly to her head. She started for the guest bath, but slammed the brakes on when she saw the mess in there. Quickly, she grabbed up all of the towels and threw them in the washing machine across the hall. She started the washer and returned to the bath. Lainy untied the knot in the curtain. The wrinkles would hang out in time, but she didn't want any unhealthy residues, so she began unhooking the curtain from the rod. That went into the wash cycle as well. She looked around. She would have to give it a thorough cleaning—walls, ceiling, everything—when they returned from Bodie. *Wow*, Lainy thought to herself. *We leave tomorrow.* She was already packed and ready to go. At first, Lainy had been a bit anxious. Now, at least, she wasn't nervous about the trip any longer. On the contrary (and with much thanks to her crack-smoking ex), she felt like she had to get away from here, and Bodie was beckoning.

"And I still have to pee," Lainy said. By now she had decided to use the bath off her master bedroom. Lainy figured she may as well get ready for bed, even though it was a Friday night and still light outside. She knew she wasn't going out again; she had microwave popcorn and a couple of old Clint Eastwood films on VHS. Besides, maybe a long, luxurious shower would make her feel better. She reached in to turn on the spacious walk-in shower, pulling the curtain back just enough to surprise an opossum scrambling to get its footing on the marble tile. It started hissing at her and scratching furiously. Lainy screamed in surprise. *My God, those things are hideous up close.* She backed out and went running for the broom. Armed and on her way back to face the opossum, she hurriedly took the security bar out of the sliding glass doors' track and opened them wide. The possum was out of the shower, but now it had backed itself into a corner by the commode. Lainy jumped atop the toilet and used the broom to coax the possum out. It took Lainy another twenty minutes to get the critter out of her house.

"*Agghh*," She shuddered violently. "Thanks Ray, for leaving the door to my house wide open," she exclaimed as she closed and locked the door and put the bar back in place. "Oh no, the shower." She ran to the back of the house and put her hand under the rain shower head; luke warm. She was out of hot water. *That's just great.* She turned the water off. She stood there in her bathroom, thinking about what she wanted to do. Her eyes fell on her packed suitcase, sitting next to the dresser.

Her car pulled into the parking lot, surprising Lara, who worried it was someone looking for a room for the night. Lara peeked out the front to make sure the "No Vacancy" sign was still hanging.

It was. Before she could check out the visitor's car from the other bank of windows, the back door screen was being rapped on.

"It's me, Lara. Open, hurry." Lainy was shifting from foot-to-foot.

"Hey, you're back." She crossed the room and unlocked the screen door for her sister. What's up?"

"Bad things happen in my bathrooms. I need to use yours," Lainy said hurriedly.

"Uh, sure. But, what's wrong with your bathrooms?" Lara asked.

Lainy made a face. "I *really* have to use the potty."

"Go," her sister told her.

Lainy walked quickly to the guest bath and closed the door. Through the door, she hollered to Lara, "I'm going to spend the night here. I hope that's cool."

"Sure. It's fine. So, what's going on at your place?" She asked.

"Bad things, Lara. Bad things happened."

✄ ✄

*Oh boy*, her brother-in-law was mad. Lainy had never seen him that mad before. She looked over to where he was sitting. *Is it just bad timing that he's polishing up his .22?*

"You know, the police are looking for him, Jeff. He's violated the restraining order for the third time. The judge told him last time that if he landed in his court again, Ray would do thirty days, *minimum*. And anyway, we're leaving tomorrow." She hesitated. "You are polishing that up for the trip, right?"

Jeff looked up and gave her one of his "molasses" smiles. Just then there was a knock on the door. "Is it my birthday?" Jeff asked, thinking it would be Ray.

Lara laughed. "No, no, it's just a kid at the door, probably selling Girl Scout cookies." She started to rise.

"*Is* it my birthday?" Jeff asked. "I love those ones with everything on 'em—can't remember what they're called."

"I'm up," Lainy said, already halfway to the door. She turned on the porch light since it was getting twilight. "Sorry, Jeff. Unless the boy scouts are selling cookies now, you're out of luck."

She unlocked and opened the door, but before she could say a word, a young man with enormous teeth started in with a well-rehearsed sales pitch.

Lainy put her hand up. "Whoa, guy. You've picked the wrong house. This is a business, and as you can see on the posted sign, right here," she tapped a beautifully-lacquered nail on a plaque mounted next to the door which read, 'No Solicitors', "we do not take sales calls, at least not without an appointment. Sorry." She started to close the door, but the young man was persistent.

"*Wait*," He yelled. "I'm not a solicitor. I'm just selling magazines," he told her. Lainy giggled.

"I already sold so many that I only need to sell two more subscriptions, and I'll win the trip to Hawaii. Come on, lady, help me out," the smarmy teen actually pouted for her.

Lainy turned and hid her face behind the glass door's wooden frame so he didn't catch her laughing at him. She made a funny face at her sister, who was moving behind her to hear what was going on.

She turned back to him, "Uh, honey, I don't even live here. I'm just managing the place while the owners are away. You'll have to win that trip with the next house." She started to close the door, but the teen stuck his foot in it.

"Remove your foot," Lainy told him, completely un-amused.

"Just wait," he rudely ordered her. "Look, I have magazines for every hobby on the planet. I even have a couple for off-the-planet enthusiasts—anything you can imagine. So, I know I have something here that you want and *you* don't even know it. Everybody has a hobby of some sort, am I right?"

"Remove. Your. Foot." Lainy had quite enough of pushy males high on testosterone for one day, and her tone was clear.

"Alright, alright. Just a sec. *Geez. Relax.* You got a hobby, right? Everyone does. So, don't be a hard-ass. C'mon, help me out, lady." Then he changed his tone from hostile to leading, "I'll take my foot out of the door," he fairly teased her.

*Amazing. Thirty-seconds in, and even this snarky little brat is disrespectful to me. What am I, every man's doormat?* She was about to holler for her brother-in-law when she heard his slow drawl behind her. "I have a hobby," he said.

The young man's face brightened immediately, and his voice took on the quality of a carnival barker. "Oh, right. That's what I'm talking about. Sir? I can't really see you, Sir? But, uh, you say you have a hobby? Then, I gotta magazine for it. So, what's your hobby, dude?"

Jeff pushed between Lara and Lainy and brought his .22 to shoulder level. "I like to shoot moving targets," he said casually, as he looked through the scope and placed the crosshairs squarely over the teeth-with-a-face.

"*Whaaaa*," The teen screamed in a very high pitch, just before he took the veranda steps in a single jump and ran as fast as he could down the highway, probably with a fresh load in his pants. The kid never looked back. If he had, he would have seen an open door and three adults belly-laughing; the two women were on the floor.

"Oh my gosh, I needed that," Lainy was laughing so hard she was crying. "That was priceless. How perfect that you just happened to have your rifle out." She saw a look pass between Jeff and Lara. Lainy's laughter subsided. "What?" She asked, suspiciously.

"Nothin.' Just…it might not have been all *that* random." He looked to his wife.

"Oh," Lainy said, understanding. "So, we're taking guns to Bodie?" She asked her sister.

"A single firearm, that's all, probably just for gopher hunting."

"Probably, for hunting gophers," Lainy said, somewhat skeptical.

"If we didn't bring a firearm, Lainy, it would probably be the first time folks ever went to Bodie looking for answers without one," she elbowed her sister in the ribs to show she was kidding around.

"And lived to tell about it," Jeff teased.

Lainy felt the conversation was taking a morbid turn, and she wasn't in the mood for it. "I think I'll turn in early," she announced. "It's been a long day." She hugged her sister and brother and headed for her room.

He watched his sister retire to her room and close the door. Jeff turned to his wife and in a soft, syrupy under-voice, told her, "There's something I want to take care of before we leave tomorrow."

"Something, or someone?" Lara asked him. He didn't answer.

# Chapter 27

Rachel did not make a habit of working on Saturdays. As a therapist, she recognized the need for adult downtime. But she'd already decided she would make an exception to her own rule today. She was excited about beginning the writing of her manuscript on the "dream sisters," as she had begun referring to Lara and Lainy in her notes. But she'd just finished a busy week full of appointments, and she'd had no time at all to dedicate to the project until now. The office was quiet on Saturday; there was probably no one else working in the whole building. Rachel locked the outer office door before continuing on to her private office where she kept her word processor. Her arms full of research materials and a huge satchel-like purse, she methodically began turning on light switches using her right shoulder. Then she dumped her load on the desk and walked to the small kitchenette located off the reception area, opposite her assistant's desk, in order to start a pot of coffee. She flipped through the white-washed basket full of foil coffee pouches until she found a Mocha Irish Crème flavored one. She tore open the bag and emptied it into the filter unit. She poured water into the coffee machine, pushed the button, and wiped up a little spilled water. The coffeemaker was fast. It could brew an entire twelve-cup pot in under eight minutes. *Good*, Rachel thought, because it was already nine-thirty in the morning, and she really wanted that coffee.

Back in her office, she flipped on the hard-drive unit and typed in the date and time. She slipped an already-formatted diskette into the A drive in order to back up her writings, tucked a plush pillow behind her lower back, and settled in. She was ready to begin work on the case study that might just be her destiny. Something of enormous import occurred in Bodie some 115 years ago; she could just *feel* it. And with every session she'd held with the sisters, the more she felt personally connected to them—and Bodie. She was starting to entertain the notion of undergoing regression therapy herself. What an explosive final chapter it would be, if she were to learn that she'd lived—and likely died—in Bodie, too.

The building corridor outside Rachel Carrell's office door was tomb-like on this Saturday morning. It was orderly and clean, and no living soul seemed to exist within miles. Confident that he was alone, he pulled a black pouch from inside his CHiPS look-alike leather jacket, and removed his burglary tools. He had a small spray can of graphite and some tension tools and picks inside his bag of tricks, but he would not be using those. The job was not supposed to look professional. Instead, he pulled out two metal files; the first, to hack at the molding which prevented access to the latch bolt's striker plate and face plate, and the other to slide the latch bolt up. Jake had already used the same rough technique on the optometrist's office around the corner from Rachel Carrell's door, stealing all the pain medications he could find as a phony motive for the break-in.

Rachel had typed in the personal data of the dream sisters, without actually naming their identities, and had begun making a quick outline of the points she would cover and the further questions she hoped to answer. She jerked her head up at a small ticking sound, then realized the coffee was done. She saved the file to the disk, and then asked the computer to save what she had typed so far to the A-drive diskette. The aroma of the coffee was overwhelmingly tantalizing. Rachel removed her glasses and set them down, then forced herself from the comfortable chair in her quest for morning brew. She yawned as she rounded the corner to the kitchenette, but stopped before finishing. Rachel's eyes grew wide and the therapist gasped when she saw the outer office door standing part way open. A cold steel ball dropped from her stomach to her toes. Her heart began pounding so hard it hurt. She knew with certainty that she had locked that door. Rachel reacted. She pivoted a half-turn and made to bolt for the open door. But she'd never had a chance. A well-built Latino man stepped out of the kitchenette and squarely in her path. He faced her toe to toe, smiling handsomely. Rachel screamed. It was the man from the building entrance a few days earlier. Mark had been right. The man had been watching her and listening to their conversation.

"I had no idea you was goin' to look so good, chica," the man said as he threw her against the wall, his forearm braced beneath her chin.

"Oh, God. Please," Rachel choked. "What ever you want. I'll give you whatever you need. There's a prescription pad on my desk." Blessedly, she could not see the large, very sharp knife the man was holding at waist-level.

Jake did not really enjoy his work as much as Vanderling presumed. He considered it a shame to have to kill this pretty lady. He would not torture this woman by allowing her terror to build. Without another word, he stared into her eyes and smiled sweetly as he plunged the knife deeply below her right breast, then quickly jerked it up through major organs. Rachel's eyes widened in surprise and sudden understanding even as her body began to slump against Jake's arm.

He whispered to her softly, "Sorry, babe, but no dame's worth thirty-five mil."

# Chapter 28

An empty beer can rolled out of the truck when he opened the driver's door to get out. "I, uh, that's not mine," he pointed to the rolling can.

"Ray," Jeff chuckled, "did you have peeling lead paint in your nursery? I mean, man, you've got some big ones showing up here...but, thanks." He began rolling up his sleeves.

"Oh, come on. We were only teasing her and, as usual," he sneered in Lainy's direction and slurred his words. "She blew it all out of proportion. So what? Now you're gonna 'even the score'?" He used annoying air quotes.

"Like you've only seen in movies," Jeff promised Ray. He took a step forward for emphasis.

"Okay, look...I'm sorry, okay?" He looked from Jeff to Lainy, and finally to Lara. "I came to tell Lainy I was sorry for smoking—" he looked at Claire and quickly finished, "you know, in the house."

Lara grabbed Claire's hand and took her and Sammy for a walk in the orchard, away from the confrontation with her dirt-bag uncle, but not before the family pet piddled on Ray's suede shoes. Ray was too inebriated to notice. *Good girl, Sammy,* Lara thought.

Claire started giggling. "Good girl, Sammy!"

Lara stopped and looked at her little girl, wondering if it was a coincidence. She did not wonder for long.

"What's a dirt-bag, Mommy?" Claire looked up at her mother's taut face.

"Claire, you're hopping into my head again. That is an invasion of my privacy, Cornflake. I don't do that to you, do I?"

"Sorry, Mommy."

"Okay. A dirt-bag is a…it's just name-calling. I am not very happy with your Uncle Ray right now."

"Because Uncle Ray is a bad man, huh Mommy? Like the bad man in Bodie."

"What? Where on earth did you hear that? And, no, Sweetheart. Your Uncle Ray is not a very good man, but he's not really a *bad* man either. He is certainly not bad in the way that the bad men from Bodie were. They killed people. But that was over a hundred years ago, baby. Bodie is just a State park now, and the bad men are all gone."

Little Claire gave her mother a questioning look. "All of 'em?"

"I already know what you're thinking, Jeff—" Ray stammered.

"If that were true, you'd already be defending yourself," Jeff promised.

Ray tried to back up, but he was already against the open door frame of his F150 truck. "But did you forget that I'm, like, a full head bigger than you? If you hit me, I'm gonna have to hit you back, man," he threatened weakly.

Jeff just laughed. So, Ray, the consummate coward, tried a different tack. "I've been taking Tae Kwon Do at the Community College. I don't wanna hurt you."

"Oh, *you're* taking college classes?" Lainy asked him. She rolled her eyes. "What a coincidence, so am I. Scrotum-punching 101. I would *love* to show you what I've learned so far."

Lara and Claire walked by the group on their way back from the orchard, with a pile of apples they picked to take on the trip. Lara hollered toward the group, "Excuse me, Ray, but did they tell you I called the cops the moment you arrived?"

Panic shot across Ray's face, and then a bit of doubt.

"No, I really did," Lara assured him. "You should get going, and keep going. And don't come back."

At that very moment, a black-and-white police car emerged on the horizon. It was still about a half-mile down Highway 101, but it was heading their way. He nudged Lainy to see the car, then turning back toward Ray, he bowed slightly and asked her permission, "May I?"

Lainy hesitated for a fraction of a second before she replied, "No, Jeff, don't." She saw Ray smirk and relax against the frame of his truck. That ticked her off. "Allow me," she grunted as she kicked her soon-to-be ex-husband in the soft marbles.

Ray gagged and dry-heaved, but finally found his voice. "Aghhhh, you bitch!" He screamed at her as he grabbed himself and doubled-over.

"Lainy! I was a kick boxer and I'm telling you, you put some hurt on that kick," Jeff told her.

"I am gonna—" white-lipped Ray began to threaten.

"—say goodnight," Jeff finished. He plowed his right fist into the left side of Ray's face. After the back of Ray's head ricocheted off the truck's frame, he slid the rest of the way to the ground, eyes closed.

"Jeff, are you alright? Did you hurt your hand? Please, tell me you didn't break anything." Lainy worried. Her eyes followed the police car as it pulled into the parking lot.

"Just the "Fun" meter!" Jeff rubbed his fist and then shook it off, laughing merrily.

# Chapter 29

By noon on Monday, every radio news show was talking about the brutal homicide of pretty Longview psychotherapist, Rachel Carrell. It was an apparent robbery attempt, the reporters said, although the detective in charge of the investigation was stressing the word *apparent*.

Peter Keefe hugged his desk top and cried incoherently, "Rachel, oh Rachel—oh my God, I didn't mean it, Rachel." The tears streamed down his cheeks and into his right ear, but he did not bother to swipe at them.

The door to his office opened marginally and the same pretty coed, Janet, poked her head in. The professor had told her to come back on Monday, and these were his office hours. She was shocked to see the professor drowning in tears and wailing some woman's name uncontrollably. She quickly closed the door and turned to leave. A fellow classmate was approaching the professor's door and Janet grabbed for his shirt sleeve.

"Don't go in there," she warned. "He's crying like a baby over some woman. *Hysterically*. It's pretty ugly."

"The professor?" the classmate responded, clearly surprised.

"I swear. He's prostrate on the desk and crying rivers. I'm just saying, *I* would not go in there."

"Wow," her classmate paused. "But, maybe I should go in, you know? See if he's all right. Maybe he needs someone to talk to or something."

"I didn't know the guy *had* feelings," Janet hushed.

"I didn't think he had 'em for *women*." The classmate remarked.

"You know what? I don't care." She tossed her longish hair over her shoulder for emphasis. "It's not as though he cares about any of his students. I was here last week during office hours because I need help with the paper—"

"Me too," the classmate interrupted.

Janet nodded. "But it's not a good time for him, he says. During his office hours is not a good time? I come back Wednesday, I had to give up my best shift, and this time he's available, but I swear he's totally plowed; roaring drunk, weaving around his office. He saw me poke my head in the door, so he waved at me to come in, to 'get a good look at the Great Professor.' He was blubbering about what a spineless failure of a man he is—his words, though I can't help but agree. There was no way I was walking in there. I could not close his door fast enough. And now this? These Monday office hours were my last chance to ask him some clarification questions. I'm so screwed. So frankly, I could not care less about his pining over some lost love. Physician heal thyself." She tossed her hair again and set her jaw firmly.

The classmate, who just kept nodding at Janet while she raged, now looked at her calmly and said, "Would you like to go over to the Commons, get a coke and work on our papers together?"

"Sure," she said. She was vented. As they walked down the length of hall, Janet stole a look back at the closed door. "You know, I really think we should talk to the Dean about all of this," she told her new friend.

Inside the office, Peter Keefe continued to wail, but less intensely now. He was moving out of the grief stage and into a state of guilt, which required some painful self-examination on Peter's part. He paced his office. He reached for books and expensive objects to throw, and he castigated himself. He may not have been the one to place Rachel on a burning cross, but he'd brought his own marshmallow to the fire.

*I should have warned Rachel. I should have done something to stop Vanderling, or stop Rachel from pursuing the damned thesis.* Peter fumed. But he hadn't. Instead, he stayed in a state of drunkenness for days in an attempt to avoid his gut instinct that Vanderling might actually do something to Rachel. *My darling Rachel was dying a brutal death while I stayed true to my family genes and avoided responsibility.*

Her death was as much his fault as if he'd wielded the weapon himself. It was a family character flaw, this running from responsibility, Peter reflected; an inclination to avoid adversity. His great grandfather, Pierce Keefe, had begun that particular legacy when he ran from Bodie, taking nothing more than his wife, toddler son, and what few possessions he could stuff into flour sacks. That was in 1878, just a few years before the Touchstone mines began to deplete. During the period of Pierce Keefe's absence, the mines were pulling out more gold than any other in the Sierra-Nevada high desert region. Of course, the Keefe family received their twenty-five percent share of profits, but it was twenty-five percent of whatever the managing partner, Aaron Renick, declared the quarterly profits were; that was a much smaller figure than what the markets were reporting. The Keefe family patriarch knew he was being cheated but did nothing. It was the very fact the managing partner was believed to be a thief and a murderer, that Pierce Keefe had fled Bodie in the first place.

Fortunately for Peter, his grandfather, Pierce's son, returned to Bodie many years later to settle the score. He'd rightly figured his father's partner cheated on others besides the Keefe family, and he ventured to find proof enough to bring Renick to his knees. Patrick Keefe was the first, and sadly the last, man in the Keefe bloodline to show such moxie. Apparently, strength of backbone must have been inherited from great grandmother Helen's branch of the tree.

To this day, many people do not realize that the cyanide process of extracting gold was actually perfected in Bodie, and is what allowed Touchstone to continue working their otherwise worthless mine tailings for record gold. A German immigrant had been employed by Touchstone to sail to Europe and learn all there was to the newly acclaimed cyanide process. When the employee returned, Touchstone refit their mining operation so they could crush and pulverize the gold ore diggings into dustlike particles. Then a cyclone classifier was built; it looked like a kitchen utensil used to separate fat from meat drippings, only it was enormous in size and made of steel. This stage of the operation separated the fine particles, called slime, from coarser ores, called sand. The German process then required a single application of a weak cyanide solution to be poured onto the sand in a leaching tank, thus dissolving the gold. Then a dust of zinc, or in Touchstone's case, lime brought in by barge from the Mono Lake area, was added to precipitate the gold from the cyanide. Finally, a filter press was used to separate the gold precipitate from the solution as a dark brown powder.

When the larger, obvious veins of gold became played out, this cyanide process allowed Touchstone to salvage vaguely distinguishable gold dust still present in the ore. And when these supplies began to diminish, another method of cyanide milling, one which the environmentally-responsible Germans would not have considered, was developed by the Touchstone Mining Company. With the new process, once the gold in the sand was dissolved in weak cyanide solution, carbon particles were added to collect and hold gold ions (electrically charged atoms) on their surfaces. These carbon particles were then removed from the pulp and placed in an even more caustic cyanide solution, which separated the gold from the carbon. With this additional, more advanced process, Touchstone was able to literally bleach ore of every particle of gold present. The process eventually distinguished the company as having recovered more gold than all other mining companies in the region combined.

Their dark secret was safe because anyone who could have told, was dead. In short order, people forgot why Touchstone recovered so much more gold than any other company. Miners who did know how Renick achieved his magic, had no understanding of the process, at least not well enough to wonder about any toxic waste-cyanide. No one ever questioned how the waste cyanide solutions were disposed of, with the exception of an unfortunate widow innkeeper by the name of Elise Swazey.

After several more years, the secondary cyaniding processes failed to produce quantities of gold. The remedy? Touchstone deliberately began tapping into their neighbor's claim. They would have had to; it was the only plausible explanation. And it was the motivation for Patrick Keefe's ride to Bodie.

Patrick had been given all of the family's Touchstone stock upon his father's death. With his shares in hand, the heir traveled to Bodie to find the owner of Touchstone's neighboring mines at Skeleton Flats. Of course the owner, an Irishman named O'Pauley, believed his mines to be worthless, and perhaps they were, save for the secondary cyaniding process utilized by Touchstone. The new Keefe heir suggested his suspicion to the old Irishman, that if Touchstone's claims were panned out, as everyone surmised they must be, they can only be digging a still-producing ore from a neighboring property.

The Irishman's temper erupted in an unintelligible string of brogue profanity upon hearing of a double-cross. As he relayed to Patrick with some drama, he had leased doubtful ground from Touchstone at an ungodly price some years earlier, but then had a fortunate stroke of Irish luck and pulled out ninety thousand dollars of gold in about ninety days. When Touchstone Director Aaron Renick learned of O'Pauley's providence, he refused to renew the lease.

O'Pauley's strike had provided him with more than enough money to purchase the adjacent property, also believed to be beleaguered of gold. The fair-luck Irishman had managed to hit consistent, moderate pay dirt, and eke out a living. Now, old man Renick preserved the audacity to prospect the Irishman's ground without permission or volunteer of rent. Patrick Keefe later testified that on that day, the trail to Touchstone Mines might have been streaked perfectly blue from the cussing that was indulged in by O'Pauley, as he stomped toward his property line.

As Peter understood the family history, an agreement was reached between the Irishman and Peter's grandfather, Patrick Keefe. They would seek evidence that Touchstone had fraudulently tapped Skeleton Flats and, if the investigation proved successful, would seek damages in an amount sufficient to gain a controlling interest in the Touchstone Mining Company. For bringing the suspected claim-jumping to light, Keefe would be granted a share in the new company—an interest equal to the shares he possessed in the existing Touchstone stock—a generous twenty-five percent. The way things shook out in the end was poetic. Nearly forty years after his great grandfather Keefe fled the town of Bodie and his active interest in Touchstone Mining, Patrick and his new partner were legally granted not merely a controlling interest in the mining company, but damages so great that the men took over the company entirely. It was Renick's turn, then an old man in his seventies, to run from Bodie in the middle of the night. Peter knew the history; he knew Renick had tried.

In 1955, Peter's father became the next Keefe heir. However, there was no longer a fortune to be pulled from Touchstone mines, nor was the stock worth much more than the paper it was printed on. The family had made other investments which were capable of providing a better-than-comfortable lifestyle for generations, if properly managed. But Peter's father hankered to seeming more than merely "comfortable" in San Francisco society. The rather well-nourished Patterson Keefe spent his money quite freely, until there was little for Peter to inherit, save the presumed worthless Touchstone interests. Then a wonderful turn of events befell Peter Keefe a year ago. First, a Canadian company by the name of Globalesque Mining offered to purchase Peter's share in the Bodie mining rights. Peter agreed to sell half of his interest for an extremely generous price. Peter burned through that windfall pretty quickly. But then, less than a year later, the total mining rights to the Bodie Bowl were being sought by another conglomerate for a price of thirty-five million dollars. And Peter still owned twelve and one-half percent interest in those rights. A single dark cloud threatened this bright transaction, however. It was named HR 230.

The Bill, which was currently before the United States Senate, would require any new ownership of mining rights in the Bodie Bowl to install a wastewater treatment facility for clean-up purposes. Of course, the Bill's authors were completely unaware of the old Touchstone Mining Company's toxic waste pollution. So, it was just dumb luck that the verbiage of the Bill demanded any mining effort to "restore" the area entirely, upon completion. That wording meant *any* waste or pollution within the claim boundaries would have to be cleaned up *completely*, no matter how ancient the destruction. Internal estimates run by Globalesque put the cost of clean-up for such a facility at more than $230,000 per month. Naturally, the new speculators in the Bodie mining rights would have no interest in paying for ancient waste clean-up. But if no one were to learn of a need for clean up efforts, Globalesque President Victor Vanderling had confided to Peter, he could have the bill quashed. He remembered

Vanderling mentioned something about a crooked U.S. Senator from California, he had in his pocket.

*And that,* sniffed Peter Keefe miserably, *is where Rachel had flirted with tragedy.* A public account of the "dream sisters'" experience could have called unwanted attention to the illegal mining practices of more than one hundred years passed. Having straight-bourbon'd the way through his reflections, Peter was now thoroughly intoxicated. But he was still possessed of enough perception to realize he had sold his friend's life for about four million dollars. In this rare moment of pity for someone other than himself, Peter mourned for Rachel. He ultimately realized too late, she had been far more precious to him than gold.

He slammed the drained tumbler glass down upon the antique secretary and snatched up his car keys from the Lalique crystal bowl that rested on the sideboard. He weaved in the direction of the door as he tried desperately to channel his grandfather Patrick Keefe. He would need the progenitor's singular grit, if he is to confess to the authorities his own reprehensible role in Rachel Carrell's murder.

# Chapter 30

"For there is a golden haze over the land—the dust of gold is in the air—and the atmosphere is magical and mirrors many tricks, deceptions, and wondrous visions."

—Carey McWilliams,
California: The Great Exception

5 April, 1993
Longview, Washington

"He's killing me," the veteran cop muttered. He turned to his subordinate with something close to astonishment on his face and griped, "That kid's slower than a banana slug on a salt bed."

Lieutenant Stan Block had been ready for a relaxing morning of shooting practice at the club and was dressed accordingly in Dockers and a sweater. He never wore his shield pinned to him, and he didn't like to carry it in his pocket, where it would be snug against his traveling deck of cards. He wore it on a lanyard about his neck, and he kept it tucked inside his shirt unless he had to flash it. He found people to be less nervous talking with him when his hardware wasn't in their faces. Even though he displayed no badge, he was clearly the detective-in-charge.

He frowned in the direction of the college student who was fiddling with the therapist's computer, while he talked out the side of his mouth to his partner. "Christ, Mac, it's two-thirty already. Those forensic guys have been dittying with that body all day. And now this kid. Hey, what is with this kid? He acts like I just told him to recite the Constitution from memory."

"I got a nephew the kid's age. He's barely out of his tighty-whities, Stan. Cut 'im some slack. Between the smell in here and, sheez, it's kind of a small space for this many people and that much gore. I might blow garbage myself if they don't get her out of here pretty soon."

"Colorful," Stan said.

Mac smiled widely. "Cut the shit. I can tell you're about ready to grab that trashcan and lose your groceries."

Block ignored him. He turned back toward the office waiting room doorway, where a young officer in uniform stood guard over the crime scene. "Patrolman, can we get some sandwiches or, at this point anything resembling food, will do just fine?"

"Yessir," the rookie cop nearly jumped. This was his first homicide case, and he'd been embarrassed to admit to his partner that he was sickened by the brown smears on the wall and carpet, not to mention the stench of a corpse that was two days old. *It was awful.* So his partner graciously parked him at the entrance to the office, and told him he was to monitor the hall. Even though he got a little nauseous, and then a little embarrassed, this day would still be among the rookie's most exciting on the job. He was working a murder scene with Lieutenant Stan Block, a man who was a legend in the department.

Stomach growling, Block fought to keep his concentration on the facts related to the therapist's homicide. It was a vicious attack on a defenseless woman, and nothing rubbed Stan raw like this kind of victim. He removed the deck of cards from his pocket and began laying them out for a game of Solitaire, which helped him to relax and think.

"Okay, it looks like the attackers cleared out her computer files," one of his detectives approached him. "Again, no prints, so, they wore gloves. Oh, and her prescription pad is still laying on her desk, in plain view. Must've forgotten to take it with 'em."

"Yeah? So, that's no prints on the hacked-up door jam, and no prints on the vandalized computer. You know, the carpet was pretty light on footprints before we all got here. We'll check with the crime scene photos, but I'm leaning toward a single guy trying to make it look like moremore. So, we're supposed to believe this was done by a bunch of crazies. They're crudely breaking into doctors' offices for pain meds. They take time to spray paint 'tags' on walls, and they have the forbearance to stop and put on gloves first. They take a shrink's computer files, but leave the prescription pad." Stan paused dramatically, "Is it just me, or does that strike anyone else as odd?" He slammed cards down in angry rhythm as the wheels in his mind turned.

"They sure went to some trouble to make this all appear like a gang member initiation, or drug theft or something. And they sure didn't want anyone to know what they were really after." Mac surmised.

Stan paused mid-throw, and looked up at his partner. "I don't know whether to be relieved our perp is simple-minded, or pissed that he thinks we are." He threw another card down. "I *will* find out what he was really after...and I *will* get this guy," Stan vowed.

*The attack was meant to look like an amateur break-in for drugs. But it was obviously about something else, because someone had sent a pro. Why? What had this pretty little lady done that was deserving of such extreme violence?* No, that was the wrong question. Block would not blame the victim. A better question is, what flaw existed in humanity that allowed for the taking of life so carelessly?

Crocodiles didn't murder each other. Grizzlies didn't murder each other. But people do, and they do it a lot. That human flaw is the reason Block dedicated his life to protecting those who could not protect themselves. And if he could not protect them, then he was damned sure going to see that justice was done in the end. Stan knew inherently that justice could take a long time. He vowed he would try to be a more patient man. He began turning cards over, three at a time.

Another hand was won. He didn't need to finish it. He shoved the last bite of a turkey sub in his mouth as he gathered up his cards and pushed his powerful frame from the love seat he'd been crammed into. Block approached the college kid who claimed to be the dead shrink's part-time intern. The kid was clearly distraught over his boss's death—*clearly*. The poor kid had such a visceral reaction, it had taken them twenty minutes to stop his crying. He'd cared for the therapist. That's tough. Plus, he'd been the unfortunate one to find the therapist at nine o'clock this morning. That's tougher. Mac was right about him being just a kid, and the grisly scene was too much to stomach even for some of the veteran cops. The asshole who'd killed the pretty, petite therapist had practically gutted her from bikini line to her generous breasts.

Block checked his impatience and made a concerted effort to be more sympathetic with the college student. He approached the therapist's desk, looked up, and read the painted wooden board hung high up on the wall behind it. It was a quote from C. S. Lewis which read, "Experience is a brutal teacher, but you learn. My God, you learn!" *The doc had a sense of humor.* Stan just had to smile a little.

"Okay, kid. Come up with a list yet?"

"My name's Mark." He looked up from the screen sheepishly. "She, uh, she worked mostly with female clients and children that were, you know, abused. Um, the ones who don't really remember the, uh, molestation but get, um, you know, flashbacks?"

"So who's new?"

"Well, Rachel was excited about a new case she started a couple weeks ago. She said it was publishable. It was going to be the basis of her doctorate thesis, but she also thought that she might get, you know, some good recognition if she wrote a book about it. That's good for generating new patients, which, I mean, she loves this, uh…loved this office, but the rent is a lot."

"What's the name of this patient she got herself all excited about?"

"*Their* names," Mark corrected. "It was two sisters who were having the same repetitive dreams about some old murder. But Rachel never told me their real names. She said they'd asked her to keep their names out of it."

"Oh, well that's just great. All right, let's have a go at it from the other direction. Who was the victim of this old murder?"

"I don't know that either. But she did say the murder of the woman took place in an old gold rush town in California; Bodie, I think she said. Anyway, the murder happened, like, more than a hundred years ago."

"A hundred years ago. In California. Swell. If it weren't for bad luck…" Block trailed off. He looked over his shoulder into the doctor's file room and called for his partner. "Mac, tell me you guys found something in there about some sisters and their reoccurring dream."

Block busied himself by flipping through the rolodex on the secretary's desk. "Why *would* someone go to all that trouble over dreams some hundred years old? Even if it turned out they're historically accurate dreams, how could they be worth killing over, today?" He mused aloud. He came upon the card for Peter Keefe and stopped. He looked over at his partner. "What about this

Keefe guy?" Block flashed the rolodex card at Mac so he could see the doodle on it's corner—a cloud with the word, "gold" written inside of it. He didn't even wait for an answer. He wrestled his robust frame from the intern's tiny swivel chair, simultaneously slamming it back across the parquetry floor mat that had been placed beneath the work area. The chair made a powerful screech, and Block was momentarily struck with a strange sensation of déjà vu. It had been happening to him all morning. Shaking it off, he walked over to the doorway at Dr. Carrell's inner office and hollered at the doctor's intern. "Hey, K—Mark, you said Professor Peter Keefe was her mentor. Is it possible he was also her boyfriend, and the doctor just never told you about it?"

"Rachel told me, emphatically, that Peter was just a friend," he looked up from the computer screen and sniffed. He shook his head sadly and his eyes began watering anew at his uttering of the therapist's name. "Uh, but, Detective Block?" The intern gulped and said, "She once told me Professor Keefe wanted their friendship to be more than that. But he *was* just a friend. And I know she was planning to meet with him again about the 'Dream Sisters.'That's how she referred to them."

"Again?" Block cut him off.

"Yeah. They'd already met once. Let me just look at her calendar here, I set up an appointment for them to meet about the case study—here. It was a week ago this past Saturday. Oh man, I just remembered something. Peter's her mentor and all, but she'd also wanted to ask him what he knew about the gold rush town the sisters were going to visit. His family, I guess, was big in the history of some famous California gold mine."

Block pointed his finger at the secretary. "Now *that* was helpful, Mark." He yelled for one of his detectives to find him Keefe.

"Keefe? Would that be Peter Keefe?" a detective asked. "I'm afraid he's already on his way downtown."

"He called the station?" Block asked, confused.

"No, I heard the name come over my radio an hour or so ago. He's on his way to the morgue. His car hit an embankment, then a sixteen wheeler. From the sounds of it, he's hamburger. It happened just a block from the station. Traffic over there's a mess."

"Crap and fall in it!" Stan threw the useless rolodex card on the desk.

Mac reached out and fingered the card thoughtfully. "So, were you thinking he might've been a person of interest or…what?"

Block paced. "I don't know. Maybe he just heard about this on the news and tied one on before driving—wait, that's not right. The County morgue would have been in the other direction for him. So, maybe he *was* heading to the police station downtown. But why, if he knew her body wouldn't be there?"

Block now wondered if Keefe had known something about the murder of Rachel Carrell, or had possibly even anticipated it somehow. *Was he heading to the station to confess?* In Stan's experience, people generally disbelieve shocking news about someone they care for, until they see for themselves. Even then, many folks were still disbelieving. *But that wasn't the case for this Keefe guy. Keefe didn't need to see her body for himself.*

All things considered, Block was not about to accept without question, that Peter Keefe crashed-and-burned a few hundred yards from the police station by mere coincidence. He never did put much stock in coincidence.

"Mac, I think this guy may have known the truth. Maybe he was expecting the murder and maybe he wasn't. But I think he knew something. It's possible he had a guilty, even if reluctant, part in it. I mean, his family was into California gold…the therapist was writing about a gold rush murder…the two were having secret meetings, now she's dead and he's dead…"

"Yeah, probably too much for mere coincidence," his partner said.

"That, and he's the only thing close to a lead we have right now. We should find out what all he was into." Stan told him.

"Business and personal. And get somebody to pull research on Bodie, California. I need some history here. Go back a hundred—wait, go back a hundred and twenty-five years. We're looking for a female murder victim."

"On it."

Stan felt he was missing something; something he'd seen or heard, something he should have questioned.

"Uh, Lieutenant?" the secretary interrupted the detective's thoughts. "I remember on Friday, Rachel said the sisters, you know, the ones I just told you about? They were supposed to be leaving Saturday to go visit Bodie, to try and trigger some more memories," he shrugged weakly. "They were going by car. Maybe they're still there?"

*That was it.* He'd heard the kid say earlier that his boss had wanted to ask Keefe what he knew about the gold rush town *the sisters were going to visit.*

"Want me to look into that, too?" Mac, offered. "I can check with the Department of Tourism in California and find out if Bodie is accessible for tourists. Maybe they have a personnel-manned information booth there."

Stan nodded. At that moment, the body of Rachel Carrell was being moved to the ME's gurney and shrouded, her hands placed in plastic bags and her throat dusted for fingerprints. The detectives didn't believe they would find anything useful. From all indications, she hadn't had a chance to struggle with her assailant. Block looked Dr. Carrell over briefly before they carted her away. She was a tidy person, good taste, nothing flashy about her or her office. Pretty face. She had decks of playing cards placed around the waiting room, as opposed to outdated magazines. The therapist was someone he would have liked to have known, Stan thought sadly.

Camera flashes were clicking all around the room as Rachel Carrell's body made its appearance in time to lead the five o'clock news hour.

# Chapter 31

They'd made it as far as Red Bluff the night before, and stayed in two adjoining rooms at a nondescript motel. They'd all shared a pizza across a queen-size bed in Lara and Jeff's room and spent the evening playing games with Claire until the adults were exhausted.

"You should have seen your sister take Dic—, er, Ray, down this morning." He turned to Lainy, "I was being serious, Lane. You've got great form. You really should take Tae Kwon Do classes. And by the way, they really do teach it at the community college, self-defense classes too. Martial Arts would be a far more useful hobby than watercolor painting. Besides, I've already taught you guys all of the basics."

"I think that would be fun. And definitely useful. Let's do it, Lara." said Lainy.

"Yeah, we should check into that when we get back. Maybe Claire could take the classes with us. How young an age will they teach, Jeff?"

"I'm sure they'd take her. I think you girls should—all of you."

They rose early and started out for Berkeley around seven o'clock in the morning. At 11:00 a.m., they ate a quick lunch at a Shari's coffee shop. When they'd arrived on campus, they were walking a bit saddle-sore, but were none the worse for wear. The weather was beautiful, and the air smelled fresh and clean. Jeff took Claire on a tour of the campus to stretch their legs, while Lara and Lainy did their sleuthing through the old Bodie newspapers that Berkeley's Bancroft Library kept on microfilm.

They went directly to the March, 1879, records and were dismayed somewhat by the long list of newspapers which operated from Bodie during that time. "I had no idea the town would be so big, Lainy. Five newspapers! This is going to be like hunting for a needle in a stack of needles."

There was The Chronicle, Daily Free Press, Evening Miner, Morning News, and The Bodie Standard to choose from. Since the Standard was the biggest newspaper, Lara began skimming its columns for March 2, 1879, the day after the murder of Elise Swazey. Lainy wound the reel for the Morning News on another microfilm projector. Within minutes Lara knew something was wrong. The only article that mentioned the death of a woman was a report of suicide. As she read, and without taking her eyes from the screen, she tapped Lainy on the shoulder and pointed at the text.

"What the—?" Lainy said, and pressed her hand to the side of her face as she read. Lara watched as Lainy's eyes widened in disbelief. The more they investigated, the more they realized Bodie's history smacked of deception.

"But, it wasn't a suicide. This is outrageous."

Lara nodded solemnly and read the column aloud,

> "Mrs. Swazey was a person of respectability and standing in Bodie until the recent death of her husband. She is rumored to have resorted to prostitution in order to support herself and her son, plying her trade among

gamblers and miners from Aurora and Bodie, where she was becoming well known among the 'demimonde.' Late last evening, friends claim, she appeared out of sorts when she suddenly bolted into the street from her hotel. Friends heard the report of a gun minutes later and rushed outside to find her body. A packet of opium was found next to her, which Doc Heilshorn surmised must have been countering her extreme depression of late. Heaven knows she is better dead than living a disreputable life. Mrs. Swazey is survived by a son."

Lainy pounded the screen with her pointed finger, "God, no wonder she's haunting us. What crap! This is the reason she's reaching out to us, Lara. If I were Elise Swazey, I'd come back from the dead to clear my name, too."

"Yeah, it definitely was a cover up for something," said Lara. "And it must have been big to have chanced not just killing a decent woman, but discrediting her, too." She smacked the screen in frustration. "Jeez, Lainy, they buried her on Boot Hill!"

Lainy pointed to the article glowing on her own screen. "Look at this, Lara. They found her handkerchief outside the front door, but her body was found on the side of the building. How did a sheriff overlook that curious detail?"

"The same way he overlooked the really obvious problem with the gun. She shot herself, right? In the head? And no gun was found? How the hell does she blow her brains out and *then* ditch a gun?" Lara started fussing with the desktop, straightening and arranging, and re-arranging…"It doesn't make sense. And no one questioned it. There is no mention of this woman's, quote suicide, in the next day's paper at all."

"Or the fire," Lainy nudged her. "Read on. Seems awfully suspicious to me that her hotel would catch fire and burn to the ground the same night she shoots herself. And where is her son? It says here that they could not find the son for questioning, but believe he started the fire and then disappeared."

"Well, he wasn't murdered. If he had been, we wouldn't exist. He was the only Swazey left. I suppose he could have witnessed what happened, though, or suspected he was in danger and fled." Lara said.

"*Someone* witnessed it," Lainy said quietly, thinking back to what Rachel had told them about Lara's transgression, and how she claimed to have been there when Elise was killed. "Someone named Frank Junior witnessed it, Lara. *You* witnessed it." She turned the knob on the projector to reveal the rest of the rather short account of Elise Swazey's presumed suicide.

Lainy must have been distraught. She was letting Jeff drive her Camry. They traveled east on Interstate 80 toward Reno, and from there caught 395 to Bridgeport. At four-thirty, they stopped in the small town of Minden for an early dinner.

They paid at the cashier's station and observed a man taking cash out of the till. Lainy asked if he was the owner, and when the man joked that he'd better be, she proceeded to compliment the entrepreneur on the quality of his restaurant's food. It caused the older gentleman to blush and stutter. "You folks ain' from around these parts, are ya?" he laughed. "I could tell right off, ya know. No one around here appreciates me. You folks vacation'n?"

"Sort of," Lainy answered.

"Where'ya headed? If you don' mind me ask'n."

"Not at all. We're going to Bodie."

"Ah," the man's eyes fairly twinkled. "She's a gem, Bodie is. Rich history there." He toyed with the cloth-covered button on his tweed Gatsby hat. "I go to visit me-self, now and again. I never tire of seeing her on a fair afternoon like today. You folks enjoy yourselves, now," he advised.

They only had about an hour of travel time to go before they reached the cabin they'd rented for the week in Bridgeport. "We're almost there, French-fry," Jeff told his little girl.

"Yay, we're going to Bodie!" Claire exclaimed.

Lainy gave Lara the thumbs-up sign, "Good-bye, God."

# Chapter 32

"You didn't tell me the shrink was gonna be such a babe. Man, I'm ramming seven inches of surgical stainless home and thinking all the while, I got seven inches—"

"Enough, Jake," Vanderling put his palm out in the air to stop the assault of further words. "Please don't apprise me of the alleged proportions of your manhood. I really couldn't care less," he smiled thinly. He was flipping through the yellow note pad Jake had retrieved from Rachel Carrell's office. "There's nothing useful here," he said angrily. "We've got physical descriptions of the girls from the diskette, so we know one of them is a redhead—"

"Man, how can you eat that stuff," Jake interrupted.

Vanderling looked candidly at the scone he'd been nibbling on as he worked. "Scones are quite tasty, Jake. You should be more discriminating." *And don't stop at the food you eat*, he thought. Vanderling knew Jake envisioned himself exceedingly desirable to women, and something of a Renaissance man to other men. Sometimes, like at this moment, Vanderling was tempted to inform Jake of all the ways he fell short. First off, Vanderling had gotten Jake cheap, so he was more a bargain-basement chap. Where Jake thought himself charming, others found him jejune; where Jake was mannerly, others found him affected; where Jake imagined he was brilliant, others found him insipid, vapid. *Ah, well, Jake thinks himself a player, and insulting him would be counter-productive,* Vanderling allowed. So long as Jake was close enough to sniff the jock of breeding and wealth, he would feel himself worthy, and he would do a good job.

"Hey, I am discriminating. That's why I don't eat stuff with names like clotted cream and mincemeat pie, or my personal favorite, blood pudding. I'd hurl if someone put that in front of me and told me to eat it."

Vanderling ignored Jake's ramblings. He was scrolling through the limited personal data that appeared on the screen, looking for a clue that would help locate the sisters. He was having trouble concentrating. "Jake, go get a tissue and blow your nose. My God, man."

Jake hadn't realized he had just snuffed down a nose full. He sheepishly rose and hunted down a box of tissues.

Vanderling's mind traveled back to the weekend he'd spent at a friend's home several years ago. The family owned a winery and fruit orchard in Washington state and had hired hundreds of Mexican laborers to do the picking. A rather serious altercation had occurred in the fields and Vanderling accompanied his friend to discover the cause of all the commotion.

Apparently, an elder sister, who could have been beautiful but for the fact she was missing most of her front teeth, had an admirer who was hankering to pound Jake for thievery. Jake had stolen the grocery money from his sister and mother in order to purchase, of all things, expensive Ray-Ban sunglasses.

It was the young man's complete lack of guilt or remorse which had inflamed the sister's admirer, and had attracted Vanderling's attention. When confronted, Jake admitted he had taken the money, but claimed he needed the glasses. The sun was bothering his eyes, making him squint. It caused premature aging, he'd offered as his only explanation. He then repeated it, while ripping the glasses off and pointing to the side of his eye for emphasis. "Premature, a*ging.*" Then the young man swaggered out of the fields. Vanderling followed and offered him a job. He needed an impenitent man who could be motivated with money and materialism to do Globalesque dirty work.

"Ahhh, here we go," cooed Vanderling to the word processor. "She has a rough outline here of things she wished to explore with the sisters. Let's see, blah-di-blah external impressions, hmmm, names from conventional records, yadda, yadda, upon their return from Bodie, Sunday, April 11—returning April 11? My God, they're probably in Bodie right now." He looked up at Jake.

"So? Aren't you gonna get God-Cilla to move the vote up anyway?"

"Yes, well, I'm going to see that she tries. But in the meantime, I simply can not afford to take any chances."

"Meaning what?"

Vanderling rocked back in his reclining desk chair and church-steepled his finger tips. "Meaning you leave for Bodie immediately, Jake."

"You're kidding."

"I'm afraid not, Jake, old boy. I can smell ashes falling on our acquisition deal. The proverbial volcano is belching for two more pretty maidens."

"Ah, how refreshing. A public servant who is actually to be found at her desk, actually serving her public." Vanderling chuckled at Roberta "Bobbie" Cilla when she answered her line.

"*Victor*," she exclaimed with surprise. It had been a month since their last meeting in D.C. She had not expected to hear from him until payday.

"I'm afraid, Senator, I must ask you to put in, how shall we say it—a little overtime?" He paused. "Our plans have acquired a few snags, Senator. We will need your assistance."

"I don't understand. You said no one knew anything."

"It is very difficult to explain, Roberta. I personally find it unbelievable, but we have discovered a psychic who has stumbled upon the dirty little secrets of Bodie."

Cilla caught her breath. "I'm on a cellular phone, you idiot. Don't say things like that over this line," she hissed.

"Sorry, my dear. In any case, we need you to go to work on this tomorrow."

"Because of a self-described psychic? Victor, dearest, I don't think your crackers are toasted on both sides. I can't change the Senate calendar now. The vote is scheduled for next week, and that will have to be soon enough. Then I'll perform the...favor that we agreed upon."

"No, there is more to the story. I won't go into it. But the vote must take place this week, Roberta. And it must be no later than Wednesday. Come up with a good story for why you can not be present for the vote at a later time. The issue concerns your State. I'm certain they can fiddle with the calendar for a senior Senator such as yourself."

Senator Cilla rubbed her temples, then slid open the top desk drawer with her left hand and blindly searched for the small bottle of aspirin she knew was hiding in there. *This was supposed to have been easy money,* she thought to herself. *Shit, shit, shit.*

"You've lost your nut, Victor." She sighed heavily. "If I make some quick phone calls I might be successful in moving it up to Friday."

"Make your calls, Roberta. But it must be by midweek. We are close to having this deal blow up in our faces."

Vanderling hung up the phone and absently cracked his knuckles. His company had filed for Chapter 7 bankruptcy in December of the previous year, and he had thus far been able to keep it secret. If the Bill passed and the buyout failed, Globalesque was out of the picture. They had no money. Jake was perched on the corner of his boss's desk waiting for instructions.

"Go, Jake. Do what you have to do."

# Chapter 33

The dream was so vivid it played like a movie in Lara's head, with Technicolor and Dolby-sound. It was glaring daylight, the sun was directly overhead, and Elise Swazey was jaywalking across the dirt thoroughfare in the direction of the newly-erected Boone general store. She was carrying a large gray cookpot by the bail with knitted hot-pads. She stopped when a handsome man leaning against a huge boulder of ore called out to her.

"Praise be to the good-hearted women of Bodie, Mrs. Swazey. How very generous and kind of you to bring supper for the grieving Boone clan."

Elise was frightened by the man. Though his words were admiring, they rang of menace which even Lara could perceive through her dream state.

The man left the rock and walked straight up to Elise. He lifted the lid and inhaled deeply and luxuriously. "Pity, them losing their little girl to such a senseless mishap. But it appears they will dine well this evening."

"Mr. Parker, I don't believe supping is a concern to the poor girl's folks right now. Really, your offhandedness is in such poor taste."

The man smiled graciously, exaggeratedly, and tipped his hat to Elise. She'd taken just two steps away when the man, Parker, replaced his hat on his head and continued after her. "You know, it's a terrible thing can happen to an innocent human being. If only the poor toddler had minded her own business," he sighed dramatically. "But, no. She had to follow old "Picks" out the door and shadow herself directly behind him when he decided to heft that old pick ax a' his and aim it right here, at this here boulder. You know, he ain't been sober a minute since it happened? Claims he loved that little girl like she was his own," he shook his head sadly. "Her parents told her she ought not to follow ol' Picks around all the time, making a nuisance of herself. If she'd a just minded their words of warning, well, she wouldn't be laid out in Perkin's mortuary this minute, with a big ol' pick ax hole in the top of her head."

The pot of stewed hens was growing heavy and Elise was growing weary of the man. "Are you making a point, Mr. Parker? This cook pot is heavy as a Spring pig, and I'll swear if I don't have a host of chores ahead of me this day."

The man continued as though he'd not heard her speak at all. "You know, my boss says we old folks can learn a lot from children. Ya think that's so, Mrs. Swazey? Think you could learn from that child's mistake?"

Elise was getting angry. "I know who you work for, Morris Parker. Your employer is a slippery dastard, and I don't reckon I'll be taking any lesson or advice from the likes of him."

"Oh, now, that ain't friendly, Mrs. Swazey. He's just concerned you might start mindin' someone else's business and earn your own self a hole in the head. It's out of concern for your well-being he sent me here to talk to you."

Elise bristled at the implied threat, "You, Mr. Parker, are a brute. And you may tell your Mr. Renick that I've no interest in any worrying he does on my account. His concerns would be better served on the good folks of this town he's poisoning with his milling. I know he's behind it all, and I intend to be making my learning's known to the news makers in Bodie soon enough. As a matter of fact, I will be seeing Mr. Phegley at the Standard before the day's end. You can tell your employer that piece of news as well. Now, off with you. Step out of my way."

Parker did not move. "Well now that's just the sort of meddling I was sayin' could land a person in hot water. You're just not payin' attention, Mrs. Swazey."

Elise stepped around him and hurried to the general store to bestow her condolences and gift of food to the bereaved parents of little Penny.

Lara watched the scene end with Parker standing in the middle of the street, embellishing his bow with a tip of his hat.

"You have a nice day now, Mrs. Swazey. You have yourself a nice evening, too," he'd hollered after her, smiling.

Lara bolted upright in bed. "Jeff," she roused him on the shoulder. "Wake up. Are you awake?"

"Yeah, what's wrong?"

"I just had the most incredible dream. I mean, I don't think it was a dream at all. I think I know why Elise Swazey was killed."

"You're kidding."

"I watched and heard an entire conversation between her and a guy she called Parker. I saw him threaten her in living color, Jeff. For knowing something about a guy named Renick who was poisoning the town somehow, with his milling, she'd said. God, it was so real."

"You mean milling, as in milling gold?""

"I would think so. We could probably verify the names and stuff, couldn't we? I mean, Lainy and I made copies of some of the newspapers. I wonder if we can find the names I heard Elise mention. She called the guy who was talking to her 'Morris Parker,' and the guy they were discussing, 'Renick'. Wait... oh my God. She said she was going to talk to Mr. Phegley at the standard. She meant The Bodie Standard, the newspaper. Goodness, Jeff, that ought to be easy enough to check out." She stopped her recounting of the dream and turned to her husband. "What do you think?"

"I think this is getting really interesting, Lara. You could really be onto something, some big cover-up that happened a long time ago; not that it would matter now. But I'm sure the historians would love to hear about it. Hey, you could write a book."

"I think Rachel is planning to write a book. She'll be thrilled. She said to call with any impressions—in fact, she'd said to call if we found anything of interest at all. What, with the phony suicide, and now this, maybe we should call her in the morning— only, I don't know where I'd call her from. I can't believe they don't even have a pay phone in this dump."

"Well, why don't you go to the state park first? Maybe you'll come up with even more to tell her. And you can probably call her from there. They'll have a public phone; you can use your calling card."

"Yeah, you're right. Okay," she lay back down, staring at the water-stained acoustic tiles above. "Boy," she said to the darkness, "this is going to floor Rachel."

# Chapter 34

6 April, 1993
Bridgeport, California

Lainy sat down at a 1950-circa chrome-and-laminate dinette set that was squeezed under the only window in the cabin's tiny kitchenette. "It's a symphony out here. Have you ever heard such roaring birds in your life?" She asked her sister, as Lara finished packing the picnic baskets. Lainy picked up a grimy, plasticized placemat and tossed it to the other side of the table.

"I think it sounds pretty," Lara said. She packed the food while she watched Jeff and Claire play keep-away with the dog, Sammy, out in front of the little cabin. She'd risen early, not being able to sleep after her vivid dream about Elise. She was just too anxious to tell Rachel about it.

The sandwiches were made; tuna for she and Lainy, peanut butter and strawberry jam for Jeff and Claire. She'd loaded the wrapped sandwiches into two baskets, setting them atop cold bottles of Snapple juice drinks. She also added two bottles of beer to Jeff's basket; it would keep him cool during the afternoon while he and Claire fished the lake. Also in their basket, Lara added a large bag of nacho-flavored tortilla chips and two huge white chocolate-chunk cookies. As usual, it was too much food. But after years of food withheld, or otherwise used for control of her, preparing "more than enough" food, was sort of her signature.

Lainy watched as Lara placed the items in the baskets. "You know, when other people say they made enough food to feed a small army, *they're* exaggerating," She giggled. Lara just gave her a silly face. She loaded the rest of the food into the Bodie basket: apples and a knife for slicing, two bananas, and some celery sticks stuffed with peanut butter. "No cookies for us?" Lainy gave her an exaggerated pout.

"Did you want me to pack cookies for us? I just figured you wouldn't eat one if I did, and then I would ending up eating two."

"Oh, you're right. I shouldn't gain any weight. But honestly, Lara, if you get any skinnier you'll have to tease your hair just to keep your pants up."

"Lainy, that is so gross!" Lara laughed. "And I did not say you shouldn't gain any weight, *you* did. You have already dropped at least ten pounds since you filed for divorce from Dipstick. You look great. Jeff says you've lost over a hundred and ninety pounds—of obnoxious fat."

"That's a good one," she laughed, then suddenly grew serious and fixed Lara with a steady stare. "You're really lucky to have found Jeff, you know."

"I know. I wish he had a brother for you." She slipped some cookies into their basket.

Lainy sighed. "Yeah. But, I just got rid of one jackass, and you know I'm a magnet for them. I think I should just swear off men for awhile. It's either that or move some place where there are more single men than women, so I can better my odds. I know I'm never going to meet Mr. Right in Neskowin, Oregon. You know what I mean?"

Lara set the finished baskets on the small table and faced her sister. "You can't move away. Where would you go?" Then Lara's attention was captured by Lainy's swinging foot. "Oh my God, you can not wear those shoes to walk around Bodie all day!"

Lainy rolled her ankle and inspected her strappy espadrille. "Can. Will. And as for your first question, I want a *real* man, one that's not tied up in a pretty bow with his mother's apron strings. I was thinking, I don't know, Texas?"

"Texas? Yep, the men are real men, and the sheep are real scared."

"Oh stop. What do you think about Alaska? I've always wanted to go."

"Ah, Alaska. Where your odds are good, but the goods are odd." When she'd said "Alaska" she'd spread her arms wide and knocked an old metal teapot off the two-burner stove. It clattered to the floor making a huge racket. "Oops," She laughed.

Lainy had to laugh too. "Way to go, Hands. So, are you going to do that word-play with every place I list?"

"No, those are the only two I had, *Toes*. Now will you please go grab another pair of comfortable shoes to take with you?" She frowned at the grimy placements laying haphazard across the table and immediately straightened them all into an orderly pile. She placed them atop the loudly-humming three-quarter refrigerator.

"Oh alright. Can we go?" Lainy whined. "I've been anxious to talk to Rachel ever since you told me about your new dream." Lainy had the dream too. Hers had matched Lara's, detail for detail.

Lara smiled widely. "Let's do this! But, you know, I think Jeff is right. We should probably walk around Bodie for a little while and see if any other memories are triggered, before we call Rachel. Remember what she said? Waking flashes of a previous life can be sparked by actually passing through a place where you've lived before, or by meeting someone you've known before, right? She said that dreams of that type can be triggered by external, *real* experiences, et cetera, prior to sleep. I think the newspaper article was the catalyst for last night's dream—or else we met someone from a Bodie past life and don't even know it." She laughed. "Anyway, if that's true, then we might start receiving more flashes when we get to town. Let's just play it by ear."

"Yeah, okay. But let's go already."

They piled fishing gear, baskets of food, camera equipment, wind-cheaters, in case the unseasonably warm weather turned suddenly, and finally themselves, into the Camry wagon. Sammy perched herself between Lainy and Claire in the backseat. To Lara's surprise, Lainy had again surrendered the driver's seat to Jeff, who drove them all to the Sierra Mountain lake. That was where he, Claire, and Sammy would spend the day fishing. Claire was animated and could hardly keep still.

"I'm going to get a lunker," she announced indisputably. "That's the biggest fish. I know how to do it. You just wait for a tug on the string—"

"Line." Jeff interrupted. "It's called fishing line, Claire."

Unperturbed, Claire continued, "You just wait for a tug on your line, and then you yell 'Hook up'."

Aunt Lainy laughed. "That's all there is to it, huh Claire?"

"Yep. And I'm going to get the lunker."

"Who has to put the worm on the hook?" Lainy asked.

Claire glanced at her dad quickly. "Daddy said we're going to use powder bait."

"Power bait," Jeff corrected. "Looks like Cheese Whiz and smells good to fish. I've used it on these mountain trout before and got more hits than Cheech Marin." He grinned at his daughter in the rearview mirror. "We're going to hammer 'em, right Claire?"

"Right. We're going to hammer them," she smiled from ear to ear.

The lively conversation on the way to the lake lightened Lara's mood. She was feeling fluttery, her lips and legs were slightly quivery. There was a child's pinwheel spinning in her stomach. She was looking forward to going to Bodie, but equally looking forward to getting it over with.

She kissed her husband lightly on the lips and said good luck. She gave Claire a big squeeze and a kiss and whispered that she had no doubt her little girl would catch the biggest fish, to which Claire giggled conspiratorially.

"What time do you want to be picked up, babe?" she asked Jeff, who was already rummaging through the silver tackle box.

He squinted up at the morning sun and pale blue sky, "Oh, how about four o'clock-ish? That way we'll be back in time for Happy Hour, and we can celebrate Lainy's official freedom from Numb-nuts. But don't worry if you're a little late. We'll just keep fishing, right Claire?" But she and Sammy had already sprinted for the lake.

"I put some beer in the lunch cooler for you, and a surprise too. For later. I love you, babe.

"I hope it's cookies. I love you, too."

"Good night, John-boy, good night, Mary Ellen," Lainy teased.

Lara stuck her tongue out at her. "Okay, we'll aim for four," she told her husband. "Catch a bunch, you guys," she yelled and waved to her little girl. "We'll have fish for dinner."

Lainy climbed behind the wheel, rolled the windows down, and opened the sunroof. It was only nine-thirty in the morning, and already the sun was blazing. Some years, the Sierras received snow as late as May. This year the sun was generous to April. They were warned the temperatures could drop drastically come nightfall, especially this time of the year. But they would be gone long before that. Lainy looked at Lara and smiled nervously. "Ready or not," she announced.

"*Ready,*" Lara buckled her seat belt. "Walton's Mountain references, huh? Jealous," she accused.

"Not."

"Are."

"Yeah, I am."

# Chapter 35

1, March, 1879
Bodie, California

"**D**amn it, Elise, he knows where I live, and he sure as shootin' knows where I work. I got a wife and children to think of. If you know what's good for yourself, you'll quit talking this nonsense and go back to tending your inn. Think of your son, Elise." Phegley was too humiliated with himself to even take his head out of the curio's cabinet drawer. He was busily rummaging. At least, he tried to look very busy.

"I am thinking of my son. I am *always* thinking of my son. But Ezra, *my* child drinks rain water and melted snow that we capture in a cistern. So, I know the water he drinks is poison-free. What do your children drink? I heard your eldest son is eight years old and has almost no teeth. Ezra, please. If you don't help me now, how will you be able to look yourself in the mirror in the mornings? You know you could stop all this. If the whole town knew what those two is up to, think about it, Ezra. I know you're afraid for your life, but if everyone in Bodie knew what was going on, they couldn't kill us all," she pleaded.

He finally faced her. "I ain't worrying about them two killing off the town. I'm worried for me and my family. And they'd do it, too, just out of spite. I heard Renick had that dastard Parker do away with Drummond over a little tiff in the stamp mill. John Drummond. He was a mountain for Christsakes. Did you know that man could snap a neck with his bare hands? I'm just a little newspaper editor." He removed his spectacles and wiped them nervously. "I'm not a brave man, Mrs. Swazey. Never said I was. I'm sorry, Elise. I will not be printing any stories about poison in the water."

She was frustrated beyond words—almost. It had taken all her courage to enter the office of the Bodie Standard, while Morris Parker watched. And now she was being refused any help at all.

"You can handle a piece for your own protection can't you? I'm a woman, and I can handle a revolver or rifle. I used to take my revolver out and shoot grouse and pheasants for our dinner, when I was just fourteen. So I'm pretty sure I can hit Morris Parker if I aimed to."

"Elise," Phegley gasped, "You're gonna get yourself killed. You're not any match for a hired gunman, and you know it. But you got a powerful weapon with your reasoning. Why don't you hit the square and gather up a crowd. They can't kill you after you make your suspicions known; that would be much too obvious. Better yet, leave town with that new beau of yours. Excuse me for sayin' it, but quit your stalling and marry Jack Gunn. Worrying about what Bodie folks think, instead of doin' what you know is right for you, is gonna lose you the man you love. And staying in Bodie after the threats you made to Parker, well, that's gonna lose you your life."

"I think you could benefit from your own advice, Ezra. I walked through that door hoping to find a man who would stand up for what he knew was right. Instead I find you, standin' here shaking as though you had buck ague. Anyway, I can't just leave town. Don't you remember? I have a son to think of."

"As do I, Elise. As do I. I'm sorry. I can't help you."

Elise stood her ground for nearly a minute staring at his backside, but he wasn't going to turn back around to meet her, face to cowardly face.

⚜ ⚜

Perhaps it would have made a difference if she'd gone directly to the town square, as Ezra had advised. And she might have packed a revolver, as she herself had hinted at. But she'd done neither. Later that evening, it was a doleful newspaper editor who was called to the Swazey Hotel to write her obituary. It ruined the otherwise ethical man forever when he was forced to print nonsense about her alleged prostitution, drug addiction, and suicide.

There had been plenty of other, earlier occasions when Phegley had printed pure dribble at the gunpoint of Morris Parker. By the time his press had slandered the lovely, pitiable Elise Swazey, the editor was barely a man at all.

One warm September day, when Ezra Phegley was busy at his post at The Bodie Standard, hand-typesetting a powder puff piece about Touchstone, his young wife suffered her second miscarriage in a year, and committed suicide. Phegley went beserk from pangs of conscience. He told Aaron Renick he aimed to use his quill to warn Bodie about the cyanide poison being dumped in their water. The headline, he promised Renick, would read, "Touchstone Poisons Bodie Water Supply." Phegley was found four days out in the desert with his eyes and entrails picked clean. In some manner of twisted irony, there was no one at The Standard to write him a proper obituary.

# Chapter 36

From Bridgeport, they drove south on 395 to the turn-off for the Bodie State Historic Park. The road, if it could be called that, was rock and desert dust that swiftly rose upwards in great swirls as the Camry bounced and pitched. Lainy hit the button to roll up the windows, but not soon enough to keep some dust from filtering into the car. Their eyes began to itch and water almost immediately and Lainy observed, "God, can you imagine living in this flea-infested armpit in the summertime? Life here must have been hell. I'll bet everything in this town, people included, was either dusted gray or bleached grey."

"Glad I was spared memories of this. I'm miserable," Lara answered as she massaged away the itch in her nose.

"Wow," Lainy exclaimed as the town came into view. "I had no idea there would be so many buildings still standing. This is neat."

"The brochure says it's the best preserved ghost town still standing in the country. That's good for us, I guess. Does it look familiar to you at all?" Lara asked.

"Nope. But, you know what? Suddenly I'm not nervous anymore. I don't know, I guess this place feels—comfortable."

Comfortable was not the adjective Lara would have used. She had the uncanny feeling that the desert dust was trying to shoo them away. It urgently whispered unintelligible warnings and swept up in gusts to rush the car as they progressed forward. This place had not been friendly to Elise Swazey some hundred years ago, and Lara did not perceive the land as particularly inviting to them now.

Their car approached a small kiosk that served as a park ranger's booth, perched on the southern end of Bodie's Main Street. Main Street was pedestrian-only after that point, barricaded to motor traffic with boulders. A bypass road veered west to a large parking area. The sunny, middle-aged park employee who guarded the historic site, wore a nameplate on his uniform that simply read, "Bob." He was a slightly balding gentleman with spectacles that rested on the bridge of his nose. He carried an air of cheerful dignity that contradicted the job, badge and holstered weapon. They saw that their arrival had wrestled him from another task.

"Hi," Lainy lightly hollered.

"Good morning to you, ladies."

"Same to you, Bob. Did we interrupt some writing there?" She asked him.

He glanced back at the desk. "Frustrated Journalist," he told them and laughed good-naturedly. Bob gave the girls a tour booklet which provided historical references and pinpointed landmarks in the town. The guard issued a congenial warning not to trespass beyond northeast Union Street, as the old Touchstone Mining Company facilities up in the hills were unstable, and considered hazardous. They paid a small fee and Lainy thanked Bob for his help before continuing on to the parking area ahead, rolling her window up as she drove. "He was sure friendly."

"Seems like a nice man, but I think he just might have fallen in love at first sight with you, Lainy. Geez, he just fawned all over you."

"Oh, sure," she answered. "Besides, icky. Too old…and too meek."

"That's right, you're looking for a real man," Lara teased.

"Shee-uddup. I know you're going to laugh at this, but I know that if I ever do find the right guy, I'm going to know it at first glance. I'm done with taking a man simply because he was willing to ask. I'm a catch, damn it."

"Yes, you are."

"No more men whose company I value less than my own—and Clint's." Lainy promised.

They parked and walked around to the rear of the car to fetch the camera, squinting up into the surrounding hills and down into the town. The mid-morning sun was high and bright.

"I need to chug-a-lug some Snapple," Lara said."

They both hopped onto the wagon compartment, facing out, and Lainy pulled the picnic basket between them. "Want to just share one for now?" she asked.

"Sounds good."

Lainy shook it, uncapped the bottle, and guzzled half of the contents down without stopping. Then she handed the remainder to her sister, who was inspecting the town's topography.

Lara downed several swallows, as her sister had, wiped her mouth with the back of her hand, then wiped the back of her hand against her jeans. She laughed out loud. "That wasn't terribly delicate of me, was it?"

"Who cares? No one's paying attention to us. You want anything else out of the basket?" Lainy asked.

Lara looked into the basket thoughtfully and her eyes came to rest on the knife she had packed for the apples. On impulse she snatched the knife, and slipped it carefully into the back pocket of her jeans, pulling her sweatshirt down to cover the handle. She didn't know why she was concealing the weapon. Maybe so she didn't worry Lainy unnecessarily. But, Jeff had asked her to be careful and to obey all feelings or inspirations. Perhaps taking the knife was silly but the impulse, or inspiration, to grab it had been strong. "I'm going to put another drink in my fanny-pack for us, just in case we get thirsty walking around. We sure don't want to drink from the water fountains here," she answered.

Binoculars pressed to his eyes, Jake diligently watched the two girls who pulled into the lower parking area in a green car. They were sitting in the open back end of the wagon, and he could no longer see their faces. But minutes ago, he saw the redhead climb out of the driver's side, and she was a dead ringer for the description Rachel Carrell had given the younger sister. *That has to be them.*

Bodie wasn't a trendy vacation spot for a lot of people, anyway. Then consider that April was a slow tourism month, and Tuesday was the slowest day of the week for the Park; Bodie was nearly dead. If there were tourists in the area, the majority of them must be sleeping late. Jake went unobserved as he scrutinized the two girls sitting in their car. He swung the binoculars due south toward the guard's cubicle and surveyed a near-desolate ingress to the park. The guard appeared to be distracted with reading something. This was going to be child's play. Jake judged the distance from his location straight down Main Street to the guard station to be less than a mile. Never a man who was shy about going after what he wanted, he slung the binoculars over one shoulder, checked the knife he had strapped in a sheath under his jacket, and set out down Main Street to have a chat with the guard. Perhaps they'd talk about weapons, Jake chuckled to himself. He did rather admire that Smith and Wesson nine mil the park employee was holstering.

# Chapter 37

State Park employee Bob Sabin was diligently drafting the May newsletter for The Friends of Bodie Society. He enjoyed the creative task. His was more than a mere hired interest in Bodie's preservation. His love for the historic park was genuine; his application toward any task on Bodie's behalf was fastidious and sincere. He took the security guard position for that reason, not because he was a brave man. He wasn't, especially.

His head shot up in surprise when he heard the tapping at the Plexiglas behind him. He turned to see a young Spanish-looking man smiling radiantly at him through the clear upper half of the booth. Bob smiled back and motioned the young man around to the booth's Dutch-door. The top half was opened wide, and Bob stepped over and rested himself against the bottom half of the door.

"Help you with something, young man?" he asked in his friendliest manner.

The stranger stepped up to the opening, much too close for Bob's comfort, and smiled largely again. Perhaps the smile was a little too big as well, Bob thought. There was something a little off about the young man's congeniality. The smile never reached his eyes. Bob immediately found him circumspect and backed himself up a half-step.

"I was just wondering why a State Park employee *here* needs to wear a gun," the younger man responded. "Are there still bad men in Bodie?"

"Oh," the guard reflexively placed his hand on the pistol at his side. "Yes, it is unfortunate, but the State Park System encounters its share of vandalism and so on. I've never had to use it here. Used to be the most violent town in Western history, but I haven't seen a lick of trouble in all my years here. They had some vandalism about ten years ago, though, and they've had problems at other state parks, so I am required to wear it," he explained.

Bob was growing uncomfortable with the younger man's presence. He kept standing too close, eyeballing the booth's interior, and grinning in a way that struck Bob as counterfeit. But more than that, the young man wasn't even paying attention to the answers Bob was providing to the asinine questions he asked.

Pretending interest in the old schmuck's job while his eyes took in the small station, Jake nodded toward the small desk the guard had been sitting at. "Whatcha writin' over there?"

Bob's hackles were beginning to rise, though he could not put his finger on exactly why. Something about the dark-featured man struck him as familiar, and not in a pleasant way, but Bob was certain he'd never met this man before.

"None of your damned business," is what the hair on the back of his neck wanted him to say, and then slam the door shut. But Bob Sabin would never do such a thing. He was getting a bad feeling about the guy, but it was likely just the surprise of having someone come up to the kiosk on foot—someone he must have admitted by car within the past few hours, but for some reason could not remember at all. Perhaps he'd been too absorbed in the article he was writing when the young man came through. It was possible. He did tend to get absorbed in his work.

He dismissed his initial distrust of the man. "Oh, I'm just an old, frustrated Journalist," he told the stranger. Ever the conscientious ambassador for the State Parks system, Bob turned to his desk and picked up a newsletter copy to show the young man. He started to explain, "I'm writing a—" Bob felt the spearing hot lance propel through his left kidney. His hand shot up to grab at the flash of unbearable pain in his rear left side. He opened his mouth in torment but no words came out. He had the sensation of dancing a ballet in slow motion, but the movement made him seasick, and he faltered into the work desk. He made a desperate grab for the counter top with his right hand to keep himself standing, but failed and sank face down to the floor. Before his eyes closed for the very last time, Bob Sabin heard the footsteps and felt the shadow of the man standing over him.

"I need to borrow your gun."

# Chapter 38

"The spell of the desert will grip you before you've left the main road five miles behind. That night you'll sleep beneath steady stars and listen to the whispers that are the night noises of the desert.

By morning you'll either hate and fear it, or you'll love it. I never knew any middle point, not with anyone. The desert engenders either fear or fascination, either love or hate."

—Erle Stanley Gardner
Golden Bullets, from Whispering Sands

6 April, 1993
Bodie, California

The girls took the trail from the parking lot to Green Street, which ran west to east through the town of Bodie.

Lara was wearing a hip pouch made of black nylon with a zippered closure, into which she transferred the kitchen knife, a bottle of Melonberry Cocktail, some change for the pay telephone when they found one, and some lip balm.

"Check out that church, Lara. I can't believe the glass windows are still intact," Lainy commented on one of the first buildings they came to. It was in pretty good shape compared to the other buildings in town.

"Look, you can tell the glass is original. See its wavy surface? They called glass like that, "floated." Lara told her.

As they walked on, they saw most of the remaining structures were dilapidated and uninhabitable. Dust and sparse weed crowded the various formations that seemed to rise from the desert like rotting baby teeth half emerged from dying tissue. In the case of Bodie, the body of wasteland had desperately campaigned to reclaim the dentitional projections and was winning the war. That is, until The Friends of Bodie Society took up arms on behalf of the town and arrested the decay.

Lara flipped open the tour booklet which the friendly guard had given them, and read to Lainy about the building. It was the old Methodist Church, erected in 1882. Unfortunately, the building had been vandalized on the inside, according to the pamphlet. The girls were further captivated by a house down the street which boasted a glassed-in sun porch. Again, every pane of glass was intact. Shelves hung on the inside of the sun porch sported a collection of bottles and glassware in clear, green, and cobalt blue. A meager picket fence defended a barren strip of ground no more than two feet deep to the front door, divulging the homeowner's pathetic bid to keep the desert at bay. This building, too, had admirably weathered the desert for more than a hundred years. The girls tried peering in every window, but could see little of the interior of the home.

"I wish I could get inside and see," Lainy remarked.

"I think I have been inside that house," said Lara. "I know it sounds weird, I mean, it's not a psychic flash or anything. It's more like a hunch, an impression. But I know I've been here."

"Really? You can feel that?" asked Lainy incredulously. "I don't feel anything."

Lara noted the sadness in Lainy's voice. "So? That's okay, we knew you weren't psychic, which you should thank God for, by the way. But even so, Rachel said you could receive messages of sorts from Elise, and that those messages are often gifted to the current life, to help with areas of struggle. You should consider yourself lucky, Lainy."

"Is that more free advice?" she smiled coyly.

"Yes. And worth every penny," Lara laughed. "Remember, I'm a visionary."

They walked a hundred yards or so to the intersection at Main Street and turned south, heading for a museum and visitor center Bob had marked on their map for them. They passed by the morgue, a tiny building on the southwest corner of Green and Main, and looked in the store-front window. Resting against the back wall were several caskets in various stages of completion. They were simple unadorned black boxes that came to triangular points at one end. Lainy noted the size of the boxes. "Wow, I've heard them say people were smaller back then, but...," she said.

They turned away from the morgue and faced the southeast corner of the intersection. The edifice standing there was identified as the Swazey Hotel. According to the brochure, the building had, during its history, housed a clothing store and a casino as well. The site of the building had a certain magnetic attraction for the girls, but upon stepping directly up to the building, that sensitivity grew cold.

Lara said, "It's not the same building. It has no relation to Elise, and it's not at all familiar. I guess when her hotel burned, it burned completely to the ground. There's nothing here to remember."

"Except," Lainy said apprehensively, "on the side of the building there," she pointed to the side facing Green Street.

"Oh," Lara agreed. "It leaves you feeling kind of chilled doesn't it?"

"That's where she died, Lara. I can feel it," she told her sister, slightly shaken. They were staring at the bare plot of ground that was the site of their great, great, grandmother's murder.

# Chapter 39

"I see public restrooms, drinking fountains, visitor center, picnic area—nope, no telephones. Lainy, there has to be a public phone in a State Park, doesn't there?" Lara stood with the tour map open, searching for a marker somewhere on the page that would denote the location of a pay phone.

"That guard was awfully nice. Maybe if they don't have public phones, he'd let us borrow his. I mean, we're going to use a calling card anyway."

"He'd let you use his phone, I'll bet. Okay. It's only about a half-mile down Main Street from here. Let's go call Rachel. Then we can go back and get the basket, finish eating, and maybe tour China town."

"Sounds like a plan," Lainy answered as she snapped a few more photos of the street before tucking the camera away.

They had mutually agreed that the spot most likely to elicit a sensory or psychic response was the place of Elise Swazey's death. Having visited the site, and having failed to receive any flashes of memory or insight other than a pervasive sense of fear, they decided to call Rachel and fill her in on the newspaper findings, their dream of the night before, and Lainy's first inkling of psychic inspiration. Then they could spend the remainder of the afternoon amusing themselves in the history of the town, just as any other tourists.

✠ ✠

A little more than half-way to the kiosk, Lara grew uneasy. Finally she stopped in the middle of the road. "Lainy, please don't think I'm being dramatic, but—"

"You? Dramatic?" Lainy said teasingly.

"I'm serious. I'm getting a nauseous, dizzy feeling, and it wasn't anything I ate."

"Do you want to sit down?" Lainy asked, concerned. "Maybe it's the sun," she offered.

"I don't think so. Jeff and I hike almost every day in the sun. Anyway, it's not that kind of feeling. Something's wrong with this spot. Something's making me feel anguish, sorrow. It's like being sick at heart. And, you know, I can't shake the feeling like we're being watched."

Lara ambled to a small knoll at the edge of the road and rested. She didn't want to explore this, but knew she should. Lainy sat next to her and said nothing as she watched her sister give into her feeling.

Lara placed her open palm on the earth and closed her eyes. She tried to let her mind wander. She imagined Rachel's regression hallway with numerous doors. Suddenly, she could see herself following Elise Swazey down the corridor. They were both passing slowly by the doors, one by one. In Lara's mind, as she began to approach the fifth of many identical doors on the right side, her tongue went heavily to the inside of her right cheek, something which occurred each time Lara had a psychic impression, her own brand of Ougi board. This told Lara she needed to explore what lay beyond that particular door. She could see herself standing in front of it as Elise continued on down the hall in a beautiful dress of emerald green and black. Lara could feel the door's magnetic pull. She slowly turned the knob and pushed.

It was a room filled with shadows. Lara began to distinguish dusty floorboards and flimsy hanging sheets fluttering quietly from a breeze coming through an open window at the far end of the room. Lara strained her eyes in the gloom, trying to adjust. Beds began to materialize between the curtains and then, slowly, forms emerged beneath coarse blankets on the beds. Pale, thin women moaned and cried softly. Young children filled some of the beds, but they remained dreadfully quiet.

One bedraggled older woman turned her head jerkily toward Lara and with an expression filled with pain, mouthed one word, "Frankie." Lara recognized the woman immediately, although the emaciated appearance caused the woman to seem much older than she was. It was Rachel Carrell. But of course, it was not Rachel. This woman's name was Amanda Bust; a name for which the double entendre drew plenty of comment for the only female card dealer in the Esmeralda Region. She'd been beautiful and buxom when she'd arrived on the Bodie stage from San Francisco in 1872. But her beauty had since grayed and her bosom had withered with the illness. Elise had been the only innkeeper willing to employ Amanda when she'd first arrived in Bodie. Hiring Amanda had turned out to be a very profitable arrangement for them both. The gamblers and miners quickly came to love Amanda and her talent for listening and sometimes offering sound advice. She radiated cheerfulness and hope, and brought increased business to the struggling Swazey Hotel. Elise and Amanda had become fast friends, and remained good friends long after she left The Swazey, for the highly-sought position as pit boss in the Grand Hotel's card room. A short two years later, however, Amanda took up permanent residence in the women's ward at the Bodie Hospital. She was no longer able to care for herself, let alone deal cards.

A whimper arose from a distant bed. "My baby," Lara heard the woman cry. The curtains fluttered slightly; the room began darkening again. The vision faded to black, and she was back inside the corridor. Another door. She opened it and saw more beds. She was drawn to the first one on the right. A withered man was billeted beneath the sheets. She approached softly and her eyes fell upon jars of clear and viscous liquids holding a pageant of grotesque intestines and more. The man raised his arm and whimpered and the arm shook terribly, but Lara didn't know what he wanted. She felt helpless. And then that image faded away too. Lara opened her eyes to the bright light of day and the sensation of her sister's hand squeezing her shoulder reassuringly.

"Are you all right?" Lainy asked with concern. "Lara, you were crying."

Lara reached up and felt the wetness streaming down her cheeks. "I saw Rachel," she said miserably. "Rachel was here. Died right here," she patted the ground. "There was once a hospital here."

"You saw all that? How did she die?"

Lara looked so sad as she told her sister about the vision, "Oh Lainy. It was terrible. Women and children, so many of them dying. They were so sick; so thin and frail."

Lainy's eyes registered understanding, "The poison," she stated.

"Yes," Lara agreed. "In our dream last night, Elise talked about a man named Renick who was poisoning the town."

Lainy shook her head in disbelief. "You really recognized Rachel? I mean, did you, or I, know her back then?"

Lara nodded. "I was following Elise down a corridor, and I stopped at this one door and opened it. She turned to me and said, 'Frankie.' She knew me as Frank Junior. We all must have been friends."

"How can that be?" Lainy murmured to herself.

Lara thought her sister looked as though she could suffer a nervous break-down. Lainy was thinking the very same thing about Lara. That these messages and relationships crossed time, crossed centuries, in fact, to be received by Lara and Lainy, had the girls re-evaluating their whole belief system. For instance, they were both wondering just how involved God was in their daily lives.

"So, does that mean there really are no accidents? I mean, is Life, or Mother Nature, following a plan? We get to make little choices and decisions every day that can affect *how* we get there, but eventually each and every one of us is going to get *there*, wherever that is, and at whatever cosmically-predetermined time it turns out to be. Right?" Lainy asked.

"I don't think everything is left to Fate, Lainy. If it were, would we be here now? Aren't we here to fix some cosmic accident or injustice?" She stood and brushed off her seat, then bent and offered Lainy a hand up.

"I don't know. Everything that's happening, people we've known, has it all been, like, orchestrated? I mean it's like everybody is seeking old friends out in a new lifetime. Of course, how we are recognizing each other is still a mystery." Lainy said.

"Or a miracle," Lara offered. She stopped suddenly. "Hey, if we are here to seek each other out again, can Jack Gunn be far away?"

Lainy stopped in her tracks. "You, you think he came back, too?"

"Well, from what I've seen of Elise and Jack, they have some serious unfinished business. Wouldn't you say?"

Lainy stared at her sister. She'd been officially divorced for a single day, and her heart just skipped a beat at the thought of another man, one she had never even met. She laughed at herself and shook her head. "Let's just call Rachel and then head back to the lake. An afternoon of lazy fishing sounds pretty good to me right now."

"Sure. And if you want, we could always come back tomorrow and see China Town with Jeff and Claire. I'm sure we'd feel, I don't know, less vulnerable, with Jeff along."

They continued walking in the direction of the kiosk. They could see more cars entering the park past the guard's booth, and more were in the parking area to the west. They walked directly up to the half-open doorway, crossing in back of a van full of young people that had just paid their admission. About a mile in the distance, another car was bouncing down the road toward the station. The guard was sitting at a desk with his back to the door when Lara said hello, loud enough to get his attention. But when the guard turned around, it wasn't the same guard they had met earlier. Lainy had just stepped up to the opening beside Lara and the two girls exchanged quick glances.

Both noticed that the guard was wearing a name tag that said "Bob."

"Oh," Lara exclaimed with surprise. "You're not the same man we met earlier."

The man smiled hugely as he rose from his chair and walked to the door. He looked down Main Street, then up the drive, noticing approaching cars. "No, I just came on duty. Lunch break for the old guy, you know," he said.

"Both your names are Bob? I'll bet that can get kind of confusing."

The new guard glanced down at his name tag to read it, as though he wasn't already aware of his identification. Lara found the gesture odd.

"What can I do for you lovely ladies?" he ignored the question.

"We would really appreciate it if we could borrow a phone. We have a calling card," Lainy offered.

"Or, if there is a pay telephone in the park somewhere and you could point us to it, we'd use that one instead," Lara said.

Jake could not believe his luck. Of course he had no idea whether there was a phone in the park or not, and did not wish to tip his hand by admitting as much. But if the girls used the office telephone, and talked long enough for the noon traffic to die down, he could kill them here and leave before anyone saw him. He reached down to unlock the bottom half of the door and welcomed them in with a sweeping gesture.

"Phone's on the desk there. Feel free," he said, crossing his arms and ankles and leaning back against a six-foot high locker-like cabinet built into the south wall.

He had obviously intended to listen to their call, but a car pulled up to the window. It was the car the girls had seen approaching from a ways off. The new guard acted as if the arrival was a big inconvenience; he turned grudgingly to take the admission fee.

Lainy noticed he failed to hand out any of the information they had received from the other Bob, and he also never mentioned the hazardous areas to the newcomers. *What a slacker. Bet he won't last here very long.*

After punching in fifty-thousand numbers the line began ringing, then abruptly stopped after three. The connection proceeded through a series of clicks, then another ring, and a strong male voice answered simply, "Hello."

Surprised, Lara said to the other end, "Is—is this Mark? Do I have the right number for Dr. Carrell?"

"Who's calling please? Are you a patient of Dr. Carrell?"

"Yes, my sister and I are—seeing her. Is she available?"

"May I have your names please?" continued the voice on the other end.

"Uh, I'm sorry, who am I speaking with? What's going on?" asked Lara, panic creeping into her voice. "I would like to speak to Rachel please. Is she not available, or? Please just tell her it's... it's the dream sisters calling."

"One moment please," the voice ended abruptly and music began to play.

"They put me on hold," Lara said to Lainy, shrugging. "I don't know what's going on, but this guy doesn't sound like that student she has working there."

A different male voice, this one deeper and richer, clicked on the line and demanded the name of the caller.

"I, uh, would rather not say. Rachel understands this. Can I talk with her? She's expecting our call." Lara was starting to get angry.

"Let me ask you a question. Are you calling from Bodie, California?" the voice asked.

Lara's eyes opened wide in surprise. "How...?"

"Dr. Rachel Carrell was murdered sometime Saturday morning. She was attacked in her office. You're speaking with Lieutenant Stan Block of the Long View PD. We have every reason to believe that you and your sister are in imminent danger, Miss..."

Lara sat stunned. Lainy watched as her sister turned pale, and she knew something was very wrong. She looked over at the guard. He was still busy at the window. She nervously glanced around the small office, and her eyes came to rest on the cabinet the new guard had been leaning against as he'd prepared to eavesdrop on them. Down at the bottom, seeming to stem from behind the door, was a thin, crooked black line leading to the floor. On the floor beneath the line was a single drop of thick, black liquid. Lainy was mesmerized by the trickle. Her scalp began tingling, and her heart nearly fluttered to a stop when the realization hit her. It wasn't black, it was deep crimson red. She looked back at the guard. His uniform hung so loosely on him; why hadn't they noticed that before? She looked back at the cabinet, at the trickle of blood, and realized they needed to get away from the phony guard before he noticed the blood too, or noticed the shaky fear that was threatening to paralyze her. Lainy tapped her sister on the shoulder and turned her toward the cabinet pointing.

Lara, astonished by the news she had just received on the telephone, repeated into the handset, "Rachel's been murdered?" as she looked vacantly to her sister, then to where her sister pointed. But then her eyes zoomed in on the offensive flow. She looked up to meet her sister's terrified expression. She quickly glanced over at the guard. He was busy with more visitors; there were four cars in line waiting. They needed to escape while the phony guard was busy and there were plenty of witnesses around. Lara carefully, quietly replaced the mouthpiece to the cradle, disconnecting a very frustrated police lieutenant, and tip-toed to the half-open door. The driver's side window of the car was rolled down, revealing a man in his early thirties, a woman beside him, and one child in the back seat.

Lara nudged the phony guard aside roughly and leaned over the ledge to be heard, "Sir, my sister pulled a muscle in her leg. Do you think you could take us back to our car in the lot over there?" The guy looked at his partner and shrugged, "Sure, we have room."

Jake was seething at the missed opportunity. Something tipped the girls off. They were acting spooked, and he was sure the redhead's leg had been just fine when they'd walked up Main Street to the kiosk. The girls pushed past him and quickly climbed into the car. As the car pulled away, Jake looked around the cubicle and spotted the blood seepage from the cabinet. His cover was blown. He leaned out the upper door and waved all the cars through, then he jerked open the door to the kiosk and began jogging down Main Street, the pedestrian route, toward the parking area.

# Chapter 40

The moment the car moved ahead, Lara leaned forward and urgently told the driver of their suspicion that the man in the guard's booth was an impostor. "He's not the same man who let us in here this morning, but he is wearing the first guy's uniform and name tag. I know it." Lara pleaded.

"We needed to use the phone in the office. We're here to investigate an unsolved murder that occurred here in Bodie some years ago. In the course of that call, we learned that our…partner has been murdered up in Washington state. And they think the killer, or killers, are after us." Lainy added.

The man looked nervously at his wife. Their eyes met and held with the silent understanding that they had just picked up two nut cases who were now in the same back seat with their young son. "Uh, look," the man started.

His wife jumped in quickly, "We'll just drop you at your car, and you can call the FBI or CIA or whatever secret organization you work for."

"Yeah, uh, you must have a cellular phone and all that high-tech stuff, right?"

Lainy threw herself against the back of her seat and expelled an audible sigh. "You think we're crazy. You don't believe us."

"Look," Lara tried again. "We thought there was something odd about that guy back there. I know this may not be enough to convince you that there's some evil conspiracy going on here. But, please listen to me. While I was making that phone call, and he was busy admitting people into the park, my sister and I noticed something leaking out of those tall cabinets in the office. We looked closer; it was blood. I think that guy killed the real guard. Very soon, he's going to be coming after us. You people have seen his face. Please believe us because I'm afraid you're now in as much trouble as we are."

Lara glanced at the little boy beside her. He was probably Claire's age. Lara was aching with guilt. By hitching a ride with these people, she had unwittingly involved them. This little boy was in danger because of them. "Please. I have a little girl about the same age as your son. I don't want any of you to get hurt. Just drop us at our car, and then keep going. Get the hell out of Bodie. And as soon as you're safe, call the police for us." She looked helplessly from the husband to the wife. "Call the police *on* us, but please go."

She did not receive an answer. The car came to a stop, and nobody said a word. The little boy was gawking at her and had nervously placed a thumb in his mouth, a comfort he probably had not indulged in for years. She reluctantly opened her door and got out. She looked back toward the guard house but saw no one in pursuit. Lainy walked around the front of the car and approached the man from his still open window. "Sir. I know you're not buying our story. It does sound pretty wild, I'll grant you. But, it is true. So, even if it's just to report two escaped lunatics, will you please drive quickly out of here and call 9-1-1 for us?"

The man looked over at his wife, who stared straight ahead. She did not appear happy. He turned back to the girls with his jaw set and his lips tight. "Alright, you girls have had your fun with us. We did you a favor, and you thank us by upsetting our child with your cockamamie story of murder and such. Why don't *you* just get the hell out of here yourselves?" And with that, he put the car in gear once again and lurched forward fifty yards or so, to a parking space well away from where Lainy and Lara were left standing.

"I'm going to be sick," said Lainy.

"They're not going to leave," Lara agreed. "They're going to get themselves killed, their child too." She looked at Lainy; her eyes were spilling over. "Come on Lainy. We don't have time for that. Maybe he'll ignore them; he's after us."

"Why? Why is he after us? How do you know that? And, who told you Rachel was murdered?"

"When I called Rachel's office the call was forwarded to a police station. A detective told me."

Lainy gasped, and her tears fell faster.

Lara continued, "He wanted our names. He didn't know them already, so Rachel must have honored our request, which means Jeff and Claire are safe. The detective knew that we were calling from Bodie, and he said they have every reason to believe we are in danger.

"Then you pointed out the blood, and we had to get out of there before the traffic died. So I hung up the phone without telling them who we are. But, like I said, they knew we were calling from Bodie, and they know we're in danger. They must have police on the way to help us, and for the time being there are just too many people around for him to try something out in the open, right? But if we get out on that desolate highway, alone with that guy chasing after us, we wouldn't stand a chance—he has the guard's gun, Lainy. We have to stay here in the park and hope that the cops come to help us in time. If we don't show up at the lake at four, Jeff might get worried and phone the park office. If he gets no answer, or we're very late, he'd call the police, I think.

We just have to stay alive until help arrives, and that means we need to hide, Lainy, before the park is empty of visitors, and we stick out like two sore thumbs. I don't know why someone wants us dead, maybe we know something we don't know we know, but we need a plan if we're going to survive."

"Let's just tell him we don't know anything," Lainy's voice escalated with panic.

"Hell, Lainy, he isn't even going to ask. He's just going to kill us. We have to get away from here and hide."

Lainy looked nervously back at the guard house. No one was coming from that direction, either by car or by foot, but it didn't look as though there was anyone manning the office either. "I think he's gone," she said hopefully.

"Well that's not good. He's laying in wait somewhere, or he's circling around. Either way, I don't want to get trapped on this side of the park where we are completely exposed. We should assume he's stalking us, circling around. What about exiting the park from the north, and heading toward Aurora. The brochure says the road is closed at that point, but what the hell. I always wanted to see what it was like to bust through a road block."

"Like Thelma and Louise?" Lainy offered, sniffing back tears and trying valiantly to smile.

"Well, no," said Lara. "Personally, I'd like to live through this."

Jake dashed up Green Street using buildings on the north side for cover. He turned north on Fuller, sprinting from structure to structure so as not to be seen by the girls standing in the parking lot above. When he reached the end of Fuller, there was nothing more than rusty machinery and an abandoned head frame between him and the parking lot. He saw the redhead look over at the guard station and say something to her sister. They talked briefly, then jumped in the car and sped north. Jake ran the distance to the parking area, crouching just below the embankment. The family in the white Ford Taurus that had given the girls a lift was still sitting in their car. The sisters must have told them everything. They were probably at this very moment debating where to go to call the authorities. Jake kept low and snaked his way to the rear of the car.

He could hear them talking inside. It sounded to Jake like the woman was angry and the man was trying to calm her down. He went for the hard target first, keeping low and out of view of the man's side mirror. When he arrived just behind and below the driver's side door, Jake removed the knife from its sheath. In a single, fluid motion, he rose, pivoted, and planted the knife in the driver's neck before the man knew what had hit him.

The driver's elbow and forearm had been resting on the door through the open window. After a moment the arm fell, fingers pointed to the asphalt, and the man's head lolled sideways. He was already dead, but his eyes stayed open and surprised, as did his mouth. Inside the car the woman was shouting his name. She never saw Jake, did not witness the attack, and did not see the blood. But she realized something was wrong with her husband, sadly, too late. By the time she reached for her husband, Jake had reached her window.

The scene unfolded with the jerkiness of an old cartoon reel. She felt, rather than heard, the presence at her side. She had just turned her husband's head to witness the gaping, spurting breach when, clicking her head back to the right, she saw a flash of a hand and a slicing glint aimed under her chin.

*Cold.* As though someone had lanced her throat with an icicle. The sudden pounding ache of impact was immediately soothed by the frostiness of the icy spear. Her head lolled forward slightly, and she was appalled to see she had just wet her pants. A man stood at the window. He was holding a bloody knife in his hand. *That doesn't make sense,* was her last thought. *He's smiling at me. That doesn't make sense.*

As the woman's eyes glassed over with bewilderment, and the blood slicked down her throat, Jake pushed the woman's sagging body forward to the glove compartment and leaned in the window, smiling over the headrest at the child in the back seat.

The little boy looked pitifully small and was sucking furiously on his thumb as the man stood grinning at him.

# Chapter 41

"Psychics, my ass. I'm trying to save their clairvoyant butts, and one of 'em hangs up on me." He complained to his partner. Mac was driving while Block sorted through the material his staffers had retrieved from the internet; thank God for new technology. They were just outside of Portland, Oregon, where they were making a flight to Reno, followed by a commuter to South Lake Tahoe. Block's office also reserved a rental car for them. He was really hoping it wouldn't be one of those little economy-sized nut-crunchers. He was a big man, after all. And Mac was a mountain.

"Get me that State Park's office in Bodie, I've been disconnected," Lt. Block bellowed into the cellular phone. He was still trying to get the hang of using the clunky device. "Unbelievable." He said to Mac.

Detective First Grade Eric MacGowan's eyes were twinkling. "Your idea of routing the doc's calls to the cellular phone worked," Mac offered. He knew why Stan was behaving so surly; Stan was afraid of being too late. Mac had to admit, there was a strange element to this case. It was a sense that the safety of the two sisters was a monumentally important matter—for all of them. Both men admitted feeling it, even though neither of them had ever met the women. "The ladies must still be all right if they could make a phone call."

"Yeah, there's that. But, I can't say I feel good about two hunted women, who don't know they're being hunted, stopping in the middle of the afternoon of their vacation, to make a long distance phone call to their shrink. I think they've hit on something. They're investigating, see?"

He'd had detectives inquire of local and state offices about any pending activity, event or legislation that might be in the news, or which could in some manner affect the Bodie Bowl area. They uncovered mention of a pending Senate Bill that would restrict sale and usage of Bodie Bowl mining rights. "That Bill has to be the culprit. Its pending passage has someone extremely anxious. You and I both know, it would only be worth killing for if—"

"—if its passage was going to cost someone a lot of money," MacGowan finished. He and Block had seen plenty of crimes against persons, and the single-most distinguished motive for committing them is money. "How *does* this Bill's passage cost someone money? And who owns those mining rights?" Mac asked.

Block took a long drink of coffee from his travel mug. He turned his attention back to the folder, where he found what he was looking for in short order. He hung the sheet in front of Mac's face for a split second before announcing, "I can answer your second question: A Canadian company called Globalesque has eighty-seven and a half percent, and you'll never guess who has the other twelve and a half?"

"That candy-ass professor?" Mac asked.

"How did you know that?" asked Stan, impressed.

"Well, we know he's connected somehow. And like I've heard you say a hundred times, it always comes back to the money."

"I might just have the answer to your first question, too," Block told his partner. "Don't ask me what made me think of this. It popped into my head almost like the thought was being *put* there. Have you ever been to that place in Colorado where you buy a pail of dirt, and whatever gold you find in it, you get to keep?"

"Never heard of it," Mac was looking for a parking space in PDX's long-term parking lot. "Keep your eyes peeled," he told Block as his eyes swept back and forth.

"Oh, sure you have. There was a kid on the news not too long ago who found a huge nugget worth more than fifty thousand dollars, remember?"

Mac just shrugged and shook his head like, *so?*

"Well, here's my point: If you don't find a nugget, one of the attendants will mix cyanide with your dirt for you. It separates dirt from any gold dust. Then, they, I don't know, they use lime or something to collect the gold precipitate. They clean up what's there, and they weigh it. Nugget or no nugget, most of the time you end up with more money than you paid for the dirt. Hence, pay dirt. Get it?"

"Not really, Pard." The bone-dry desert, Death Valley, talk of gold and hitting pay dirt, it didn't tempt Mac. He felt no passion for it whatsoever. He didn't understand the fascination, and he'd be just as happy if he never had to leave the northwest and his wife and children, ever.

"The point is the cyanide, Mac. It's extremely caustic poison, and the park has to be real careful about how they dispose of it. EPA hoops and all that. Their enterprise doesn't even use that much, you know? Like a couple of tablespoons here and there, yet the guy being interviewed said it was one of the biggest expenses the park faces, the disposal of the waste cyanide." He searched frenziedly through the research materials and found what he'd been looking for. "Now consider this." He looked up to make sure Mac was listening. "Bodie perfected the cyanide process. I'll bet no one's ever given a thought as to how all that gold was mined way back when. And I'll bet my badge nobody's ever checked into what they did with waste cyanide back in 1880." He smiled like a kid on Christmas morning.

"I get what you're saying about the cyanide. They were probably just dumping the stuff down mine shafts or into the creek or something. But what has that got to do with mining rights in Bodie Bowl today? What is it they are willing to kill people over? We find that out, I think we'll find our bad guy. Hey, are you looking for a parking spot? We're going to miss our flight."

"Sorry. Is that a spot there on the other side of the Range Rover? Anyway, there are some very strict environmental safeguards written into this Bill that could put a damper on any potential sales. I'm betting they have a sale pending, and this thing has them scared shitless." His cellular phone rang in his lap and Stan almost jumped. "Yeah?" He answered, blushing slightly.

"It just keeps ringing," the clerk in Stan's office reported. "Should I check with the phone company?"

"Yes do that. And check with that State Parks' general information line. Ask them if the Bodie Park would be unattended today. If someone's supposed to be there, ask why their guard would close early or leave his station. If they don't have a good explanation, notify the local authorities that our hired-assassin suspect may be in their backyard. He *may* be a young Hispanic male, according to the therapist's secretary, and that is all we know. We're, uh, we're pulling into the long-term parking and Security's allowing us to board directly, so we're gonna have to turn this thing off for a while." Block said. He leveled his gaze at MacGowan. "We've got to hurry, Mac. Something tells me those girls are running out of time."

"There. There's a spot." Mac scored a tight little space with a light truck on one side and a landscaped curb on the other. "E, third row over. Don't forget it," Mac warned. He lifted their two bags out of the trunk and set them down to pull the handles up.

They were ready. Mac looked at Stan for a second and said to his partner, "We're really doin' this. We're going to Bodie."

"Yeah," Stan chuckled sardonically. "Good-bye, God. We're going to Bodie."

# Chapter 42

Jack Gunn knew something was wrong. He had kept one eye on Elise through the swinging doors and one eye on the game being played before him. But he'd turned his head away, only for a moment, and Elise was gone.

Something nagged at him. Phegley had hollered at him when he'd passed by The Standard earlier in the evening. Ezra had been locking up, but he turned and yelled to Jack that Elise was treading in deep waters. "If you really love her, throw her a life-saver," he'd yelled at him.

"What deep waters, Ezra? Speak English."

To which Ezra had replied, "Dirty waters, Jack. Black, and very, very dangerous."

Elise told him Parker had threatened her just that morning. But, surely those two malignant miscreations at Touchstone would not *actually* harm a woman. No Bodieite would make the mistake of killing a decent, single woman. *And Elise is an eyeful.* With men outnumbering the marryin' gals and whores by better than forty-to-one, to do so was a hanging offense, and everyone knew it, so they wouldn't *actually*—

Perhaps he should take a stroll outside and keep a watchful eye on his woman. He excused himself again and made for the doors. The loud bang was so close his ears buzzed, and he ducked reflexively, thinking someone had taken a shot at him.

"*Elise.*" Jack yelled.

The shot had been fired close by. He rounded the hotel's cross-street side, and beheld the love of his life laying crumpled in the dust. His owl-like sight could see a dark figure running away, and instinct had him drawing a gun, which he carried in his pocket. He fired at the retreating suspect. The shadowy figure fired back, the bullet just grazing Jack. Then whoever the shooter was, he was out of sight. Jack knelt over Elise. He lifted her torso to hold her in his arms one last time. His love was already gone.

"You must have been so frightened, darling. I should have been here with you. I never should have let you out of my sight," he cried. The gruesome sight of her once-beautiful face was too much for him, and something in him died, too. Jack would always blame himself for Elise's death, for not being there to protect her. As he knelt grieving, before the commotion was stirred over another death in Bodie, something made the hairs stand up on the back of his neck. His peripheral vision detected movement in the darkened street with him.

"I see you there. Show yourself—else I'll fire and ask questions later."

He stepped out of the darkness in back of the hotel. "It's me."

"Frankie, how long you been standing there?"

"I saw him, Jack. It was Morris Parker."

"Your ma is dead. I'm sorry, Frank." Jack was crying openly. "You certain it was Parker?" He wiped at his eyes, unashamed.

"I am. I saw him. And I'm gonna kill him."

"No, we're going to get you the hell out of Bodie. And then I'm going to kill him."

❧ ❧

Bodie was a town of general lawlessness. So when Jack Gunn entered Sam Leon's Bar wearing a star on his vest, it set off a bout of rowdy laughter. But they stopped laughing when he drew his gun lightening fast and shot up every bottle over the bar.

"Okay, Jack. You got our attention, and you're paying for the damages. What is it you want? There's no trouble here, 'cept maybe you've managed to trouble my liquor supplies pretty good," griped Leon.

"You know I'm good for it, Sam." Jack addressed the entire room. "I'm looking for Morris Parker. You see him, you tell him I'm gunnin' for him. I'll take him dead or alive, but I fancy him dead."

"You've got to be mad as a March hare. Menacing a hired gun like Parker? It's deranged. You're walkin' pretty heavy, Jack." Sam warned him.

"You tell him he can die by hanging or he can die by my bullet, but either way he's going to pay for the killing of Elise Swazey. You see him, you tell him that."

"Wait, I'm real sorry about Elise, Jack. She was a good woman, and her passin' on is a damned shame. But the paper said she was a suicide. Why do you think Parker did it?"

He had the room's attention, such as it was. Jack looked around the intoxicated group, aiming to make eye contact with each and every man. "I got an eye-witness, first-off. Second off, I was at Elise's side, and there was no gun. So how was she supposed to have shot herself in the head with no gun?" The men stared at Jack, numb, dumb or awed.

"Speaking of fatal, Parker's grown fatally careless with his killin'. He's not getting away with this one." And with that, Jack Gunn reloaded his weapons and walked on to deliver the message to the next establishment. He hoped the brashness of his act would provoke Parker into a confrontation.

# Chapter 43

Parker didn't think there was a gunfighter equal to him in Bodie, and certainly not Jack Gunn, who had been heard more than once declaring his loathing for firearms. And it was true, he didn't like them, but that didn't mean he wasn't an expert in handling one. And he'd spent the better part of the year since Elise's death practicing up his aim and handling. Jack figured Parker was stupid once, he could be stupid again. In fact, Jack was counting on it.

Morris and French Joe were thoroughly drunk when one of the other whores came weaving past their partition. "Oh, excuse me," she giggled. "Why, Mr. Parker, how do you do?" Her eyes held an altogether different meaning as she scrutinized his crotch.

"Get out'a here you drunken whore." He tossed a boot at her head, and it crashed through the window behind her when she ducked. "God damn it, why'd ya have to go an' duck for?"

She smiled at him provocatively. "You know, if'n you had treated me better, Morris, I might'a told you somethin' you'd have wanted to know. But, now, go to hell!" She broke up with laughter. "And you will too, you will!"

"What the hell are you cacklin' about? I swear all you whores carry on like hens."

"Oh yeah? Well men ain't payin' us for our conversational skills." She spat at him.

He was up in a flash and holding her by the roots of her hair before she could wipe the saliva from her mouth. "*Ouch.* Damn you, Parker, you're hurtin' me."

"What are you talking about, whore? What ought I to know about?"

"*Ow.* That Jack Gunn fella is lookin' for ya. He's wearin' a badge, and he say's he's gonna shoot you down or hang ya—your choice. Now let go 'a me." She twisted angrily from his grip. She glared at French Joe. "Joe, you got crap for taste." She spit and ran out the door.

"*Ooooooh,* he's gunnin' fer ya. Ain't you a little bit scared Morris?" She teased.

"Hell no." He pulled one boot on angrily, realizing the other was probably sitting in mud. "Jack Gunn is a Sport, not a gunman. And that ain't a very smart bet, telling people he's gunning for me. I wonder what he's up to." He stood up and tucked his shirt in, grabbed his holster from the bedpost and buckled it on.

Joe sat up eagerly. "Are you going out lookin', Morris? Can I watch?"

"Do what you want, stupid whore." He left in search of his other boot.

⤫ ⤬

Strangely, there seemed no one in town could tell Parker where Jack Gunn lived. The man was elusive, showing up in all the right places but disappearing as quick and as quiet as an Indian. Parker would have been surprised indeed to discover that Gunn had learned many lessons from fighting Indians, and some white men who were worse than savages. He had traveled from Illinois to Oregon, along the trail. He had cut his teeth on warring Indians in the Colorado foothills when he was just twenty years. The fighting was so bad, their party had to veer toward New Mexico instead, saving Oregon for a later date.

When the time came to try for Oregon again, they had made it as far as Curry County. It was unfortunate that the Curry Indians had decided at that time to join up with the Rogue River Indians for a massacre, and *none* of the white men who had been forewarned, believed it. By the time Jack's wagon train entered Curry County, the Indians had already killed most of the settlers in the area, thrown their bodies in the river, and burned their cabins. It was the smoke from all of those burning cabins that alerted the immigrants. They changed course and headed for a fort they knew to be located just a mile or two north of the mouth of the Rogue River. The fort was well-stocked with supplies, and the party wound up garrisoned for several weeks.

Every night, several of the men would creep out and pick off Indians as they found opportunity. It was no easy thing to sneak up on an Indian, and one learned quickly their tricks or died trying. Jack was only twenty-one years old when fifteen men, including an Indian agent whom the Indians despised, had gone from the fort to dig potatoes for their stores. The men walked into an ambush and half were killed. The agent's heart was cut out.

Eventually, soldiers arrived from Crescent City under Captain Ord. The Indians had since taken refuge of sorts in a house facing the river. In a fairly brilliant and brave plan conceived by the army officers, they waged an attack and killed all of the warriors known to have participated in the massacre at Big Bend. It was Jack Gunn who had run down many of the warriors as they tried to escape down the river. One of those warriors had not taken part in the massacre, and Jack intended to take him prisoner. The warrior surrendered to Jack, telling him he would like to eat Jack's heart, so that he might be brave like him. The Indian had meant it as a compliment, and Jack had taken it as one. But a settler had overheard and shot the Indian dead. They took no prisoners that day.

There was a lot of Indian trouble in the West during the late 50's and 60's, and Jack Gunn had seen more than his share. He understood the importance of accuracy and speed as he learned the trade of Indian fighter. He also learned you had to act like an Indian if you hoped to kill one. And so it was the Indian part of him which allowed Jack to sneak into Morris Parker's fancy house like a redskin in the woods, and switch the bullets in his peacemaker for molds of soap, which held no lead at all. He could have killed Parker in his sleep, but Jack was clever. He had other plans.

"I got other plans," Parker complained to his boss. Renick wanted Morris to negotiate with a couple of lucky strikers who staked a claim six miles south of Bodie Creek.

Parker was still fuming over his breakfast this morning. He'd sat down to his usual black coffee, bread, and hard cheese, when he spotted the fancy invitation perched against the lantern in the middle of the table. He wasn't certain how long the envelope had been sitting there, since he had broken his own cardinal rule the night before and allowed himself more than one drink. It could have been sitting there before he'd turned in last night, and Parker just hadn't noticed it. The invitation was from Jack Gunn. It read,

> "Come out and play.
> Place: You pick it.
> Time: Your time to die.
> Don't be yellow. Jack Gunn."

He petted his self-cocker. "Something came up, Aaron. I got some personal business to settle first."

"You've been getting sloppy lately, Morris. You can't do me much good if you're in a jail cell. That idiot who think's he's gonna Marshall in this town, just might be fool enough to try and arrest you."

"Yeah, Jack Gunn. *He's* my personal business. I'm gonna go take care of it right now."

When Morris Parker rode down Main Street whistling, *My Darling Clementine*, it seemed people greeted him a bit guardedly. He was growing a little uneasy, still fretting over just when and how Gunn had left that note inside his house. He dismounted at the Grand Hotel, and as he tethered Clementine, someone called for him from the railing up above.

"Today is a good day to die, eh, Morris? Say, you ain't yellow after all. More a delicate shade of pale, I'd say." The insult was accompanied by laughter from a couple of the lovelier whores in town— which was not to say they were rare beauties, to be sure— who plied their trade at the best hotel. Parker seethed.

He squinted up. "Jack Gunn," he said. The man looked to be in fine spirits for someone who plays with fire. Morris was getting pissed off. "What's your quarrel, Gunn? I got no quarrel with you."

Gunn laughed with the ladies and gents on either side of him. "Sounds like 'Menacing Morris' is a little groveling today."

The son of a bitch was talking about him like he was a baby. "You're makin' me ticklish, Gunn. You keep mouthin' off and I'm gonna have to settle a score."

"Well, what do you know, folks? Parker got my message. I was afraid as drunk as he was last night, he might miss it altogether."

Parker had to lean his neck way back and squint into the sun with a splitting headache, in order to converse with Gunn. He was clearly at a disadvantage, and Parker was beginning to think maybe Gunn had planned it that way. *Had Gunn been waiting for me on that balcony for a time?* He wondered.

"So, you're admitting in front of these fine folks, that you make a practice of breaking into others' lodgings while they're away and leaving notes?" Parker accused.

"You were home, Morris. None too inviting, a might sour-smelling too. But you were home. Sleepin' with your boots on. And now that reminds me, would you like to be buried with them boots, Morris? I believe I'd be agreeable to granting one last request. It's more than you gave Elise."

Morris tried to summon to mind if he was indeed sleeping with his boots on last night. *Yes, I was. A lucky guess? That Jack Gunn is a cocky fella.* Morris learned to be careful around those cocky types. Every once in a blue moon they were quick as they thought themselves to be.

"You begging me for a fight, Gunn?"

"Well, damn, Morris, I left you an invitation. What more do you want? We can do this more formal if you like." He bowed graciously. "Sir, after murdering my fiance, will you grant me satisfaction?"

"What the hell for?"

"For Elise, dumbass. And if you won't come out and play, then I'm coming down there after you." He turned and made for the stairs slap-dash, surprising the hell out of Morris Parker.

Parker had never shrunk from a fight, but this crazy son of a bitch vexed him. No, he'd never shrunk from a fight, but he wasn't well known for fighting fair, either. The instant Jack Gunn emerged in daylight, and before they could be paced off like gentlemen and counted for, Morris drew his gun and started firing. Every person on Main Street was awed, including Parker, when Jack Gunn kept walking right steady on up to Parker, in spite of the fact he'd just been shot eight times.

"Morris, that's just not fighting fair."

And, so the story goes, he pulled an Allen pepperbox revolver from his pocket, pressed it right up to Parker's forehead and fired. Renick had tried to warn him he'd gotten sloppy.

Jack fessed up to Sam Leon how he'd done it. "I only knew three things for certain about Morris Parker: he wasn't as smart as he thought he was, he was over-confident, and he would not fight fair. So I paid him a visit late last night, and I replaced all the bullets in his piece with blanks I carved out of soap. And what do you know, Sam? We had ourselves a good, clean fight."

The history books are full of men like Jack Gunn. Maybe his name is even mentioned in a few. Who knows? After Jack's shoot-out with the 'baddest man in Bodie,' he wasn't viewed as just a Sport anymore. Post-gunfight, Jack became sport. Every would-be gunslinger wanting to make a name for himself was itching to take a shot at Jack Gunn. And the name didn't help. He quickly became too romantic a figure for a town like Bodie.

Jack had quit Indian fighting and trail guiding ten years earlier because it was dangerous work. Men in that line of business lead shorter lives, and Jack had wanted to find a good woman and settle down. He'd found her. He'd waited a piece for her. And then he'd lost her. There would never be another woman like Elise, not for him. She'd been meant for him, and he for her. He prayed his love would find him in another life.

Jack eventually went back to his earlier line of work. He fought some fabulous battles, and he'd spawned a string of new legends. And somewhere between New Mexico and Colorado is a small grave marked with his name. A simple mark for a plain man with uncomplicated dreams that were simply not to be.

# Chapter 44

She'd managed to pick every last detail of Honey Raisin polish off her left hand. That crumpet-eating son-of-a-bitch was going to cost her Senate seat for her. As she waited for the Chairman of the Senate Subcommittee on Mining and Natural Resources to get rid of another call, she worked on perfecting just the right note of concern in her voice. "It's my mother," she said sadly, then sniffled. *No, that's too lamentable.* "I hate to ask this favor of you, Dick, but, it's my mother."

"I'm sorry Bobbie," a voice broke in suddenly. "An old friend from the Bureau of Land Management. Now, what can I do for you?" It boomed from the other end of the phone line.

Startled into an authentic degree of shakiness, Senator Cilla blurted, "Uh, Dick, I'm, uh, sorry to uh. Oh, it's my mother. Dick, I need that vote for HR 230 moved up A.S.A.P. I've got to hitch a plane to John Wayne in Orange County so I can be with her. She's broken her hip, and she can't be alone."

"I see." He pondered the idea of Roberta Cilla playing the dutiful daughter. "I don't have to tell you, Bobbie, moving up a Senate vote is on the *difficult* side of impossible. It requires a good deal of shifting and shaking."

"I know, Dick. And I'm really sorry to have to ask," her nervousness inflecting the quivery quality she'd been rehearsing for earlier.

"What exactly were you hoping for, Bobbie?" He cut in.

"I know it's quick, but, I was hoping for tomorrow morning, Dick. So I can be on the next flight out of Sacramento."

The Chairman whistled low. "That's a taller-than-tall order. The Secretary of Interior plans to be present for the vote. There are the EIR's to be assembled. What about your state's other Senator? I'm certain she has intended to be counted in the vote."

"Yes, of course," the Senator began picking at her right hand, drawing further away from the phone intercom as though a snake were about to strike from its core. "I'm certain I could take care of that, Dick. Look, I really need this vote moved up. I mean, it's my mother. She needs my help."

*She nearly had me until the last two whiney sentences.* Dick Burnside pictured Roberta Cilla on the other end of the line. *And why are we pretending pseudo concern for your dear sick mother today, Senator?*

Oh, she was lying. But he couldn't fathom why bumping up this Bill would have such importance for her. "Alright, look. There's a void in the Agenda tomorrow immediately following lunch. That's 2:00  p.m., Senator Cilla. Notifying your sister-Senator will be your responsibility. That is the very best I can do."

God-Cilla drew in a deep but silent breath. "That's super, Dick. You're a dear. See you tomorrow. Ta-ta."

*Ta-ta?* the Chairman thought as he replaced the handset. You must be joking. How did that twit ever get to be a United States Senator?

# Chapter 45

6 April, 2:00 p.m.
Bodie, California

Lara quickly grabbed for her shoulder harness as they picked up speed toward the road block. Lainy hunkered over her steering wheel, gripping it with steadfast determination. The neon orange-painted saw horses came into view first. But what could be glimpsed on the other side sent the Camry skidding and fishtailing to a stop just before the barricade.

"God, I don't believe this," Lara exclaimed. "We can't get a break." She slammed her fists on the dash board.

"What are we going to do?" Lainy fretted.

"I don't know what to do. We can't go back the way we came. And we obviously aren't going through that."

The road on the opposite side of the barricade had experienced a rock slide during its recent history. An effort had been made to push fallen rock to the sides of the road, at the base of the surrounding berms. The piles of rock were then braced with what appeared to be netting made of chain link; however, the tons of loamy dirt that had traveled down with the boulders still remained, rendering the road impassable.

"Can we just drive through the town? Right down Main Street and out the front gate?"

"It's too dangerous, Lainy. There are hardly any visitors still here. The ones that are here think he's a real guard. He is wearing the uniform. If we go driving through this State Park, nobody is going to blink if he pursues a couple of vandals. And he has the real guard's gun, remember?"

"Oh yeah. Plus," Lainy added, "we have no idea where he's hiding, but he knows where we are. So, that's—super."

"Right. He can see us." Lara tapped her fingers on the leg of her jeans as she surveyed the area around her in all directions. "We have *got* to get out of this car and hide. We're sitting ducks." She turned to her sister. "Lainy, we might beat up your car a little."

"Oh, Lara, do you think I give a crap about this stupid car?"

Lara stared at her sister for a moment, and then she smiled wide. "That's, uh, okay, so drive as far as you can out to that hazardous area." She pointed. "The *real* Bob said there were lots of abandoned buildings and wells and mine tunnels in that direction. Add the buttes, washes, and rock outcroppings—just the ones I can see from here, and we can drive that assassin crazy with hide-n-seek—all night if we have to."

Lainy kept nodding, but she emitted a tiny high-pitched wail every now and again.

Lara reached out and grabbed her sister's hands. "Lainy, it's going to start getting dark in a couple of hours. Jeff will call the police if we're still missing. The policeman who tried to warn us on the phone is still trying to locate us. Honey, all we have to do is stay hidden long enough for help to arrive."

Lainy made a three-point turn and headed back down Main to the first left turn at Union Street. That road came to an end after a few hundred yards, where a large wooden board painted by an unsteady hand admonished, "Closed to Public."

"We should probably split up, make it harder for him," Lara suggested.

"*No*," Lainy trembled.

"Look, Lainy. The only way we're going to get out of Bodie alive, is if we keep our wits about us. We *are* smarter than he is. We also have to be silent, and we have to stay alert; we can do that. We survived an entire childhood spent in foster care, and we still turned out pretty darned good. Haven't you ever wondered if there was a…a divine reason for it? For why God allows some lousy things to happen…to children? I have. And now I think I get it. Foster care gave us the grit we're going to need in order to survive this night.

"We were pretty scrappy girls. But we both tried to bury that part of ourselves along with the painful memories. Lainy, honey, I need you to dig down. I need that scrappy little girl right now." She surveyed the foothills. "There's nothing out here but Sand and Rock and Ravine—three desert sisters, and they are on our side. I can feel it. I know that sounds crazy, but this desert is alive. And she wasn't being hostile to us when we arrived, she was trying to protect us. She was trying to shoo us away. I know she'll help us hide from that killer. But not if we hide from ourselves. Lainy, we don't have to forget our past. We're stronger for it. It's made us who we are, and it's what is going to help us survive. I feel we have a sort of kinship with this place. I think Bodie suffered untold cruelties in her childhood too. She's like a sister to us."

"Okay." Lainy answered simply.

Reaching into the zippered hip pouch, Lara brought out the bottle of fruit drink and shook it. She opened the bottle and drank half of it, then handed the bottle to Lainy, advising her, "You should finish that off."

Lainy surveyed the stretch of dust and thirst before her, then she glanced behind them for any sign of someone following. She could not see anyone. She could not see very many people at all.

Urgent whispers in her head cautioned that trouble was on the way. She downed the juice. Lara took the empty bottle from her, screwed on the lid and replaced it in her pack. Later, if she needed a weapon, she could break the end off on a rock. She handed Lainy the knife.

"Oh, God," Lainy stared at the wicked blade.

"Just…you may *have* to use it. He may give you no choice. If it comes to 'do or die,' I know you can do it."

Lainy said nothing. She took her camera out of its case and placed the knife inside instead.

"Good thinking," Lara told her.

Lainy smiled. "Can you reach those windbreakers in the back?"

"Got 'em. Change into your other shoes and let's get going," Lara urged.

"Uh," Lainy reached back for the "comfortable" change of shoes she brought along.

"Oh, no. Toes, your Old Navy flip-flops?" Lara groaned. "*Those* are your comfortable walking shoes?"

"Okay, but if you had told me we were going to be playing cat-and-mouse with a killer and hiding in the 'unsafe buildings and mine shafts,' I probably would have packed my running shoes."

"Well, they're going to have to do. You can't wear those heels." Lara told her.

For the time being, they tied the windbreakers around their waists. Each sister stuffed an apple, banana, and large cookie into the zippered pockets. "I doubt very much I am going to get hungry for an apple." Lainy remarked.

"I know, but it might come in handy if we have to shoo away a coyote or weasel or, oh, who knows? We don't have much of an arsenal for our defense, so take everything. Speaking of critters, remember that rattlesnakes tend to spend their evenings curled up in a good crevice or on a rocky ledge, so look before you reach. Also, it's going to get blacker than ink for about a half-hour after the sun goes down, and before the moon comes up. So watch your step." She looked at Lainy thoughtfully, then she suddenly yanked off her ball cap and swapped it for Lainy's visor. "Your hair is going to make you stick out like a sore thumb. I think you should pile it under the cap; it's almost the identical color of the sand; good camouflage."

Lainy gave her sister a wry smile, as she tied her pony tail higher. "Thanks, *mom*. Aren't you going to remind me to wash behind my ears and wear clean underwear, in case I end up in the hospital?"

"Keep it up, Chuckles, and I can guarantee you'll end up in the hospital." Lara quipped. Then she grabbed her sister and hugged her fiercely. "I love you, Lainy. People think I have no taste, but I love *you*," she laughed, tears threatening. She stared her sister in the eyes and her voice quickly sobered.

"You and I are not going to share Elise's fate. We're tough, and we have something she didn't—each other. We'll determine our own destiny. So, be careful and be smart. Your Jack Gunn is near; *The One*, Lainy. You *must* survive this time around. For him. And for me."

Their eyes had misted over; they grabbed hands and squeezed. They each looked around the town below them. The sun was no longer overhead. But neither had it sunk behind the mountains. The streets were beginning to fill with purple patches near the scattered structures. They did not see the killer, but he was there—somewhere.

"Time to go," Lainy said. The girls hurried around the front of the car and hurled themselves over a shallow draw into a dry wash. The wash was cut through by a trail leading to the first of the old mining company buildings. Lainy silently pointed northeast where the structures backed up to a string of buttes and rocky outcroppings, and there were more signs stuck in the sand. The girls couldn't make out any discernible writing, but correctly assumed the sorely-weathered signs had been posted as warnings. Now they knew the location of the old mining tunnels.

"This is where we part ways," Lara said. "We should use the buildings for as long as we can. It's going to get cold tonight. But if he should get too close to you, head for those tunnels."

Lainy gave her sister a look that said, *you're joking*.

"Hey, any port in a storm," her sister responded.

"What if he follows me into one of those old tunnels?" Lainy asked.

"Then kill him." said Lara matter-of-factly.

# Chapter 46

"Nobody knows all that happens, right at the finish, when the desert has her way with a man. It's a grim secret that only the desert herself and the buzzards can tell."
—Earl Stanley Gardner
Blood-Red Gold, from Whispering Sands

6 April, 3:00 p.m.
Bodie, California

He probably had a half-ton of sand in his Dingos, and his feet were killing him. The genuine leather shoe-boots, which had set him back more than a hundred dollars at a Vancouver men's shop, boasted western stitching and genuine leather uppers. But they were not ideal footwear for the desert.

Jake had already piled the three tourists' bodies into the back seat of the Taurus and covered their bulk with a blanket he'd found in the trunk. He then drove the car a few hundred yards up a dirt track headed for the Masonic, a seldom used road from the looks of it, and parked it behind a butte quite close to the road. Jake would have preferred to hide the vehicle and its grisly contents further away, but the tires had bit into deep sand after just a few yards. Jake couldn't push the vehicle any further, either. He'd tried. Now his shoes were ruined, he'd taken way too much time disposing of the family, and he'd lost track of the girls. He cussed in Spanish as he trudged toward the higher ground of Main Street. *God, how he hated the desert, hated it with rarely-felt passion.* Why anyone would freely choose to come to such a God-forsaken place, Jake would never understand. And he was no stranger to the desert. Jake had been raised in Mexicali.

As he made his way past surroundings of ramshackle buildings half consumed by a barren, ferocious wilderness, Jake was assaulted by bitter childhood memories. He had been deprived of the boundless opportunities which the United States offered its citizenry, even though Jake was one of those citizens.

His American birth had been carefully orchestrated by his mother. She had endured more than eighteen hours of labor prior to scurrying across border patrol lines and calling for a cab that could take her to the hospital in El Centro. The plan had almost failed. She had been spotted by two patrol inspectors before her taxi arrived. The men had snatched her up and lay her in the back of their desert car, intending to dash for the Mexicali side of the border before she could deliver her baby. They were too late. Jake's mother had waited until she was ready to drop her baby, even before she had reached the phone booth to call her cab. Once she was laid down in the relative comfort of the jeep's back end, she screamed, heaved, and pushed one terrific time, and was rewarded with instant delivery of her American-born baby boy. Jake was born in Calexico, California, even before the patrol guards could put their vehicle into gear.

When Jake was old enough to end his dual citizenship, he put hand to paper and chose his country. This was merely a formality, for there was really no choosing for Jake. He had waited his whole life to be called an American. He had spent twenty-one long years in the slums of Mexico just waiting for his twenty-first birthday.

His parents had Jake selling flowers and sandals to rich American tourists when he was five years old. By the age of ten, Jake had been promoted to washing the windows of fancy American automobiles for quarter tips. His parents had thought their whole family would gain access to the U.S. because their son was born there, but they soon learned their efforts permitted the family no such right. They were disillusioned, but not discouraged. His father vowed he would find them a way. Jake could hardly remember a family discussion that did not focus on a means of gaining U.S. citizenship for the whole family.

When Jake was eleven years old, his father and two older brothers, Enrique and Ishmael, paid five hundred dollars each to a couple of border runners from Arizona; it was all the money the family had. For the outrageous sum of money, the aliens were promised perfectly forged papers, along with fool-proof entry into the States. But something had gone wrong. The swindlers had gotten spooked and abandoned their truck in the desert. Perhaps they had suspected their illegal actions were being observed. Or, perhaps the payment in advance was just too tempting, and they choose to take the pay but not the risk. Whatever the reason, the Federales recovered the border runners' wagon eight days later. Ten dead Mexicans were found locked in its trailer. Eight days of desert sun, in a metal box with no ventilation, had literally slow-cooked the men to death. The smell was so terrible the police burned the trailer where it lay. Jake never saw his father and brothers again. At the time, Jake had thought his family's situation was as bad as it possibly could be.

Looking up at the declining sun over Bodie, Jake clenched his teeth involuntarily. He wished the memories of his childhood would stop haunting him. He surveyed his immediate surroundings and remembered how he'd killed his first man, or rather men, in a place much like this. A creepy sensation slithered up Jake's spine, a feeling that he'd been here before. But that was impossible.

Shortly after Jake's father and brothers were reported dead, the family's financial situation grew critical. Jake knew of a man who trafficked marijuana and hashish to rich kids in San Diego. The man needed a runner with papers. The money he offered Jake would be enough to keep his family fed. He returned to the hovel they called a home late in the afternoon, eager to relay the good news about the job. He found his beautiful sister curled up on their mother's cot. Her face and tee-shirt front were splashed with dried blood. Juanita was stuperous with pain and unable to speak clearly. Someone had pummeled her face and knocked her front teeth out.

Jake begged ice from a street vendor and held the pack to his sister's hideously swollen face, petting her gingerly as she tried to tell Jake what had happened. Juanita told her little brother how she had offered her virginity for sale to a couple of college students from California. She only did it because she was afraid her family would otherwise starve, she told him, humiliation evident in her eyes.

The college boys had been quite drunk, and Juanita had encouraged them to drink more still. She'd hoped they would pass out before they could take her up on her offer of sex, giving her a chance to rob them as they slept. But the college boys did not pass out with more tequila. Instead, they'd turned mean and began hitting Juanita for sport. The beating seemed to arouse the men, and at some point they'd decided Juanita could service them both at once, and more efficiently, if her front teeth were out of the way. They'd pinned her down on the filthy motel mattress, and banged on her front teeth with a half-full tequila bottle until the teeth caved in. The boys were immediately dismayed, and somewhat sobered, by the amount of blood that gushed

Anne Sweazy-Kulju

forward with the final yanking of her teeth. They were doubly turned-off by the damage the removal of her teeth had made on Juanita's handsome face. They threw the girl out of their motel room without her clothes, or the money they had promised. Just before they slammed the door shut on her, one of them shouted at Juanita that they did not pay for ugly whores.

The Mexican woman who minded the shabby motel had been kind enough to wrap Juanita in a white sheet and help her home. She swore at Juanita, saying she was too young for prostitution and to stay home.

*Ugly whore.* And they had made her so. Jake remembered how the retelling had seemed to hurt his sister almost as much as the beating had. He could remember that afternoon with such vivid detail, that now his fists balled up in vise-like grips, just as they had done then. That was the final indignity. Those two American boys treated his once-beautiful sister as though she were born for no other reason than to be an instrument for their twisted pleasure. It was as though being Mexican meant she was not even human to them.

Jake had arrived at the motel room Juanita indicated, and he'd found the door unlocked. He could hear snoring inside. He removed a solid-steel scratch awl he'd taken from his dead father's leather tooling set. The wooden handle and seven-inch punch blade made the tool a serviceable weapon. Jake turned the doorknob quietly and crept inside. Dirty pleated drapes were drawn over the window and a noisy, useless ceiling fan vibrated overhead. Jake saw the men had stretched out on the two sagging beds. They were drunk enough to ignore the sweltering heat within the shabby room. Both snored away with mouths open. The room reeked of sweat, tequila, and bad breath *so vile* that Jake had to breathe through his bandanna. He could see wide-spread spots of crimson on one of the beds, and his jaw clenched tightly so that his cheek twitched. He stole to the outside of the first bed and looked down with contempt at the sleeping American. Just

240

being American gave them the right to do anything they wanted. Jake suddenly broke out in a huge grin. He was American, wasn't he? It was his right, then, to do what he wanted. Feeling good about what he'd come to do—feeling liberated, he planted the seven-inch blade into the waiting throat. It was like stabbing soft butter. The boy's eyes had popped open and the veins in his temples popped too. He grappled for the blankets, trying to sit up. Blood poured from his mouth as he turned wide-eyed toward Jake. Jake just continued to smile hugely and whispered to him, "Es por Juanita." The dead man dropped back to the blankets, his hands released the balled-up fabric and went slack. The eyes remained open in terror.

Jake had killed them both that afternoon and returned to tell Juanita she had been avenged. He handed her half the money he'd stolen from the boys' wallets, explaining she had earned it. He'd also taken the boys' boots, camera, shaver, and a suede vest that one of them had hanging in the bathroom. Jake rather liked the way he looked in the fine clothes. If those two *cabrones* deserved such finery just because they were American, then so did he, Jake reasoned. One day, he would be able to dress in finery all of the time, he'd promised himself. It was the week before he'd turned twelve years old.

Soon after Juanita had recovered, Jake's mother and sister were granted green cards and were permitted into the U.S. to perform farm labor. The small family spent the next ten years picking their way from farm to farm throughout the West, and later Northwest. Each time Jake or his family incurred a sneer, a cheating, or a racial slur, he promised he would have revenge on such Americans. And he promised himself success, no matter who he had to kill to achieve it.

Jake had been reflecting on his past as he rested himself on an old barn-wood bench, and emptied the desert loam from his wasted shoes. Looking around again, it did not appear to Jake as though there were many, if any, visitors left in the park. The lot he'd left behind was empty now. Straight ahead to the east, Jake could make out the back end of a dark-colored vehicle. It must be the car belonging to the girls. He cocked his head and studied the area around the car. Maybe they didn't suspect they were being stalked. Now that Jake thought about it, those tourists he'd disposed of had just been sitting in their car like they had nothing to fear. Now the girls appeared to be touring the historical sites instead of bolting for the nearest exit—not the actions of people who know they're being stalked. *Maybe the redhead really did pull a muscle. She's walking all over these rough dirt roads in high heels, no wonder.* Jake smiled sadistically. "No problema. This is too easy," he chuckled to himself. He quickly replaced the tired shoes on his aching feet and rose from the bench. Time to pick up the pace.

# Chapter 47

It was just a matter of time before the hired gun inspected every structure in the mining camp. Trying to think like an assassin, Lara reasoned he would likely begin with the nearest structure and work his way back toward the dunes. It occurred to her that if they wanted every single structure available to them, when and if they needed them, they had better make sure the doors would open, and quietly. She looked around. The phony guard was nowhere in sight. This may be her only chance to kick in the doors of structures that were stuck, without the noise of it all giving her position away. They might need those structures for warmth and shelter after the sun went down. From across the abandoned mining camp, Lainy heard Lara kick in the door of the biggest building. She turned the corner in time to see the door fly inward. Lara looked her way and yelled to her, "Let's get them all open now."

Understanding they could not risk making such noise later on, should the man pursuing them start closing in, Lainy gave her sister a thumbs-up and started kicking. They met in the middle.

"So, this is what a mining camp looks like," Lainy said, smoothing damp sections of coppery red hair back from her face.

"Did you get any of that smell?"

"Oh, you mean that smell like something's died in your attic, but you can't tell where it's coming from right away because the smell of animal piss overpowers it?"

"That's the one. It's a dead something—*Blahghh*." She shook her whole body. "That dead air must have been sitting in that building like a putrid fog, and I kicked in the door and stirred it all up. I got blasted with it—*Blahghh*. I thought I was going to barf."

"And you want us to hide out in there?"

"Well no, not yet. It's still too light, and these structures are too small. We might be able to use the biggest of them as a last resort."

"Okay." Lainy turned to survey the expanse of desert that was behind them. The landscape was monotonous, save for a few prospector holes which dotted the rise-and-fall terrain. One could easily break a leg falling in to one of those in the dark, Lainy thought. "What now?"

"I guess maybe we can stick together for a while longer while we explore what's out here. What do you think?"

"I'm up for a stroll in the desert," she made lightly. "Let's head out to that little coulee. If we crouch-over, he'll never see us."

"Let's go."

They ran from spot to spot, until they knew small hills blocked any view of them, and then they slowed to a paced walk. Things were a lot further off than they first appeared in the vast openness of desert. They'd walked two miles before reaching the coulee. Lara's denims were heavy and pressing into any creases in her skin they could find; her panties felt like they were fused to her skin with sweat. She felt stiff and lethargic. Add dusty, hot, and thirsty, and she was miserable. When they finally got to the coulee's edge, they pitched over the side and slid down its sloped bank to the bottom.

"I am so thirsty. Maybe this will lead to water," Lainy suggested hopefully.

Lara just looked at her.

"Oh, right." She lifted her shirt away from her skin, shook it, and blew on herself. "I'd give anything for a sparkling clear swimming pool right now," she said yearningly.

Lara groaned, the imagery making her all the more thirsty. She wiped at her face. Her skin felt gritty and dry. Her hair was plastered to her head, and her cheeks were flush and glistening with the glean of perspiration. The sunscreen she had put on her face in the morning was running into her eyes, and it burned. "I'd be happy for my sunglasses," she said woefully.

Instead of water, they found one rolling hill after another, until they no longer knew where they were in relation to the town or the old mining structures, or to the killer. They had walked for over two hours in the late afternoon sun, until they were both so tired out that neither girl knew how to go on. Lainy was almost ready to give up in despair, when her sister stopped with her back resting against the slope of the dry stream bed. "I'm not conditioned for this, Lainy. I'm worn out."

"Me too. We can't give up, Lara."

"Do you have any idea where we are? Jeff always complains I have no sense of direction, and he's right. I'm completely lost."

Lainy was about to answer when they heard a voice echo down the coulee. "Might as well just drop bread crumbs, chicas. You left me a trail a blind bat could follow."

Their heads darted every which way. There were so many twists and turns in the cut-through that the killer could be just around the last one, or a mile away. Voices carried in open space. Lainy poked her sand-colored ball cap above the rim of the ditch and looked around. She saw a couple of coyotes skulking around the base of the foothills. The coulee must have wound around in almost a complete circle, because they just materialized about a half-mile out from the mining camp they had thought they'd left behind them. She could not see anyone, but he must be on their tail. She dropped back down and placed her back against the slope next to her sister. She whispered, "Oh Lara, we are in so much trouble."

"Why?" She whispered back. "Is he right out there?"

"No, he's not. He's behind us, and we just went around in a big circle. There are coyotes loitering around out there, just waiting for dark, I'm sure. We must smell pretty tasty to them right now."

"Shit." Lara said quietly.

"Exactly. The camp is in front of us now, maybe a half-mile away. It might be a good time to use those buildings and hide. It's going to be dark very soon."

"Okay. I guess this is where we part ways. Oh, Lainy, I'm so…just remember, honey, all we have to do is buy time. Help is coming."

"Soon, I hope. I really don't want to be on anything's menu tonight."

Lara gave her sister a quick, nervous smile. She ticked off three fingers, then said "go" in a hoarse whisper. They scrambled out of the ditch with as much hardihood as they could muster, and ran for all they were worth. When Lara reached the side of the largest structure, she turned to Lainy, but her sister wasn't anywhere in sight.

"Oh God, Lainy. Please be careful," Lara whispered a small prayer.

Lara crouched in a corner of an upstairs loft, in the largest of the old structures. It must have served as the stamp mill, Lara surmised. A steep slide, which looked as though it were constructed of five-gallon metal cans cut in half, led to a mine shaft from a rectangular orifice the size of a pantry door, on the east side of the building. About midway down, and just to the left of the slide, Lara saw what looked like an abandoned well covered with flimsy corrugated sheet metal. The only illumination in the second story filtered in through this slide opening. Any minute, when the sun went down, the room would be plunged into pitch blackness. *Perfect.*

She inspected her surroundings. She picked up a length of board on the ground and poked around in the corners where scrap metal, wood and cloth remnants had been left piled. Nothing rattled or scurried. That was a relief; she didn't need to get into a turf war with a rattlesnake. *Thank you, Lord*, she mouthed to the ceiling. She removed the empty juice bottle from her fanny-pack, angled it, and rapped solidly against the wood floor. Two perfect triangles of glass broke out of either side of the bottle. Lara tossed the sharp triangles down the slide and out of her way, so she would not accidentally cut herself on them in the absolute dark later on. She held in her hand a formidable weapon. It had a comfortable grip that flared into two long sharp peaks. She wound some of the cloth scraps around the jagged ends and replaced the weapon in her pack, not bothering to zip it closed; in fact, she viciously ripped the fob off of the zipper so it couldn't make a sound that might give her away. She wriggled herself into a deep corner and sat, arms hugging her knees, waiting for her hidey-hole to sink into protective darkness. Lara mouthed a silent prayer that Lainy found a good shelter to conceal herself.

Lainy's heart was racing. When they leaped from the coulee, she'd veered far left of her sister. She figured the building nearest the road would logically be the first one the assassin would check. She hoped if she could dig herself into a corner, and was fortunate enough to be overlooked on his initial search, it would be hours before he would check back. And time was what they needed to survive this night. In just a short while, she would have the advantage of nightfall. But as Lainy walked the interior of the structure, she discovered several of the windows facing south and east were broken out. She would not last long in the building once the cold desert wind began to blow. She fought back the tears that wanted to well up in her eyes—she could not give into them. Stepping out the back, she looked toward the largest of the buildings and could feel that her sister was there. She wanted to run over there so badly. But she understood why Lara suggested they stay apart; if the killer did find one of them, odds were less that he would find them both.

Panic was beginning to set in as Lainy looked to the remaining buildings. They were so small. None offered a decent hiding place. Her palms were clammy and her heart felt faint. She didn't have to be the psychic here to know she was running out of time. The killer may already have guessed they left the coulee. If so, he could be in the camp and working his way toward her at that very moment. She had to make for the tunnels. *Any port in a storm—Crap. Pray for me, Lara.* They were her only hope. She'd be sheltered from the night and hidden from a killer, if she could find one of those tunnels.

Lainy broke a flip-flop and had to ditch them. Running through the deep sand was easier barefoot, anyway. She kept herself low as she stole toward the buttes, dashing between clumps of chaparral and boulders. She really hoped she would know a mine entrance if she came upon one. The sun was going down, and it was easy to find shadows of cover amongst the drifts and declines. She steadied herself with her right hand against a wall of rock and peaked around its edge. Slopes of sand. Stacks of stone. Endless, but not without design. Lainy was mesmerized by the spectacle of colors across the terrain at sunset. Blue in places, pink to lavender in others. Pale buff of sand and sparse shoots of dusty green sage grass. The sky overhead was a darkening detergent blue. Only a sliver remained of the great orange fireball on the horizon. *The desert was beautiful,* Lainy amazed. Rounded contours and pastels were beguiling window dressing for the desert. There was hardness and intensity beneath the landscape's deceptively gentle appearance. Lainy realized with wonderment that she alone was audience to this desert show. She had barely moved an inch around the ledge when her hand moved from its resting place to an unfamiliar texture, one of old boards. She hadn't seen them because they were bleached and blasted by years of sun and sand, so that they were the same color as their surroundings. She pulled up at the base of two boards in the center. Their pegs pulled free of the trestle soundlessly. Lainy would have preferred the boards had not pulled free entirely, but the rusted nails had crumbled at her slight tug. She turned herself sideways and slender, and moved through the opening into the shaft. She could not discern its depth, but it was warm inside, and appeared to be free of bats.

"Good enough for me," she declared to the shelter. She turned back for the boards. She was going to try and rest them back in their original places, so her niche would remain camouflaged. *Don't move!* her mind screamed. Lainy froze. The phony guard was walking the perimeter of the largest building, looking up at the second story windows. If he were to turn and happen to look in Lainy's direction, the tunnel would stand out as a large black hole.

She wondered if he'd already noticed it. If not, maybe she could still replace the boards. But if he had already seen the hole, or if he caught her movement…? Lainy abandoned the idea and backed up deeper into the excavation, keeping one hand on the wall for guidance, and both eyes on the motions of the man who had come to kill her.

Lara could hear him calling for them. His voice bounced eerily through the abandoned camp, teasing and taunting. Every few minutes she heard the thunderous slam of aged doors splintering into collapse, upon impact with the walls behind them. He was systematically searching each and every structure, just as they'd anticipated. He was just doing it faster than they'd ever imagined.

He cried out again. A question. "You're up there, aren't you?"

Lara pressed her back tighter into the corner. *Not good enough.* It was dark in the room, but not yet dark enough to go unnoticed. She lay herself face down and scooched up against the back wall. Then she strew the abundant scraps of cloth and debris about her. She pulled some lengths of board to lay in front of her. Now if he walked around in the dark, he wouldn't accidentally kick her, feel something soft, and give her position away. She fought to keep her breathing shallow and her body still.

*Slam!* The ancient planks of the structure reverberated with the impact of the door bursting inward. Lara flattened herself even further to the floorboards. She could taste the oppressive mustiness of passing decades; her nose and lungs urged her to expunge the pervading dust. She squeezed her already-closed eyes tighter still, willing herself to endure it. Footsteps trudging harshly on the lumberous steps grew louder, and then were suddenly quiet. She'd erred, and erred badly, Lara realized. She was hiding in plain sight of a killer, within a room maybe twenty-by-twenty feet at best, and the room had not fallen into complete darkness as she'd hoped it would. For the first time in her adult life, Lara felt beaten. She was despaired to the point she wanted to roll into the fetal position and cry. But she didn't move, and she wouldn't give in. She did not dare turn her head to look for him, because she feared her eyes would draw his like a magnet. Anyway, she did not need to look. Lara could feel evil. It was in the room with her now.

# Chapter 48

Detective Stan Block slid into the passenger seat of the Cutlass, fastened his seatbelt harness and lay his head back on the rest provided. Mac climbed behind the wheel, took one look at his partner and rolled his eyes.

"Hey, I saw that." Block told Mac. "Don't you worry. I've got directions to Bridgeport's police department here. I'm the navigator. I'm navigatin', buddy."

The car rode smoothly, but Block was finding it awfully hard to relax. He was nervous; uncharacteristically so. He took to trick-shuffling some playing cards he carried in his pocket, with just one-hand. Going through the motions helped him to concentrate. The car was so quiet; the only sound was an insect-like buzz in his ears, like some electronic high-pitch only he and dogs could hear. Mac's voice seemed to boom like a cannon out of nowhere.

"So, you think it's that British pantywaist at Globalesque, don't you?"

Stan rubbed his eyes resentfully. "Yeah. Some tough-guy. His bio reads like a cream puff. He's not the kind to get his own hands dirty."

"He hired someone, obviously. I'm going to love putting these guys away for murder." Mac told him.

Stan's dark brows went askew over eyes that were as large and as black as an Indian squaw's. He looked more like a handsome movie star *playing* the role of cop, than the real deal. "I sure hope that's just the one count of murder, and two counts of attempted." His fingertips massaged his forehead. "You know, Mac, here's the kicker: the guy has all this money—"

"He didn't earn it, though. Inherited it," Mac interrupted to qualify the statement for him.

Block grunted, "Yeah, it is easier to get to heaven if God's your father."

"That's a fact. I know you're being facetious, but guys like him don't have a God. They worship gold," Mac asserted.

"Yeah, they do. So, the guy inherited a *lot* of money. Didn't have to earn any of it. All he had to do was…not lose it. But the dipstick manages to lose it all. So, obviously, we're not dealing with a mental giant. I mean, the guy can't be playing with a full deck—" Stan realized he was still one-hand shuffling and stopped. He put the deck away. "Anyway, this is the guy who thinks he's going to mastermind a big, multi-million dollar deal?"

"So he's a criminally-*stupid* pantywaist. I'll tell you who I want," Mac told him, "I want the Senator. I never could stand that broad. Always thought she was crooked as a dog's hind leg. That other female Senator, too. You know who I mean? She looks like a pixie?"

"Oh Yeah."

"And that Congresswoman from San Francisco who's had so many facelifts she probably *does* have eyes in the back of her head, she's the worst of the bunch." Mac was getting himself riled.

"Must be something in the water here," Stan said sarcastically.

"He-he. Her husband is a venture-capitalist, whatever the hell that is." Mac said.

"That's a man who's wife is a crooked politician, and he has to explain the windfall from bribes and shit, as legitimate investments."

Mac chuckled. "So, anyhow, I talked to the Chairman of the Senate Subcommittee on Mining just before we left. Nice guy, you'd like him. He thinks Senator Cilla is a twit, by the way. He hinted pretty strongly that her "need" to get the vote moved up smelled suspicious as hell. I'll tell you what, Stan, that woman may not have any enemies, per se, but none of her friends like her. You know, they all call her 'Godzilla' behind her back."

Stan rubbed his temples for another moment. He could not get rid of the tension in his neck and shoulders; if anything, the tension was building. Every fiber in his being was spurring him to go faster. They *have* to be in time to save those two women. Stan almost felt as if *his* life depended on it. "Go faster, Mac."

"I'm doin' seventy, Stan."

"Go faster."

Mac stepped on the gas. "It's been almost seven hours since those girls made their phone call. You really think there's a chance they're still alive?"

Stan stared out the side window thoughtfully. The night had become obsidian and it was getting downright cold. "Two women, unarmed, in the desert, at night, stalked by a professional killer, and they might not even know there's an assassin after them, so he has the element of surprise, too. You could probably fart bigger than their chances, Mac."

"Why me?" He reached over and chucked Stan on the shoulder.

"I don't know. You're the biggest guy I know; bigger... flatulence?" Stan postulated with humor.

"Are you kidding me?" Mac loudly protested the logic. Stan merely treated him to one of his wise-ass smirks.

Well, he was glad he was able to lighten the tension for his partner a little bit, for however long it lasted. Mac shook his head sadly. He sure hoped they weren't going to Bodie to find two dead women.

Jake knew he'd screwed up when he reached the top step and the last bit of daylight blinked out, propelling him into total blackness. He carried no flashlight, having assumed the moon and stars would offer passable illumination. He'd been away from the desert too many years. He'd forgotten about the half-hour or so of infinite blackness that occurred between the setting of the sun and the moon's rising. Although he'd been born and raised in the desert, he'd never made an effort to get to know her. He hated her.

He'd reached the second-story landing just as the last of the sun vanished, and a curtain of black had been dropped over the building. Jake had only a glimpse of the room before his vision had been inked out, but he was relatively certain he was alone. That wasn't the same thing as the alcove being empty, though, was it?

The place stunk like decayed animals and mouse piss. It was suffocating. Walls were lined with abandoned lumber and metal scraps that Jake did not wish to cut himself on, break an ankle on, or disturb for any potential inhabitants. He ran a hand down the planks nearest him and, satisfied the spot was clear of debris, settled against the old tongue-and-groove and waited for the stars to come out.

He was so close that Lara could hear him breathing and fidgeting. He smelled like he splashed on Aramis in lieu of taking showers for a month. That was lucky, because she was certain she must smell pretty ripe herself. Her knees and the tops of her feet were collecting bruises by the minute from the hard boards she was pressed against. She could feel something crawling up the leg of her jeans. It stopped where her jeans creased at the back of her knee, thankfully blocked by the folds in the denim. The sensation of something crawling unfettered up her skin gave rise to goose bumps and involuntary shivers that Lara tried hard to control. Trembling skin must bother spiders because the damned thing bit her. It burned way worse than the time she was bit by a horsefly. Lara had to chomp down on her lip, hard. The idea of a huge spider crawling along her leg, biting her at will, made her feel queasy. She hated spiders anyway. *What if that one is poisonous? Oh crap. It just bit me again.* This time the burning pain was truly nauseating. She was biting her lip so hard she was tasting coppery blood. But she did not dare move.

Jake thought he could make out the outlines of the walls and debris in the room. Either his eyes were adjusting to the dark or the moon was rising. Probably both. He figured thirty minutes or so had passed. Jake started to push himself up off the floor when something scuttled across the back of his neck and down the guard uniform shirt. Jake jumped up with a shriek and slapped furiously at his backside. He was rewarded with a pinching, burning pain just inside his left shoulder blade. He smacked at it viciously with the back of his hand and felt a big oozy squish against his skin. Jake unleashed a string of profanities in both Spanish and English. There was a colossal wet spot on the cotton shirt. *That damned thing was big as a mouse, for shits-sake.* Enough of this hiding in the dark, he admonished himself. "I'm not gonna sit here and be spider food," he growled to what he thought was an empty room.

He picked up a thin board he noticed when he'd first arrived on the landing, just before everything went dark. He used it now to sweep back and forth in front of him as he headed back for the stairs. Each sweep stirred up century-old dust and ghost poop that made Lara want to sneeze. One wide swing of the board caught Lara in the back of the head, but she never made a cry. Jake never suspected he'd had the company of anything more than debris—and some big-ass'd spiders.

When she was sure he had left the building, Lara scrambled upright and shook and patted her pant leg until she was quite certain the cursed spider was gone. The heavy fabric now felt a little cold as well as damp, and Lara hoped that it was evening seeping into the fabric, and not spider guts. She was not terribly anxious to sit back down, especially after having heard the killer carry on about being bit by a spider as well. There must be spiders all over this room, Lara decided. She would just stand in the center of the room and shake her feet. At least for awhile she was safe, and her sister must be, too.

Chapter 49

6 April, 6:00 p.m.
Washington, D.C.

"What the hell do you mean this is merely insurance?" Bobbi Cilla screamed into the telephone, in her luxurious condo overlooking the river. Everything in the room was white leather, marble, or chrome. Art was chosen on the basis of price tag, no expertise or eye for congruity was employed. The only common theme was expense-minus-taste. She slammed her Chivas straight-up on the marble end table and paced back and forth like a tigress in her terrycloth bathrobe. She'd been called out of the shower by the ringing of her phone, and hadn't an opportunity to dry her brittle, yellowed hair. She stood in the center of the room with a towel wrapped around her head. The white towel was most unflattering against her uneven, thick and wrinkled complexion. It was the skin of someone who slept in full make-up more often than not, over years. It's heaviness tattled of skin cells filled with Chivas Regal and faux-collagen. She distorted her small but abusive mouth. "Listen to me, you rotten little pecker, I could lose my office if I'm connected to you or this gold deal in any way. They could have my head for this. What the hell have you done?"

"Relax, Senator. I have only taken said measures to ensure our success. If there isn't anyone left to question about the environmental integrity of the Bodie Bowl, there is no danger of your efforts failing. I'm making certain no one is left to question. That's all."

"That's all? That's *all?* You idiot, are you telling me you're having people killed? What if they've told others what they are looking into, and then they show up dead? Vanderling, you stupid ass. You're more ignorant than I ever imagined. Call it off." she hissed.

Vanderling rocked back in his chair and smirked. God, he hated that horsey-faced bitch on the other end of the phone line. But he needed her.

"Bobbie. You should not get yourself so worked up. You need to give a convincing performance, er, argument, to the Senate tomorrow, remember?"

"You don't have to tell me. Stop it—can you stop it? Call whoever. Look, I don't want to know any names or anything else about it. Just cancel the order, Vanderling. It's insanity. I never said I would involve myself in murder. Christ, you're an idiot."

Vanderling turned his wrist and took a long few seconds to examine the time on his Rolex. "Simmer down, Senator. Right about now, all our problems should becoming to an end."

Senator Cilla felt a migraine coming on. Not from guilt, hell she couldn't care less about two shit-kickin' podunks from Oregon. She was in trouble. Urging a move-up on this vote may not have looked suspicious before, but now? What if the Chairman got it in his head to make inquiries into the health of her mother—and were to learn she is on holiday in France? God, that Vanderling was such a buffoon. And she'd gone into business with him, so what did that make her?

She'd needed the money, damn it. She was no good without money. She had no friends without the money. She didn't get along well with other women because she was too manly. Men weren't attracted to her either, for much the same reason. Her husband has an apartment in Manhattan that she's never seen. And she hasn't seen *him* in almost six months. Her flat, pancake buttocks had not pounded the sheets in a very long time. No lovers, no friends. She had followers; brown-noser's who hung around her power and her wealth, which she wielded like an expert extortionist. But there was never enough money to go around.

*Damage control, Bobbie. Think.* She shot the rest of her Chivas and went to the wetbar for more. *Think, Bobbie, think.* When the idea came to her, it was like a shot to the head—probably because her head was hurting her so damned bad by that point.

There were other abandoned gold boom towns in the California desert for which similar environmental bills had been proposed. So far, only Bodie's made it through the House, because of the strong grass-roots group that had championed it. So, what if she were to have a sudden change of heart, and switch sides; become a champion of California's environmental, instead of financial, concerns? She was elected on an environmental platform, after all. This would finally clear her of suspicion that she might have been paid by the mining concerns for her stand on the issue. And if she was not in league with the mining concerns, she could not have had anything to do with murders committed by them to better their position. But she still needed Vanderling's money. The answer to achieving both was really so simple, she didn't know why she hadn't thought of it before: Change the name.

Tomorrow, Senator Bobbi Cilla would turn tree-hugging environmentalist, and would give an eleventh-hour, impassioned plea to include all of the other threatened mining areas within the California desert into the Bill. She would rename it, "The

Desert Protection Act," or something like that. Naturally, before passage by the Senate under a new name, it would have to go back to the House of Representatives for re-ratification. By the time it got back to the Senate, the congressional season would be at an end, and the Bill would be stopped short for a second, and therefore final, time. But she would be recorded as having gone against the mining concerns. This may turn out to be her most brilliant scheme yet.

Bobbi Cilla looked out over the river view that she had clawed her way up through life to make possible, and lifted her glass in mock salute. "You're good, Bobbie. Here's to the death of HR 230. Long live The, *hmmmm*, The California Desert Preservation Bill."

# Chapter 50

When they had first started walking back to the cabin, Jeff was well on his way to fury over being left stranded at the lake. Yes, he'd said four-ish, but "ish" does not mean 6:00 p.m. He could not believe Lara would leave them out of doors in the Sierra's, with desert winds and near-complete darkness closing in. It wasn't like Lara to be inconsiderate of others, let alone be dangerously thoughtless. She was the one person Jeff knew who could *always* be counted on to follow through. She never left a job incomplete, she never failed on a promise, and she was *never* late for an appointment.

They'd had to stop walking when the sun went down. Now they waited for the moon to shed some light on the landscape ahead of them. They were warm enough when they'd been walking and the sun had not gone from the sky, but standing still in the darkness was cold. Jeff sat himself against a boulder and sat Claire between his knees. He draped himself and his jacket over her as he rubbed his hands up and down her arms to help keep her warm. He'd ordered Sammy to lay across Claire's lap. This area could be treacherous in the dark. They had no choice but to wait for scant light from the moon before moving on.

Adding to Jeff's burden was the Playmate chest full of nine good-sized mountain trout. They'd had a good day of fishing and he hadn't wanted to throw the fish away, but after all that time in the cooler they were beginning to get strong with the odor of blood. *We can always bake them in the oven and pour some stew over the top—they'll still be good.* Jeff thought.

Claire was shivering, and Jeff was starting to worry. There was no good situation he could think of, where Lara would have left them in total darkness and utter cold. He rubbed his hands nervously up and down Claire's flimsy jacket one more time, and told her they should start walking again. "We're only about a quarter-mile from our cabin now, Sweetheart," he said, coaxing her.

He kept asking himself how his wife could leave him and Claire out in the cold like this. She knew how the temperatures fell in the desert at night. *Jesus, Lara! What are you thinking?*

Little Claire must have zeroed in on his worry, because she squeezed his hand and whispered that her mommy was in trouble.

"No, no, Sweetheart. I'm sure Mommy's okay. She and Aunt Lainy probably had car trouble, or maybe they got lost, or something like that."

Claire looked up at her daddy's face but saw only a white outline of his head in the dim moonlight. "And that's why Mommy is so scared?"

Jeff looked down at his daughter briefly, as he continued to lead them carefully around and over boulders and rises in the landscape. He had witnessed before the strange connection Claire had with her mother. He didn't pretend to understand it, but Claire often seemed to know what Lara was thinking.

"You think Mommy is scared about something Claire?"

"Uh-huh. I saw her," Claire moved her head up and down emphatically.

A chill passed through Jeff. "You, you saw your mommy? I don't know what you mean. When? How?"

"When we were sitting on the rocks waiting for the moon. I'm not supposed to hop in Mommy's head anymore because it's a a-vazshan of her privacy. But I didn't, Daddy, I promise. It was Mommy. She hopped in my head."

Jeff knelt in front of his young daughter. A feeling of dread was building but he refused to give in to it. "Where was Mommy when you saw her, Claire?"

"In a really dark place. And she was really scared. Honest, Daddy. I'm not lying."

*Maybe they had managed to get themselves locked inside an old building or got lost in a mine tunnel or something, but they're fine,* he tried to convince himself. He could not, would not, imagine going through life without Lara. "Claire, tell me everything you can about the place where Mommy and Aunt Lainy are."

"Aunt Lainy's not there."

"Where is she?"

Claire shrugged. Jeff stared at her for a moment. "Tell me about Mommy."

Claire pinched her eyes closed and frowned in determination. "Ummm, she's in a dark room, and it's old and smells bad, and it's really dirty, and there are icky spiders and junk everywhere."

Jeff exhaled heavily, and he relaxed a bit. He even allowed himself a tiny smile. *Of course Lara would be frightened if she were locked in an old building with spiders everywhere, but at least she wasn't in mortal danger.*

But then Claire said something else, which caused Jeff to pitch his prize catch of trout, grab up his daughter in his arms, and run the rest of the way to the cabin, Sammy leading the way. She'd said, "and that man, Daddy. The bad man from Bodie is in the dark place too, and Mommy's really afraid of him."

Jeff borrowed the phone at Doc and Al's cabin, which served as a meager office for the rentals. He apologized again for disturbing their dinner but explained it was an emergency. He did not explain further, though. He didn't know how.

He dialed 9-1-1, and told the dispatch operator that he was reporting two missing persons. His wife and his sister-in-law did not come home, he explained quickly, fully expecting to be pooh-poohed. How was he going to make people understand? But to his amazement, they transferred his call to a police detective, who seemed truly interested and concerned. Good to know there was so little criminal activity in Bridgeport, that his missing persons report would actually be given consideration.

He explained to the detective that his wife and sister-in-law had gone to visit the Bodie State Park in the early afternoon. They were supposed to have returned by four o'clock to pick up him and their young daughter at the lake. They never showed.

The detective first asked for the women's names. Then the detective asked Jeff if the women were visiting Bodie to investigate a series of dreams. That's when the room started tilting for him. And then the detective asked Jeff if he knew of a psycho-therapist, named Rachel Carrell, who was murdered yesterday morning.

That turned Jeff's world upside down.

ake felt his way back outside. By the meager light of a half-moon, he could just make out shapes and shadows in the trackless wasteland. The scant moonbeams oozed through and over the mountains in the distance. Jake narrowed his vision to the area where he had seen the black opening of a cave earlier. Here and there the desert took turns exposing white dunes and concealing black cubbies. It was no use, he would have to approach the dunes in order to find that cave.

The women weren't stupid. Jake was at once impressed and annoyed by the two women who had eluded him thus far. They'd gone to some trouble to bust open every door, just so he wouldn't know which building to look in. He'd had to search them all. They hadn't been in any of them. Then they'd made tracks in the ravine to throw him off. He didn't know how they'd figured out the coulee ran in a big circle. They'd made tracks in both directions, so that Jake had walked the entire circumference before realizing they weren't hiding there, either. His feet were killing him. He jammed a destroyed Dingo half-boot in each pocket, tore off his dripping, sandy socks, and dug his bare feet into the soft, cool sand. He hoped he wouldn't step on a scorpion. Those things hurt.

The sisters had obviously found a cave to hide in, and all that other stuff was just to tire him out or keep him busy. *Shrewd.* He'd thought they might split up; make the search for them more difficult by forcing him to find them separately. He'd suspected one of them might be hiding in that cave he'd spotted, but he must have been wrong; they were obviously both in there. *Cabrone.* Now he had no choice but to go in after them.

The idea didn't appeal to Jake. Neither did killing the two women. *Strange*, Jake thought. He'd made a lucrative career of killing obnoxious, lazy, nonetheless well-to-do Americans, but he did not look forward to killing these two women. And he hadn't wanted to kill that doctor or those tourists either. But a job was a job. His eyes searched the dunes for the black hole. He knew it was southwest-west of where he was standing, or his one-o'clock. "Shit-caca," he muttered. Well, if two little women had nerve enough to enter that cave, then he would 'cowboy-up' and go in, too. He stopped to withdraw the guard's gun from the ill-fitting holster and checked his ammunition. Full. He doubted the gun had ever been used for more than practice shooting, but the guard had kept it cleaned and tightly oiled. Jake clicked off the safety.

When he looked up again, his peripheral vision caught a quick shadow of movement rising up out of the desert just to his right side. He rapid-fired two shots in that general direction, feeling foolish when a deer bounded for the nearest outcropping. "Loco," he spit. The desert had spooked him again. This was the one place where Jake did not feel confident or in command. The desert was like a jealous lover. They'd been intimate once, but he'd left at first temptation for the love of the city and all her finery. Now he was back, and there was no friendly reunion from his maiden, scorned. Jake could almost feel hatred being leveled at him. He shook it off.

"Ready or not, here I come," Jake said.

Lara heard a tattoo of shots and tensed. Then she heard him shout something. Just one word she couldn't understand, because it had bounced off the terrain several times on its way to her ears. He was probably startled by an animal, she tried to convince herself. Lord knows he sure danced the Macarena over a single spider bite. He was probably cursing in Spanish again. All that mattered to Lara was, whatever he'd been shooting at, he'd obviously missed.

Lainy had heard the shots too. But from inside the cave they sounded like little pop-pop's. Party favors. And it looked like the party was coming her way. She backed further into the tunnel. It was nicely warm inside the shaft, safe from the winds that were picking up outside. She'd taken out one of the cookies to eat, but dropped half of it. Lainy called the five-second rule on herself. She didn't know when she would eat again, so she felt the sand floor to retrieve the cookie. Her hand brushed against something firm, warm, hairy...and moving. She gasped. She was not alone. She threw the rest of the cookie as far as she could toward the cave's opening. She hoped that would tempt the animal away from her. Lainy thought she could hear the sound of feet crunching over the gravelly sand. She waited. There was the sound of an old board breaking beneath the weight of something cumbersome. She held her breath.

"*Hello*...anybody home?" His voice taunted her through the entrance with incongruous levity. She heard him chuckle with cruelty. She waited, listening hard but hearing only a soft shishing; a breeze stirring soft sand somewhere nearby. She backed up another foot, pressing her back against the stone of a slight nook in the tunnel wall. She slid herself quietly down to a squat and waited. The cave had no smell at all, so Lainy could tell the exact moment the killer had walked passed her. His hostile cologne and mean body odor announced his arrival.

Jake had needed to pull off another board to get through the opening. He stepped inside quickly and hugged the wall, just in case the girls had a gun of their own. They did not, he surmised, because he would never be as good a target as he was when he stepped through the moonlit doorway.

"I know you're in here," he hollered. He walked deeper into the tunnel, touching the walls here and there. He could hear— something. The sound of sand rubbing against, what? Like the rustle of a woman's undergarments against a heavier cloth. *Had he made another mistake?* He wondered fleetingly. The girls could have left the park, he supposed. Maybe they talked some other tourists into giving them a ride. But, if that were the case, wouldn't the cops be here already? *Naw.* They were here. He could hear them moving. The further he progressed, the more the sound of their stirring grew. His hand landed just a few inches above Lainy's head. The sounds became more urgent. *Was that the sound of two women scurrying from their ultimate impending doom?* The thought caused a smile to form on Jake's face. He did so enjoy the game.

He went several more yards into the tunnel, and his toes bumped into stone. The smile vanished. He'd reached the end of the tunnel. He'd walked right passed the girls. Jake turned himself around and faced the cave's opening. The sand was much deeper here. It swirled around his ankles. He could barely discern the side walls of the mine shaft. Maybe there was a tunnel which branched off of this one. He would need some light to see. He didn't smoke, but that guard whose uniform he'd stolen may have. If so, there was a chance he had some matches on him. He patted down all the pockets and found some. His fingers fumbled to the bottom of the match, and with a quick strike the match was lit. The instant the space around him was illuminated, he heard the girl scream. She was the first thing Jake saw.

Squatting against the wall of the cave some fifteen feet before it stopped, her eyes were turned toward Jake and wide with fear. He grinned. He loved the power that fear over another person gave to him. But that grin evaporated right-quick when he realized her eyes were not focused at him, but rather around him. The match went out.

Jake could still hear that hoarse, gravelly rubbing sound. *What is that?* The sand was growing higher, swirling faster around the shoe boots he'd donned once again. *How was that possible?* Jake's hands began shaking so badly that he nearly dropped the match book. He forced himself to remain calm, but it still took him three strikes before another match was lit. This time Jake screamed. They were everywhere around him! Rats! Mutants! Gigantic desert wood rats! Their red eyes laser-beamed from worn crevices in the walls around him. Yellow teeth were gnashing, claws were tick-ticking against stone, bodies were swelling in maniacal panic around his feet. One leaped directly at his face, falling inches from his nose. Jake didn't know the matches were enraging the normally shy and docile creatures. In that split second, Jake saw the pointy claws of a fifteen-inch long wood rat grasping for purchase in the air in front of his face, its yellow teeth clicking hungrily. The match went out.

He ran like hell, screaming all the way, with arms flailing and batting at monstrous rats he imagined to be crawling all over him. He threw himself at the tunnel entrance, busting off the remaining boards, and landing with his nose in the sand. He jumped up and down, dancing and brushing at himself, feeling phantom rats all over him. He gasped for breath, then screamed and jumped some more. He hated rats. He hated this desert. He hated those girls. And he vowed to make their deaths every bit the hell they'd just put him through.

Lainy had closed half the distance to the stamp mill when the impact of his body thwacked her from behind and sent her sprawling. Sand got in her eyes and mouth, but her hands could not assist her. She was temporarily seized by a terrible cramping, splitting pain. The small of her back felt like it'd been slammed into by a wrecking ball. Her labored breathing caused bright flashes of pain through the length of her spine, as though it were made of glass that had just splintered into a thousand pointy pieces. Thankfully, the paralysis was temporary. With difficulty she rolled over onto her back and rose up far enough to support her weight with one elbow. A face loomed into view directly over hers. The silhouette was outlined in moonlight but the features were shrouded in blackness, with the exception of teeth. Big, white teeth. The son-of-a-bitch was smiling at her.

Lainy groaned and tried to twist out of his reach, but he was faster. With a single strike, Jake broke her nose. Blood poured forth immediately, a real gusher that looked like black ink in the vague moonlight. *That's funny, there's no pain*, Lainy thought. Her nose just went kind of numb. The sensation of blood streaming through her nose made her gag. The next punch landed on the outside of her jaw. That punch hurt tremendously. More bones made of broken glass. The fractured feeling traveled to her inner ears, where a burning pain took over and shot up into her temples and down across the base of her skull. Her elbow gave out, and she sighed as she fell back to the sand, her blood coursing.

# Chapter 52

Stan knew they were announcing themselves by leaving the headlights on, but they had no choice. Bodie State Park was an enormous black hole without their headlights to blaze the way. The police cars jarred single-file down the rough access road. Claire buried her little head in her father's chest as they bumped and rocked their way onward. Sammy began whimpering. Suddenly, Claire lifted her head. "Daddy, Daddy! The bad man has Aunt Lainy. She's bleeding, Daddy!" the child screeched and then started crying for her Aunt.

From his place in the shotgun seat, Detective Block turned sideways and looked to Jeff in the back. "What's she talking about Mr. Reynolds?"

Jeff patted Claire's curls softly and held her to him, though he wasn't certain who was comforting whom. "I told you, she sees things. She has a sensitivity, like her mother."

Stan didn't know if he bought into that clairvoyance stuff. But it begged a question: If the women really had such ability, wouldn't they have known to stay away from Bodie? So, maybe this had less to do with psychic ability, and more to do with destiny.

Maybe that's why Bodie, and even these people Stan knew he'd never met before, seem so familiar to him. Maybe all of this was pre-determined. It would be easy to confuse deja-vu with ESP, Stan reasoned. Familiar people, places, feelings; Stan had to admit he'd received such impressions himself.

So, what was he doing here? Someone upstairs had decided it would be the fate of two Washington cops to locate two dead Oregon women in a California ghost town? The whole thing sounded so silly. A belief that destiny, and nothing else, guides the lives of people, requires a huge leap of faith. Stan Block wasn't ready to buy into that explanation. The only thing he was absolutely sure about, was that it was a real bad idea to bring the kid along. But Mr. Reynolds had insisted his daughter could help. And they could use all the help they can get.

"Can she help us find them?" he asked.

Jeff stroked Claire's soft, shiny hair. "I hope so."

Stan turned back around in his seat and squinted toward the historical town. A sad, heavy, inexplicable feeling was pouring over him. He suddenly felt like he was trying to breathe water. *Was this an omen? Will I be too late once again, to save the woman? Wait, Again?... Again? Where did that come from?* He still held hope, but it was fading fast. He'd been one-hand shuffling his trusty deck of cards to work through his nervousness. All of a sudden, he lost the rhythm and cards strew all over the front seat and floor. *Now that is a bad omen*, Stan thought. Mac glanced curiously over at him, but Stan could not meet his eyes.

"God, please help us find them in time," he prayed.

Everyone chorused, "Amen."

# Chapter 53

H e climbed on top of her in the sand. Jake drew his fist back for another punch, but something held him back from doing it. She lay there, bleeding from places all over that pretty face, and Jake was assaulted with the unwanted image of Juanita, his sister. Juanita's cascading black hair had temporarily replaced this woman's lovely red trestles. He saw his sister's smooth olive skin instead of Lainy's creamy buttermilk. And all the blood that had been his sisters, as a result of those two brutish Americans, was now the blood which drained onto this girl's blouse as a result of his own brutishness.

*Hell*, he thought dismally. *I'm a professional assassin. It's not my job to torture women.* He had no misgivings about a quick, clean homicide, if that was the job. But he'd never intended to beat these women to death or make them endure suffering. His fist dropped with impotence. His fury over the foot-long rats had worked him up to this, and it made him feel ashamed and sick. Or maybe it was just this place, this cruel desert that had turned him into a cruel man. He could not see her eyes clearly, but he knew she was watching him just the same. His voice hushed from the darkness in front of her, "I'm sorry. Real sorry. I didn't mean that."

Lainy said nothing. She cradled her slack jaw in her hand and turned her head toward the desert floor, not wishing to see the knife or gun he would use on her.

"I got pissed. Those rats, man. They were bigger than cats. I'm sorry..." he trailed off. She remained motionless. Jake sighed. "I didn't mean to hit you. You probably don't believe me since, you know, it's my job to kill you. I know you know that's why I'm here. Look, I don't really want to, but it's my job."

Lainy turned toward the shape in the dark. "Why?" She asked softly enough to nearly break Jake's heart. She sounded so much like Juanita, on that awful day.

Jake was amazed to realize he had a heart. He'd been wading in hate for so many years, he thought the cancer of hatred had eaten his heart clean away. "It's the money, Sweetheart. Thirty-five mil, to be exact, for the mining rights. You and your sister know too much, or you soon will. You know, from the dreams. And your shrink was gonna write all about it and expose the contamination of this place. If all that leaked before they could sell the mining rights, it would blow the whole deal for us. A thirty-five million dollar deal."

Lainy struggled to remain coherent, but her surroundings were taking on a dreamlike quality. She had no idea what "deal" the killer was talking about. He had a handsome face, she thought ironically. Nice looking, but not nice. His features grew clearer as her eyes adjusted to the scant light, but they were swimming out in front of her. It was like being really drunk, and for a moment she almost felt like laughing. She was slap-happy. Or was she punch-drunk? So this is where those terms came from. She was losing it. Maybe she was in shock. *Get a grip*, she scolded herself.

"It's just old dreams," she tried to explain. Her words came out mumbled as she tried to keep her jaw from moving too much.

"No, it's no dream. It's real. You gotta understand, if the right people found out about those dreams, they'd dig up all that history, and they'd find out something my boss needs kept secret."

He sighed again. "C'mon you gotta get up." Jake pulled her to her feet. She swayed with her loss of blood and unintentionally leaned against him.

Jake had to admit, he liked the feel of this woman needing him for support. Love, he discovered too late, could be as satisfying as the power he gained through fear. If he'd been raised an American, he might have had a chance with a girl like this, he thought bitterly to himself. But that wasn't the road he'd taken. It bothered Jake more than a little to know he would still have to kill this sweet girl and her sister, and soon.

"Okay, you can lean on me. But, I still have my job to do, you know? I don't want to, but I still have to, you know, you and your sister. I promise I'll make it quick, okay? And it won't hurt." He said more to reassure himself than to comfort her.

They walked to the strip of old mining camp buildings. "Where is she?" he nudged Lainy. Her head was limp against his chest, and she did not respond. She wouldn't tell him anyway, he knew. "Yeah, okay, that wasn't cool of me. You're not going to give up your sister." He lifted her chin a little and said, "I think she's in that big building over there," he tried. No answer. He looked up at the building and cringed slightly. *Spider den.* But the other one had to be up there; there was no place else. Unless there was another mine shaft. *No way.* He wasn't even going to think about that possibility. He glanced at the girl on his shoulder. He had to respect these two smallish women. They were brave, tough little birds.

He pushed open the door with his foot and ushered Lainy inside. Her head, with its luscious red hair, still rested on his shoulder. "Oh lady, I just can't let myself get soft on you," he gingerly pushed some stray curls back for her. Jake could not remember the last time another warm human being, who he wasn't paying, hugged their body to his…fifteen years or more? God, it felt so good. And she wasn't even hugging him, really. Jake suddenly became overwhelmed with a need for a human hug, and a tear rolled down the assassin's cheek. He didn't realize the Holy Spirit was straining to give him one last chance. Instead of grabbing hold of the preserver, Jake shook his head viciously. *What the hell am I doing?* he ridiculed himself. *Finish this job and take a vacation, for shit's sake.*

It had been awhile since she'd heard all the yelling and screaming from a long way off. It sounded like a man screaming and Lara dared hope her sister had killed him with the knife somehow. She'd been standing there waiting for Lainy to come for her, stamping her feet now and then and brushing the air over her head periodically. She didn't want any furry eight-legged critters landing in her hair. She shook her hair vigorously at the thought. The sound of the door opening downstairs took Lara completely by surprise, and her heart skipped a beat. She quickly stepped into one of the dark corners and waited to see if the visitor was her sister, or the other one.

Footsteps on the stairs, heavier this time. She could almost feel the weight of every tread. There were whispers and shuffling. A wispy, sticky strand of spider web tickled the side of Lara's long slender neck. She remained perfectly still. Finally, she could distinguish a shape at the landing. Then two shapes. *Oh, Lainy.*

"We know you're here, and you might as well come out of your hiding place," the voice called out calmly, in heavily accented Spanish. "I have your sister, so don't try anything stupid." He waved his gun in the air to show her, then placed it behind Lainy's right ear.

Lainy's whole self tingled with the déjà vu of the moment. It was the dream being relived. She stood in the dark, helpless at the hands of a hired killer, with a cold, oily muzzle pressed to the side of her head. Once more, she was unable to do anything to save herself. *So this was destiny*, she thought. Any second now the gun will be destined to discharge and send her mind and soul into oblivion. And her sister would be forced to watch. *Destiny sucks.* A tiny giggle escaped her. She was hurting so bad, and yet she was still feeling that slap-happy buoyancy. How could she feel like laughing when they were in so much trouble? Apparently, the lessons she was to learn from Elise's demise were wasted on her because here she was again. She sobered. "Lara, I'm sorry. If you're in here, please don't come out. You don't have to save me, Lara."

Lara's heart sank as she heard her sister's mumbled warning. The bastard had hit her, obviously. She would make him pay for that. She took two steps out of the corner and the moonlight picked up her shape in the murky space.

"Ah, there you are. And all this time," Jake remarked with barely concealed admiration. These were incredible women. *Rats the size of house cats. Deadly spiders. Assassins. Didn't anything frighten these two?* he wondered.

"What do you want with us?" Lara aimed her question at the larger silhouette, angering with the realization that her sister needed his support to stand up. "What did you do to my sister, you bastard!"

He shuffled himself and his wounded prisoner a few steps closer, "I want you to know, this ain't personal, sis."

Lara did not back off. She stood her ground. "Of course not. It's just your job, right?"

"That's right." Jake defended himself.

"Save it. No snowflake in an avalanche ever feels responsible. Anyway, little snowflakes like you beat women like us to feel macho, right? You do it because you can," Lara accused.

"No, that's—*no.* I didn't hit her on purpose. And I don't want to have to kill you. It's not up to me." Jake wondered why it was even important to him to convince them of it.

"Then why?" She had used her dialogue to mask any noise, as she withdrew the jagged bottle from the hip pouch, and brushed away the cloth strips.

"The dreams," the two words that were supposed to explain everything sounded directly in front of her, just a couple of feet away.

"And we have dreams that pose a threat that's worth killing over?" Another shuffle of feet. She heard Lainy groan. It echoed in the empty room, and regret hammered Lara's ears until she thought she couldn't stand it. She wished the killer had beaten her instead of Lainy. It would have been easier to take, she thought. Was she losing her sister? He seemed to be fairly dragging her along. Lara thought she might vomit. *Be strong,* she urged herself. She opened her mouth to breathe in silence, tasting rust and dust and the salty sour smell of the killer. She could hear her own heartbeat, could he hear it too? Where was he, exactly?

"Why won't you answer me?"

Though the effort caused the muscles in Lainy's face to spasm, and violently yank the invisible cords to her temples, her painful jaw issued the warning, "Lara, *run*. He has a gun." But Lara did not move. The loft was as still as a mausoleum.

Jake lowered the gun and lifted Lainy's head from his shoulder. He shook her lightly. "You tell your sister to give it up, and I swear to you I'll do it fast. You won't feel any pain at all, I promise."

With her arms at her sides, it was easy for Lainy to reach the knife she'd removed from the camera case earlier and now had wedged securely between her jeans waistband and leather belt in back. She tried to camouflage her swift movement by conjuring up enough spit and hurling it in the killer's face. The knife was at her side. And her pain was becoming a blessing in disguise. The silliness was gone, and in its place was left an edge of acute sensibility, so that for the past few minutes her docile dependency had been nothing more than an act.

Jake might have perceived some movement from the girl at his side, but he let it pass when he felt the presence of the other girl inching too close. She could find them from the sound of their voices, if he wasn't careful. He didn't know if she had a weapon or not. He'd wiped the saliva away quickly and turned his head in the direction of the sister's voice, but too late. The peaks of the broken bottle glass reflected the briefest glint of moonlight as it streaked through the air.

The razor edges slashed high across his right cheek and all the way down that side of his face, narrowly missing the eye. He heard the bottle clatter to the floor as a white hot pain seared Jake's face. Reflexively, he dropped his gun and pushed Lainy away from him as he grappled in a panic to seam the two widely separating edges of facial flesh back together. *His face, it was separating!* It was all he could think about. *What use were fancy clothes and expensive jewelry to a man with a horribly disfigured face?* Warm, sticky fluid seeped between his fingers. Jake grew enraged as he considered the image that would stare back at him from a mirror until the day he died.

"*You bitch,*" he seethed. "I will *kill* you. I'm going to kill you *ugly.*" He lunged in Lara's direction.

She'd moved. She stood in front of the slide's doorway in order to seal off even the scant moonlight that was available to the loft. She knew she'd cut him badly. The vacuous dry air inside the loft hungrily clutched the warm wetness and carried its metallic odor over to her.

She'd had the briefest of seconds to rejoice. The killer was enraged, and he hurled himself in her direction. Lara sidestepped quickly, and even gave his backside an added push on his way passed, hoping to propel him through the opening. To her dismay, he didn't fall. She did.

The killer threw his hands up when he saw he was about to plunge through the opening. He made a grab for the threshold just in time to stop himself at the frame support. He wavered precariously for mere seconds, regaining his balance as Lara picked herself up off the floor.

Lainy was taking the whole scene in while she struggled with herself. She could run and plunge the knife into his back right now, and their problems would be over. She wasn't sure her hands could do it, stab him, wear his blood. The thought sickened her, even though she knew he'd come to kill them. It was just that— he hadn't, and he'd certainly had opportunity.

He was raging now, though. All the while Lainy worked up the daringness to use her weapon, she was positioning herself in line with the chute doorway. Hopefully her movements were undetected; the killer was blocking most of the slivers of moonlight, as he wavered at the edge of his abyss.

Jake finally found his footing and whipped himself around, flapjack quick. He faced them with his menacing smile. Time slowed down to an impossible, agonizing pace. Everything that was occurring in mere seconds seemed to take an eternity. First, Jake's mutilated face cracked languidly into a ghastly smile, and Lainy knew he would certainly kill them now, if he could. She lifted the knife to her shoulder's height, and deliberately, forcefully, heaved the blade toward his chest. She may as well have missed by a mile, since the spear hit him mere centimeters above his left knee. He cursed and raved and carried on about it, but he was able to jerk the weapon free and now it was his.

He looked rabidly in Lara's direction. *What? Who the hell was that? Where did the woman go?* Standing where the taller sister should have been was a young man of perhaps sixteen years of age, dressed funny and sporting a murderous look in his eyes. Confused, the killer squeezed his eyes closed, shook his head, and opened them again in Lainy's direction. She was gone, and a strangely dressed woman in a blue dress had replaced her, too. He squeezed his eyes closed and opened them once more.

This time he saw the man. A big, brawny tree of a man. Jake feared he'd lost his mind; he was seeing ghosts. *"Who are you people? What are you?"* Jake screamed.

---

280

The man raised his revolver and fired. Jake saw the flash. He watched as the bullet approached him dead on. *Impossible.* He let loose a tortured scream, and emphasized it by throwing himself backwards, forgetting he'd been balancing on the portal of a fifteen-foot drop. Jake hurled through the opening and into the black.

He landed some distance down the makeshift slide, directly onto a sharp triangle of glass from Lara's bottle. He could not stop himself from sliding, and the piercing wedge was being driven deeply into his shoulder by his own weight. One hand had grabbed at his left shoulder where Stan Block's bullet had pierced him. Reflexively, he'd wrenched himself the other way to take his weight off the glass embedded in his back. That was too much for the ancient oil-can chute. It gave way.

# Chapter 54

The instant Jake landed atop the corrugated metal cover for the old Touchstone Mining Company well, time sped back up to normal. The girls ran to the opening and looked out. Only, to the killer, those were not the faces of the sisters he had come to kill. They were faces he felt he knew, just the same. And he'd known the man who shot him, too, from somewhere.

"Who are you?" was his final tormented cry.

First they heard the groan of agonizing strain, then the screeching of metal as it twisted. *Shriek-clamor-yawl.* The corrugated sheet which covered the well gave way, too. Inside the loft, they could hear Jake's screams for half a minute before the well's depths could digest them within its bowels.

Lainy tucked her head in her arms and cried in horror, relief, and pain.

Lara looked at her oddly. "Lainy? Is it you? Are you okay? Oh no-no-no. We have to get you to a hospital."

"I know. I'm okay, though. All the blood is from my nose. I think he broke it. And my jaw, too." She cradled her jaw as she spoke, and she sounded like she had a mouth full of marbles. "I feel dizzy…" she trailed.

"Oh, Lainy! Oh, honey—"

"No, it's okay. I'm okay. I want to know what just happened here? Because I, wait a minute." She couldn't wrap her head around the experience that had just occurred; the one that *caused* the killer to be hurled to his death. She'd felt a strange sensation, and when she'd glanced down at herself, she wasn't herself any more. She was dressed in clothes of the 19th century. She'd thought her mind, the stress was playing tricks on her. And maybe it was. But the killer had seen it too, hadn't he? Lainy started to sag.

Stan realized he had been standing there, frozen. He'd been stunned to realize he recognized the assassin from somewhere. He just couldn't say where. Stan prided himself on never forgetting a face. Well, maybe in that guy's case he'd make an exception. He ran over to the girls, grabbed for Lainy and supported her.

"Who are you?" Lainy asked the tall, handsome stranger.

"Well, ma'am, I guess this makes me The Law, in Bodie." He affected his best John Wayne.

Lainy gave him a weak smile and struggled to stay conscious. "Are you married?" She mumbled softly just before she fainted.

He chuckled a little and roused her by patting her cheek. "I'm Detective Block, with the Long View Police Department. Are you ladies alright?" He lifted Lainy's face a little to observe her injuries using indirect light from his flashlight. "You're not—but you're gonna be just fine. Yeah, that nose looks broken. Don't you worry, Sweetheart. We're gonna get you to a hospital."

She was dazed. Stan was pretty sure she was in shock. But, then what was his excuse? He couldn't explain what he'd just witnessed. He was dumbstruck, and that had never happened to him before. He had no idea what he was going to write down in his report. Something that would not be going into his report was a fantastic, incredible phenomenon; he had seen this woman with the gorgeous red hair before. He was certain of it. Even through her ruthless injuries, he knew he'd seen her before. In his dreams. Stan Block didn't know how to reconcile that with his long-held beliefs, but after tonight he guessed he was going to be seeing his world a little differently.

Eric MacGowan rushed into the room, gun drawn. He had ordered Reynolds to stay in the car with the child when they heard the shot fired. Mac had the Reynolds' dog, Sammy, at his heels; the dog and the child lead them straight to the women, just as Reynolds insisted they would. That whole thing in the car, with the little girl telling them what her mother was seeing and the rest, Mac was a simple man. That was all way beyond his conventional worldview.

The men helped the girls down the steps with the aid of flashlights. Lainy looked up at the detective who shot and killed the assassin and saved their lives; she knew his face. He was the man of her dreams.

"I dow...I dow unnertan." Lainy said. "I fehw dith, wike, futhy womth aw ower an den dat man wooked at me, wike he'd seen a ghosth. An you? You, you weh...twansfomed, woont you?" she asked the detective.

"Ah." He just nodded, *still* at a loss for words.

Mac gave his partner a hard, curious look that said, *What the hell were they talking about?*

"I saw it, Lainy." Lara told her sister. "Her son was here, too. I looked down at myself and saw I was Frank Junior."

Mac had arrived a moment too late to join their Mad Hatter party. But he looked like maybe he'd seen enough anyway. He'd helped Stan get the girls out of the building and into the waiting car. Mac drove. Stan was in the backseat with Lainy. Her head was tipped back in his lap, and he had his handkerchief suppressing the flow from her nose, just as her paramedic brother-in-law had shown him. Jeff had also looked at his wife's bites; he'd told them he wasn't sure they were made by a spider, at least not a poisonous one. Those would be checked out at the hospital, since she had to have a nasty bump on her head looked at anyway. Their would-be killer had unknowingly swung a two-by-four into the back of her head. The wife climbed in next to her sister, and the little girl sat with her father in the front.

Lara leaned forward and touched the driver on the upper arm. "I don't know how to thank you, but, thank you. Thank you for getting here when you did. You saved our lives."

Mac smiled widely. "I'm Detective Eric MacGowan, Lara. Everyone calls me 'Mac.' And, ma'am, I'm real pleased we got here when we did, too. Just so you know, I'm not sure we would have, had it not been for your family, including your Spaniel there. Great little dog." He added. He was glad they had arrived in time to stop the murders from happening, instead of arriving just in time to clean up the mess and hunt down another bad guy.

"Yes, well, my family saves my life each and every day." She blew her little girl a kiss. "Isn't that right, Cornflake?"

Stars cast tiny beacons of light over the evening desert arena. "Isn't she gorgeous at night?" Lara commented as she spread her arms to indicate she was talking about Bodie. The back of her left hand happened to connect with the Detective's cheek. "Oh, I'm so sorry. I can't seem to talk without my hands," she apologized, glad the car's dark interior hid her red face.

"Hands," Lainy teased.

"I know, I know. Those martial arts classes my husband suggested we take, probably would be a good hobby for me." Lara told the detective.

A chorus of voices shouted, "I have a hobby." They all laughed, leaving the two policemen confused.

"Yes, I'll…" Lara trailed off. She'd noted a police car beacon by the guard's booth, and another one parked a short way down a different road leading out of the lower parking lot. It looked like they were readying to close the park down with cones, saw horses, and rope with orange flags. She asked Mac, "You found the security guard in his booth, then?"

"They found him. And the family in the Ford Taurus—"

"We are so glad they called you," Lara interrupted. She caught a look from Mac in the rearview mirror. "They *did* call?"

"I'm sorry," was all he could say.

Jake had plenty of time to arrive at realization before he hit bottom. In fact he'd been given time to review his whole life and then some. He knew those oddly-dressed people from somewhere, or sometime; impossible, but true. He knew it as surely as he knew he was born to live this night and these events.

The moment his Dingo boots touched Esmeralda dust, he'd felt as though he'd been there before. Maybe he'd been sent back for a chance to change his ways. Well, he hadn't. By age twelve, he'd already chosen the path he and his judgment would travel. He could have crossed over to a different road. He'd had opportunities to amend his life—several, right on up to tonight, in fact. But he'd allowed hatred to get the best of him. It occurred to Jake he'd been falling for an awfully long time—forever, it seemed. He wondered how deep the well was, and if he would feel much pain when he finally landed. His body had already been dead for ten minutes.

# Chapter 55

Stan Block allowed himself to smile, and smile big, for the first time in at least twenty-four hours. Things had turned out okay, this time.

He'd wanted a career which allowed him to help people, especially people who could not help themselves. But his career had become a bit of a contradiction for him. Ever since he'd passed the detective's exam, his role had become one of avenger, instead of protector. Last night, though, last night was different. He looked down at the well-handled brochure he'd gotten from the Community College weeks earlier. Maybe this was a good time to pull the trigger on his law enforcement career, and open his own gun shop. He had his twenty years in, and he wanted to become a gunsmith. He also wanted to teach self-defense to women and children, and operate a shooting range; he had lots of ideas. Block stuffed the brochure back inside his shaving kit.

He'd forgotten how good it felt to—*be there in time.* He had the bathroom window wide open. Sunshine and desert heat flooded the tiny bath. Block breathed deeply and took in the painted mural around him; the sounds, sights, smells of the desert, all were perfectly in sync. He had a sense the world had been righted, in at least some small measure. And he had helped to do it. Mr. Reynolds *might* have saved the women. He had his dog, rifle and 'gifted' daughter, and he'd been ready to ride. He might have saved them. But Stan *did* save them. At the moment it counted, he'd been just in time.

"What a dream," Stan Block said to his reflection in the skimpy motel mirror. In all his forty years, he could not recall ever having a dream more vivid, or more exciting, than the one he'd had last night. And the funny thing was, he thought he'd never get to sleep, what with Mac's snoring and the lumpy bed with a dippy sag in the middle. Every time Stan relaxed, he'd roll to the middle of the bed and land up against the backside of his partner. They were close friends and all but there's a limit, and both men agreed, that crossed it.

Stan was smiling too much. He nicked himself, cussed under his breath, and ripped off a snippet of toilet paper to stem the bleeding. He smiled into the mirror again. Nope, nothing could ruin his day today. Yesterday, he'd stopped a killer *before* it was too late. One of the women he'd saved was literally the woman of his dreams. And then last night, he'd starred in a vivid dream as a professional gambler, Indian fighter, and legendary western hero. It just didn't get any better than that for an ordinary guy, *did it?* As he finished up shaving, he recalled parts of his dream; he remembered every detail. First there was that Indian who'd told him he'd like to eat his heart, to be brave like he was, the Indian had said. That must be a hell of a compliment to be paid by a warrior, Stan presumed. Then there was the woman. He'd met Lainy Swazey yesterday, and he'd been intoxicated, smitten, infatuated, spellbound, completely—captivated. In lieu of all that, Stan guessed it wasn't so extraordinary that she showed up in his dream. But the dream itself had been extraordinary.

---

He had been so polished, and she was so beautiful, with her royal blue dress swinging seductively around her shapely calves. They had been so in love. Stan knew it, even though he had never actually known love like that. He'd made attempts, but he'd ultimately come to the conclusion he just hadn't met "her" yet. Well, now he had. He prayed like an acne-struck teen-ager that she felt the same way.

*Don't go getting your hopes up, Stan. She was barely conscious when you dashed in, right in the nick of time, and saved her life like a Western hero from a Louis L'amour novella.* Okay, he really did need to tone it down. And stop grinning like a fool.

He eagerly conjured up more of his dream. *The gun fight in the street.* Stan splashed water to rinse his face. Well it wasn't *really* a gun fight at all, since the dream's bad guy couldn't wait for things to be paced off, like a gentleman. He'd started firing as soon as Stan had come out of the hotel into the bright of day. Stan had wanted the guy to fly off the handle. He'd goaded and heckled his enemy in front of some women, who stood on a balcony above, just to ensure that he would. And then Stan, wearing a silver-starred badge, presumably shot eight times by his enemy, walked casually up to the fella, put the muzzle of his Allen pepperbox against the guy's forehead, and fired.

Reliving the dream was like watching a motion picture he'd just starred in. He splashed after shave over his dopey grin. *Wait—what the hell was a pepperbox? And how would he know what one looked like?* He toweled absent-mindedly behind his ears. Oh, hell, it must have been something he'd heard of somewhere. He could go look it up and find nothing. Or find there was a revolver called a pepperbox, but it wouldn't look like the weapon in his dream. How could it, if he'd never seen one? The important thing is, he had dreamed he was in love with Lainy Swazey, and he had been immeasurably happy.

"Hey Mac," he yelled for his partner. "You ever hear of an Allen Pepperbox?"

"Sure. It's a small revolver. They made 'em up until the turn of the century, I think."

Stan stared at himself in the mirror. Speechless.

"*Hey*." Mac banged on the bathroom door. "Are you camping out in there? Or have you fallen and can't 'giddy up', Mr. Eastwood?"

Stan broke into smile again. He looked into the mirror a last time, "I get no respect," he said.

"Hey Smurfette! How're you feeling today?" Lara teased. She was up, dressed sensibly in khaki pants, a white scoop-neck and extra-long cardigan sweater that Jeff brought over for her. He and Claire packed up Lainy's suitcase and brought the whole thing along for her, so she would have whatever she needed.

"Dats nop phunny."

Jeff looked at the carton of milk he held in his hand and said, "then why did chocolate milk just shoot out my nose?"

"Huh-huh-huh. Ow." Lainy scooched herself up on her pillows.

"Smurfette's better than Toes, right? Hey, you think you feel silly? I had to stay overnight in a hospital because of some bug bites. They said it was an Assassin Bug—how fitting is that? It's really common for them to co-habitat with pack rats, and apparently I *disturbed* them. I thought for sure it was a black widow—I almost wish it had been. The doctor said their bites don't hurt anywhere near as bad. Anyway, I had an allergic reaction. But now I'm all good to go. Are you? Your nose looks good."

"I mus' wook puddy funny," Lainy said as best she could.

"I'm going to set your suitcase over here for you, okay Lane?" Jeff pushed it over to the small closet in the corner, out of the way, then took one of the visitor's chairs to sit in. Claire ran over to Lainy's bedside and reached out to touch her bandages.

"No-no, Claire," Lara warned.

"She's okay," Lainy said. She gave her little niece a squeeze with her hand.

Lara sat on the end of the hospital bed waiting for Lainy to *drink* her breakfast. Fortunately, they hadn't needed to wire her jaw shut. Even so, she looked so swollen Lara wasn't sure a straw would fit. She had dressings the size of winter ear muffs placed on either side of her face, covering the tiny bloody holes the surgeon used for his arthroscopic repair job. Blue ice packs, like Goofy's ears, were draped and tied over the top of her bandages. The only visible facial flesh had taken on a brilliant shade of blue. I.e., 'Smurfette.'

"How long is all your food going to have to be pureed so you can take it through a straw?" Jeff wanted to know.

Lainy shrugged and then held up three fingers, then four.

"Weeks?" He asked. She wagged her head for 'no.' "Months?" She nodded. Jeff looked at his wife. "If I had to puree my beef stew and suck it through a straw, it might just put me off Dinty Moore for life."

Lara laughed lightly. "I know. Poor baby." Lara made a frown and patted her sister's leg, then went back to straightening the covers and the items on Lainy's bed tray.

Stan Block strode through the open door, still wearing the previous night's rumpled clothing along with an award-winning smile. *He's an awfully attractive man*, Lara thought. *Now this guy is the sort of man Lainy meant when she said, 'real' man.* And then Lara was struck with a thought. *Detective Block held an astonishing resemblance to the man in their dream.*

⚔ ⚔

"Well, darlin', you should see the other guy. You two did a tap dance on him."

"Oh yuk," Lara exclaimed. "Tell me you didn't pull him out of that well."

"What was left. We had to I.D. the guy."

He plopped down in a hard chair designed, Block decided immediately, with short visiting hours in mind. He leaned forward eagerly. "Would you ladies like to know what all this was about?"

"*Yes,*" Lara exclaimed. Jeff pulled his chair closer.

Lainy sat up higher on her pillows and strained to hear through the bandages. She pointed to the ear muffs and mumbled, "Could you talk loud?"

Block raised the level of his voice for her, and caught himself wondering once more if she'd be willing to date him when this was all over. *She has to be the most breathtaking woman I've ever laid eyes on. And brave. She is, without doubt, the woman of my dreams,* Stan thought.

"Sure. Okay, first we checked into this mining firm called Globalesque." He looked to Lainy to see if she was hearing him. She gave him the thumbs-up. "They have the original mining rights to the Bodie Bowl, but they don't have any money to excavate with. They're broke. The company filed for the Canadian-version of bankruptcy over a year ago, but they'd managed to keep it quiet.

"Anyway, an interested buyer for the rights comes along, interested to the tune of thirty-five million dollars," he paused to let that sink in, slightly disappointed in their lack of excitement over the information he'd come by."

"The hit man told me about the money," Lainy mumbled.

Block smoothed his hand over his hair self-consciously. He stole a glance in Lainy's direction, and continued. "Everything was coming together nicely for them, and then these two sisters come into the picture with this unusual dream about a murdered woman. How did they know about you, you're wondering? Rachel Carrell had a mentor. Her Advisor. She'd gone to him about the paper she was writing on you two. She never mentioned you by name, by the way. But they figured it out, obviously.

"See, Rachel knew the professor owned twelve and a half percent of the original Bodie Bowl mining rights, so he must have seemed the perfect person to go to. She didn't know about Globalesque, or that the professor was hemorrhaging money. He tells the company about the pretty therapist's plans to explore the cause of a woman's murder of 115 years earlier, in a town where historians well-know single women were more precious than gold; *and* that she intended to publish.

"His idea was to get the vote moved up, but they decided to kill the therapist instead. When he hears she's murdered, he feels so guilty about it that he gets tanked, and gets himself killed in a car accident a block from police headquarters. Globalesque is still riled over the cyanide poisoning, unsure whether Keefe told the police anything before he died, or if their secret is about to be discovered by the dream sisters, so they order the hits on you two."

"Cyanide poisoning. We were right, Lainy." Lara told her sister.

"You knew about the cyanide, too? You girls are stealing my thunder." He smiled at them. "Well then, as you *may* already know, industrial pollution and illegal dumping practices weren't an ordinary concern for too many folks, in 1879. This company called Touchstone helped perfect the cyaniding process for mining gold, right there in Bodie. Mac and I got some research from Berkeley and located that piece of information, but we couldn't find a record for its disposal. It's usually treated and diluted with tons of water, of which the desert is a little shy, right? So, we had some of our people back in Long View take a good look into the town's old records. They learned Bodie's history is missing some real interesting details. Like for instance, Bodie didn't average a *murder* a day. It averaged a *death* a day. It was just journalistic semantics, but a big difference, see?"

"Uh-huh..." the sisters sang in unison. That earned them an award-winning grin from Block before he wrapped it all up, nice and neat.

"The bad guys had some sort of control over the newspapers, who blamed the high death toll on bad whiskey, bad weather, and bad men. So, the high death stats remained unquestioned. That's both the power and the danger of a coerced or partisan press. In the case of Bodie, I personally think the newspapers were accessories to her murder."

"I don't understand. Why would this Globalesque company care about some old pollution, when it was planning to sell anyway?" Lara asked.

"Excellent question. And the answer is, The Friends of Bodie. This is where the guard proved useful."

"But he was killed." Lainy mumbled.

"Yeah, he's dead. But he'd been writing something when it happened. Turns out he was the editor for the Friends of Bodie Society's monthly publication. He was reporting on a piece of legislation that made it through the House, called HR 230. My staff contacted several groups, including State and Federal Assemblypersons, to ask them about any current events concerning the Bodie area, and in particular, about this Bill before the U.S. Senate. They came back with the name of a Senator from California, who has recently been trying to get environmental protection requirements eased for portions of the California desert, theoretically, so that mining could re-emerge in the state's economy. You get one guess as to what portion of the desert she's concerned with.

"So, apparently this was a hot topic that generated television commercials and all, mainly because the Senator was elected on an environmental platform. Her base is feeling duped. But being from Oregon, you girls wouldn't have known about it. I spoke to the Senate Subcommittee on Mining yesterday, while we were on our way out here. The Chairman didn't spell it out, exactly, but he thinks the Senator's up to no good. So, with a little coaxing, he authorizes a wire tap on her telephone in D.C. I'm telling you people, it was amazing to see how much red tape a Senator can cut through with just one phone call. *Amazing*. Well, we wait to see if she gets any interesting phone calls the night before this emergency vote she's requested, which takes me back to what this guard was writing about before he was killed.

"This Bill would require any mining concerns going into Bodie, to guarantee *total site restoration* upon completion of any mining effort. So, see, that's not just clean-up of any environmental mess *they* make. By not writing the Bill with more specific language, they made it a requirement to build and maintain a treatment plant, in order to mine in Bodie. The expense would be considerable. Plus, a geologist's survey is required upon completion, and that would unearth the pollution that we all know already exists in Bodie. They'd have *that* mess to restore. All added up, we're told the clean up costs would be astronomical." Stan couldn't stop smiling.

"So, the company wanted the Bill to pass when they thought their secret was safe, and they could sell the company. But when they thought their secret might come to light *before* the sale, they needed it killed. Along with Rachel and Lainy and me. How did the senator explain her flip-flop?" Lara asked.

"That's what's so interesting about her phone call last night, and you've got it in a nutshell, Lara. I've always said, a crooked deal without a crooked politician is like sex without foreplay, it just don't stand up."

Everyone laughed, including Lainy, who was trying really hard not to.

"Don't make Smurfette laugh, Detective." Lara tried to stop giggling.

"Oh, ah, I'm so sorry. I've been around the boys too long." He looked sheepish. "I, ah, so, like Lara said, if no one knew there was a problem, and the Senator touted economy as the reason for wanting the Bill, that thirty-five million dollar sale would have gone through without a hitch. But the cat was out of the bag before the vote…she's cooked anyway. Know what else we have on tape? The woman was told about the murder contracts on Rachel Carrell and the both of you. Does she call the police and report a crime, or two crimes that are about to be committed? Nope.

That's one count of Accessory-after-the-fact to Murder in the first degree, and two counts of Attempted first degree Murder—pretty stupid for someone who is supposed to be a self-described intellectual. But back to how she managed that flip-flop—that *was* pretty smart. And really, if she hadn't been taped discussing the two of you, she might have gotten away with it."

Stan explained how Cilla had flimflammed the Chairman into moving the vote up on HR 230. Noting their expressions of alarm, he continued, "but you'll be happy to know that an arrest warrant was issued this morning for Senator Roberta Cilla, in connection with the case. The Senator's office has already released a statement saying the Senator, with her attorney, will turn herself over to Capitol police at an undisclosed time and place.

"And, you don't have to worry about the Bill. 'Good Morning Reno' broke the news on a national level this morning, and every major media outlet has picked it up and re-broadcast it. It's pretty big news when a U.S. Senator is arrested in connection with multiple counts of murder, you know. The Senate Subcommittee's Chairman has assured me HR 230 will pass. In fact, he told me it's as good as gold—if you'll excuse the pun!"

"But the company hired the killer." Lara stated.

"That's Right. We're taking him down as we speak. It's a Canadian company, so we're coordinating his arrest with the authorities over there. The President of Globalesque is a wiener named Vanderling. His personal Assistant is the guy you two swan-dived into the well last night. He was packing a pretty lethal-looking knife, which our forensics are sure will match the weapon that killed Rachel Carrell, and yesterday, that guard and the family in the Ford Taurus."

"You keep trying to give us all the credit, Detective. If you had not arrived when you did, I don't think we'd be here right now discussing it. If I haven't already said how grateful I am—we are— thank you, Mr. Gunn."

"Sorry, who?" Stan knew he had heard that name very recently. Where? *The dream.* In the dream he had last night, Jack Gunn was *his* name."

"I'm sorry, I mean Mr. Block."

Stan stared at her a long moment, then stole a glance at Lainy. The girls were trading looks like they knew where that name had come from, too. How was that possible? He was kind of an old horse, but he was trying to accept the psychic stuff. He couldn't deny that these two ladies do little mind-tricks like Lara just did on him, *a lot.* And the Reynolds' little girl was amazing.

Lara had noticed how the Detective's gaze lingered whenever he looked at Lainy. She prayed something good would come from all of this. She reflected for a few moments on Bodie's long and violent history; a history so vicious that a woman's soul could not rest until history was put right. *Would Elise rest now?* she wondered. Would the dreams stop for her and her sister? And then, almost like the cartoon comic strips, a light bulb in her head suddenly surged, and Lara knew there was still one thing they needed to do.

"Lainy, we're going to let you eat—or drink, I guess, and get yourself ready to be discharged. I'll come back after lunch, but I need to help Jeff get the car packed up and all." Her sister nodded she understood. Lara then turned to Stan. "Detective Block, could I get your help with something?" She motioned toward the hall with her head, and he followed her out the door.

After she told the Detective what she had in mind, and Block had offered to do everything he could to help, there grew an uncomfortable silence. Stan shuffled his feet a bit nervously. *Oh, what the hell. I'm going for it.* Stan squared his shoulders and fidgeted with his cuffs a moment. Then he asked Lara, "So, you really are psychic?"

"Eh…" Lara put her hand out, palm down, and wagged it back and forth. "A little bit."

"Think your sister will go out with me?" He smiled.

# Chapter 56

> Away with the flimsy idea
> That life with a Past is attended.
> There's now—only now, and no Past.
> There's never a Past; it has ended.
> Away with its obsolete story
> And all of its yesterday sorrow;
> There's only to-day, almost gone.
> And in front of to-day stands to-morrow.
>
> —Eugene F. Ware
> Rhymes of Ironquill

Spring was always the best time in Bodie. Every person in attendance could tell you it was absolutely true. But none of them could tell you *how* they knew it.

The double-memorial service was well attended. An announcement had been broadcast by television stations in the

Cal-Nevada region, and Lara, with The Friends of Bodie, took care of all the arrangements.

It was to be a double memorial: for Rachel Carrell, who was known in her Bodie life as Amanda Bust. Bodie was Amanda's only family; and, for Elise Swazey, who had been fallaciously laid to rest in the shame of Boot Hill, 115 years earlier, and who had never found peace. That day, the two women would be laid to rest righteously, and with an enormous escort of friends.

The preacher spoke eloquently, first celebrating Rachel's life and then praying for Elise to find a tranquil home with God. Lara placed a bursting array of flowers atop each mound and the guitarist sang a sweet song.

"I'd like to say a few words," began Lainy nervously, as she moved to the side of the preacher. "Rachel showed me that I was not just plain old Lainy Swazey. Thanks to her, I know I am the mysterious and unique sum total of past lives and experiences. And of course, Elise Swazey is one of those past lives, and I am so grateful to her for allowing a piece of her soul to shine through in me. She died a hero; she was trying to save Bodie when no one else would. She has, in large part, made me what I am. And what I am, is proud to be part of something bigger. I am proud to be a part of Bodie, and I know that Bodie will always be a part of me."

Lainy stepped back and Lara stepped forward. "There is a time to die for each and every one of us. No one knows when the hour will strike for them, and no one should; it's not for us to know, not until death touches us on the shoulder and whispers kindly, 'it's time.' We all know we must accept this eventuality. But to die before one has had the opportunity to live, to die before one's time, that is a sin against God and nature. Rachel died too soon. Elise died too soon as well.

"Their sacrifices saved Bodie. I know they saved me. And it occurred to me that we all owe something to Elise. We owe her the restoration of her reputation; we think this is the last piece of her 'unfinished business', as Rachel had termed it.

"Elise Swazey was a favored daughter of Bodie. But, she was buried in shame on Boot Hill. Formal recognition of this woman's bravery, heroism, and *decency*, by her Bodie friends and family, whom she so loved and whose approval meant so much to her, is long overdue. We pray this recognition will allow Elise, finally, to rest.

"I have worried my whole life over roots. My sister and I thought we had only each other in this world, and I was fairly desperate to find where we belonged. Thanks to Detective Stan Block on my left, whom many of you with past Bodie lives may recognize as Jack Gunn, we'll finally know what happened to our great, great grandfather. *I* was Frank Junior, Elise's son, who Mr. Gunn whisked away from Bodie on the night Elise was murdered. We'll be undergoing regression to learn the rest of *our* story. The funny thing is, knowing our family tree has become something more of an interest, and less of a need, now that we have our Bodie family. Her roots are plenty rich and deep enough for this one-time orphan."

Lara watched the faces in the procession. As they filed by the resting places for Rachel and Elise, they dropped tulips atop the mounds. There was the owner of the restaurant in Minden, where they had enjoyed some outstanding fish and chips. Frankie knew him as Svenson. She nodded at Mac, Stan's former partner, who returned the strong determined smile of John Drummond. There was Charlie Baker, the old miner Elise had shared fried chicken with, and Sam Leon, the bartender. There were a few faces Lara, a.k.a. Frankie, didn't recognize. There were also a few of their Bodie family who could not be there today, because they'd already given their lives for Bodie a second time. Lara knew that Bob, the guard, had been Phegley of the Bodie Standard newspaper. And their would-be assassin had been none other than Morris Parker. In his case, Lara supposed, some folks just wouldn't pay attention to the lessons of a prior life.

"Do you recognize me?" A middle-aged woman asked Lara, catching her by surprise.

"I, hmmm. Gosh…"

Lainy and Stan moved over to them.

"You used to help me groom my horses," the petite woman told her.

"I know who you are," Lainy said.

Lara stared at her for a moment and suddenly broke into a huge grin. "You, you're Mr. Conway. Right? You use to give me rides in your wagon, and you used to pay me sometimes to brush your horses down. I remember you, and Boston."

"My favorite horse." She smiled sadly.

"This is bizarre, far-out stuff," Block said. But he was a believer.

A few days earlier, Block had casually asked Mac if he'd ever heard of a pepperbox. Sure enough, Mac had. Mac told him the Allen pepperbox was a revolver from around the turn of the century. Well, in lieu of all the weird, psycho-mumbo-jumbo stuff that he'd experienced over the last few days, he wanted to locate a picture of the gun and just *see*; it appeared to be the exact gun he'd used in his dream. Then Lara found an account of a shooting in one of the old Bodie newspapers. It said Elise's boyfriend, Jack Gunn, shot Morris Parker dead with just such a weapon.

"Do you hear that?" asked the woman who was Robert Conway, looking around.

"Hear what?" asked Mac.

"Yeah. Yeah, I hear it," someone said. "But I can't tell where it's coming from. It's like, coming from everywhere."

The procession stopped and everyone started looking around for the source, searching the skies for the sounds they now *all* heard.

"It's the fire bell tolling the ages of the dead," the man who had been Sam Leon, told them. "It's coming from the fire house in town. Bodie always rang out for her dead."

"Well that was pretty cool of the Friends of Bodie, arranging the bell toll for Rachel and Elise." Jeff said. He stepped closer to Stan and the two men faked like they were going to box each other, then laughed and shook hands. "Hey, Stan," Jeff greeted him. He noted Block's arm around Lainy's tiny waist, and couldn't resist an opportunity to tease. "So, Lainy, you missin' your ex much?"

Stan laughed. "Yeah, but her aim's getting better every day."

The woman who was Conway in another life, supposed Stan and Lainy were in love. She'd already known they were Jack and Elise in that earlier time, because she had undergone regression therapy a year earlier. She prayed this go-around Jack and Elise would have their love-of-a-lifetime. She turned to the couple. "So, you two lovebirds are happy together in this life, then?" She asked.

"Oh, yes." Lainy beamed.

"You kiddin'?" Stan asked her. "We're livin' the dream."

*Guests of the Bodie Memorial would later learn the town had not had a working fire bell to ring in more than one hundred years.*

# Epilogue

This novel is a work of fiction and any similarities to actual persons living or dead, is purely coincidental, or accidentally psychic. The *story*, however, is based upon a real dream experience shared by two sisters. At the time of this novel's first draft, in 1993, the sisters report they have not had the dream in years.

Researching via conventional methods, this author learned of a small boutique hotel that was operated at the end of the nineteenth century, in Bodie. The name of the hotel was, "The Swazey."

The Bodie Bowl mining rights were, in fact, up for sale at the time this book was finished. The mining concern interested in buying out the Bodie Bowl rights, with plans to open-pit excavate, was still determined to see the plans to fruition. The owner of those mining rights, having previously filed bankruptcy, was still very interested in selling.

House of Representatives Bill 240, the *actual* Bill that went before the Senate, would have required environmental restoration of *any* mining efforts conducted within the Bodie Bowl. It was scheduled for Senate vote in the Spring of 1994. It was, however, incorporated into a larger, more inclusive Bill (HR 518) named, "The Desert Protection Act," in the eleventh-hour, by U.S. Senator from California, Diane Feinstein. It necessarily was sent back to the House of Representatives for approval.

On July 27, 1994, the new Bill was tabled by the Senate. In layman's terms, this means the Bill is dead.

Congratulations are in order to Ms. Feinstein, on her win.